Aftertaste

NAMITA DEVIDAYAL

PENGUIN BOOKS
An imprint of Penguin Random House

PENGUIN BOOKS

USA | Canada | UK | Ireland | Australia
New Zealand | India | South Africa | China | Singapore

Random Business is part of the Penguin Random House group of companies whose addresses can be found at global.penguinrandomhouse.com

Published by Penguin Random House India Pvt. Ltd
4th Floor, Capital Tower 1, MG Road,
Gurugram 122 002, Haryana, India

Penguin Random House India

First published by Random House India 2010

10 9 8 7 6 5 4 3 2

ISBN 9788184001877

For sale in the Indian Subcontinent only

Typeset in Berling LT Std by InoSoft Systems, Noida

Printed at Repro India Limited

For Chaitanya

Tulsi jag me do bade
Ek paisa ek Ram
Ram naam se mukti ho
Paise se sab kaam

Prologue

Two days after Diwali...

THE UNIFORMED SECURITY GUARD IN the hospital waiting room nodded at the couple with the empathy that comes from spending year after year watching people battle mortality. He watched the visitors with detached curiosity, overhearing dribbles of their conversation and allowing his imagination to script little stories.

There was always an interesting cast of characters sitting on the orange bucket chairs. Today, a young man with rimless glasses paced the room waiting to hear from the maternity ward. There was the woman who sneaked past the guard every day, thinking she was the first to smuggle in home-cooked food. A middle-aged man sat in the waiting room with a much younger girl in a short skirt. Her alabaster white legs variegated with pale green veins made the guard shudder involuntarily. Was she the daughter or the lover? The guard decided on the second option out of sheer boredom and conjured up a quick vision of her white legs dangling in the air, the man huffing hopelessly between them.

And then there were the people who had just walked in—a dark woman in a parrot green kurta and salwar and a tall, good-looking man with a thick moustache wearing a white shirt and jeans. The guard's eyes followed them as they went to the other end of the waiting room.

The woman in green went and sat next to an older, stout man who was slouched in a bucket seat near the window. He was fair and fleshy, had curly hair, and wore a shiny black kurta pyjama.

'What is the doctor saying, Rajan Papa?' she asked.

The man called Rajan got up wearily and squeezed her hand. 'It's the same. The same, Saroj. The doctor should be out soon, so we will get the latest news.'

The guard sensed something different about this lot. He'd watched them over the last two days. There were quite a few of them for one patient—there was the man whom everyone called Rajan Papa. He must be the patient's son. He jumped up every time the doctor passed by and followed him through the swinging doors. There was the younger man in jeans, Sunny, who smoked a lot and guzzled sweet betel powder, slitting little packets with his teeth and pouring the contents into his mouth. Probably the other son, he thought. There were two women—the dark one in green who was called Saroj and the other whom they called Suman behenji. The patient's daughters, the guard reckoned, because of their resemblance to each other and to Rajan Papa. They all had the same fleshy lips. Saroj looked a bit dishevelled, while Suman was always tip-top. She rustled in and out in crisp white organza saris and wore a long string of rudraksha seeds interspersed with gold beads around her neck. Her eyes were slits in a pallid doughy face. She looked like a fashionable nun, the guard chuckled to himself.

Suman suddenly clutched Rajan Papa's hand, digging her sharp red fingernails into the flesh.

'What should we do about the papers, Rajan Papa? Have we thought about that? Sunny, you'd better think of something before it is too late,' she said sharply.

Rajan Papa's face turned pale. He held his forehead in his hands.

Sunny did not reply. He turned away and walked up to an empty seat under a laminated poster of a frightfully pink rose garnished with enormous dewdrops. It carried the caption, 'Life is beautiful. Death is inevitable. Celebrate both.'

An hour later, they continued to sit there. Suman kept looking at her watch. Rajan Papa dozed off, his mouth slightly open, his fingers interlocked on his bulging stomach which heaved rhythmically, in slow motion.

Sunny got up and went to the balcony outside. He took out a packet of Gold Flakes from his pocket, lit one, and took a deep drag. A thread of smoke wound its way up sluggishly, disappearing into the smoggy evening. He glowered at the grey ocean in the distance. Downstairs, an ambulance bleated its way into the hospital gates.

The women looked at each other and raised their eyebrows. Suman shook Rajan Papa who woke up with a start, frowned, and ran his hand through his curly hair in quick motions.

'I don't know why this Sunny must behave like this, Rajan,' she said in an angry whisper.

'Forget it. Just forget it, Suman,' he replied, looking vaguely stricken.

'I mean why...'

'Let it be, Suman,' Rajan Papa snapped. He sank back into his chair, holding his head in his hands. It was getting close to that time when he needed to get home and reach into the rosewood cabinet with the bevelled glass door and hear the comforting clink of ice cubes against crystal. He wanted to bolt out, but the doctor had not yet come.

The guard couldn't put his finger on it. It was mystifying. What was it about these people? They should have been like any other family—an anxious, exhausted group of people trying to manipulate modern medicine into fighting what destiny had already ordained. But there was something else going on with this lot. It was almost as if they wanted the opposite. Was it his imagination playing tricks or did they really want the patient to die?

Part One

Three days before Diwali...

HOSPITAL WAITING ROOMS HAVE A peculiar odour about them—a cloying, persistent smell of antiseptic. That was what Mummyji's room had started smelling like after she had the stroke.

That morning, nine long and painful days ago, Bimla Kulbhushan Todarmal, universally known as Mummyji, had embarked on her usual rituals. It was still dark when she woke up to her internal alarm clock. She lay in bed for a few minutes until her body got used to the stiff aching leg, then slowly got up and pulled her brassiere down to get it back in position. It was an old habit and she insisted on wearing one even though there was nothing to hold up but two soft, shrivelled marshmallows sucked dry by her four children. She shuffled towards the mirror, picked up two aluminium curlers and clipped them to the sides of her hair. She walked to the front door, unlatched it and picked up the milk that had been left in the cloth bag on the doorknob outside. Why hadn't the newspaper come? That idiot delivery boy must have got drunk again last night. She limped into the living room and switched on the tube light. As it flickered on, she sat in her big round chair and picked up a frayed copy of the Bhagavad Gita. A few loose pages fluttered on to the carpet like ancient moth wings. She picked them up and slipped them back in, not worried about whether they were in order. She knew that with this book, you could start reading from anywhere and it didn't matter.

This was her most cherished time. For the last fifty years, it was the only half hour she got entirely to herself. Many years ago it was worse. By the time the sun was up, Cozy Villa had turned into a circus. It was either her mother-in-law demanding her hot neem water or her children tugging at her sari for attention or her husband complaining about the tea, or the servants lazing around insolently, and of course the perpetual visiting relative who needed this or that. Now they were all long gone, safely incarcerated in picture frames where she could enjoy them from a distance. So she spent this time of the morning in quiet contemplation, before the house stirred slowly into action.

Mummyji sensed the sun rising by the warmth that was creeping into the second floor room and silently seeping into her shoulders. But it was still bearable. The fierce October heat had not yet pushed its way through the blinds to linger on all day like an unwanted guest. At least the heat was better than the cold, when her joints would stiffen and crackle and she had to have them massaged with apricot oil every day to get them to function.

After a few minutes, she got up and went into the room next to the front door to wake up Rajni and Ratansingh, her servants. That donkey Ratan always has an erection.

Must be thinking of Sridevi in a swimming costume, she thought with a silent chuckle. 'Ah, men.' She sighed to herself. Sex, for her, had mostly been distilled into a sharp abbreviated act, conducted in hushed whispers, so that the children sleeping on the floor next to them didn't wake up. It was a response to a man's primal urge. There was no communication, only the hand that would fumble for a breast and signal that she must lie flat and lift up her petticoat. Sometimes, he made her lie on her side and entered her from behind, though that stopped after his belly started coming in the way. When he died, she felt the void, but did not miss him.

'Rajni, go see if the *Navbharat Times* has come. And then get me my tea.' She went back to her meditative seat and continued to read while the morning light slowly filtered into the room and settled on the dusty brown upholstery. Her left leg started its familiar throb and she winced before shutting it out with practised grit.

Mummyji was faintly conscious that even these mundane morning motions would be difficult to pull off in a matter of time. But that was later. For now, she was fine and there were things to be done. She had now decided that she would raise Rajni's salary—after all next month she would complete almost eighteen loyal years. Maybe she would give her that pair of gold bangles instead; that would mean the world to her, since her only pair had been stolen by the wretched Nepali who had worked here as a temporary replacement last summer.

Rajni set down a tray with tea, two Marie biscuits, and the newspaper. 'Here you go, Mummyji,' she said.

Mummyji was everyone's Mummyji, whatever the relationship. She was not a memsahib or an auntyji, or a bhabhiji. She was a full-blown mummyji. That was the name that she had grown into—a benevolent, flatulent witch, who knitted sweaters for everyone, could bargain like a banshee, and never ceased to remind her daughters-in-law that their husbands had sucked on her sumptuous untoned milk for many years before finding succour in their nipples.

Her mind drifted over to her eldest son Rajan Papa. He had told her that he wanted to talk to her about something. She knew what it was about. The whole Bhatija matter. The question was how she should deal with it. He was her devoted first-born, her strapping son, she had to help him, but it just wouldn't be right. The shop would surely be affected. She then thought of Saroj, still fast asleep, curled up like a sad child, and her heart sank. She had tried her best to take her shopping for new clothes and convince her to change her old worn slippers, but nothing seemed to bring the colour back into her life.

She didn't want to dwell on difficult thoughts so she switched to more immediate matters. Today was Dhan Teras, the first day of the festival. The house had been scrubbed clean to welcome the goddess of wealth. The navy blue velvet jewel boxes had been organized—two for the daughters, two for the daughters-in-law—and filled with strands of rubies, pearl earings, and bracelets crusted with diamonds for the lucky ones. Now she had to sort out the ones in the secret locker. Manik Jhaveri would be back from Valsad soon, so she could get the diamond set polished. That was for the bride brought home by dear Rahul, her first grandchild. Yes, she had no qualms admitting it. He was her favourite, even if he looked like his mother. She was convinced that Rahul would give her a great-grandson while she was still alive.

She picked up the newspaper and scanned the headlines. It was more of the same. One of the high priests of the Golden Temple had received an anonymous threatening letter because he had prevented a group of extremist youngsters from shouting pro-Bhindranwale slogans within the temple complex. Below that, there was an article about insurgencies in the North-East. Was there no peace anywhere? Mummyji thought, and turned straight to the obituaries to see who had died and what their children had to say about them. That was her favourite section.

The morning light had now flared into the room and it was getting warm. She pressed the buzzer that dangled from a wire next to her chair and heard it ring distantly in the kitchen. Rajni came in and Mummyji pointed to the fan. She reached up to the switch behind a porcelain statue of Mirabai and turned it on.

Ah yes, and then she had to prepare for the big Diwali dinner later in the week. She smiled inwardly, for this was her real pleasure point—eating and feeding. Ever since her husband had died, she had been made the chairman of Bimz—the family business. But even before he went, she was the critical inspiration for the sweet shop and the chain, and she was constantly adding new recipes and great ideas for sweets, the latest ones being the Bournvita Barfi and Maggi Noodle Bhajia, both unprecedented hits. This was her passion, the sweet business. What she missed most was not so much her husband, but that scent of clarified butter that he carried home with him from the shop in Kalbadevi where he spent his day.

She must make sure there were enough carrots for the halwa. The dry fruit—several kilos of almonds, cashew and pistachio—had been brought home from the shop and now wrapped in neat compartments under golden-yellow cellophane, perfect for those who want the world to see what is being given. She had to tell Ratan to see that the refrigerator was stocked with Thums Up, Gold Spot and Kwality's vanilla ice cream. It was the day the entire family came over and ate with her. Her life revolved around these visits.

Her eyes ran over the room. Maybe she could ask Manju to change the upholstery, to bring in a lighter shade. It had not been changed since Daddyji's death. Her thoughts drifted to her husband, his sudden death in the Fairy Room, the horrible sight of his protruding belly under the indifferent pink cherubs on the ceiling, which came back to her in dreams for months after. How much Rajan Papa had begun to resemble him. She drifted into a slow panic at the memory.

It was there, in the midst of the faded paisley couches, that Rajni found Mummyji. She was slumped on her big round chair, her head tilted forward, and looked like she could have been napping, but Rajni knew instantly that she would never fall asleep at this time. Frightened, she rushed to Ratan who was still a shroud under the sheet, nursing his early morning fantasy, and she shook him. She then ran to the telephone and dialled the one number she knew by heart.

RAJAN PAPA

Four days before Diwali…

THE CYMBALS HAD ALREADY BEGUN crashing with Wagnerian gusto in the prayer hall that morning. A man sat in front of a harmonium, banging at the keyboard with violent purpose. Next to the singer, an old man, with grey eyes and a white stubble, played the cymbals. An assortment of men, women, and children sat around, their eyes shut, clapping to the beat. The prayer songs had been composed to popular Hindi film tunes. The good saint Kabir's philosophy was being rendered in a tune which instantly evoked a coquettish Asha Parekh running up a hill.

Religious singing is a potent medium. The rhythm and haunting half-notes inspire mystic moods that get forgotten in the humdrum of daily motions. But sometimes, in their enthusiasm, the devout forgo the rules of melody. This is what had afflicted the singers of Shraddhashram, who met every other morning at a public hall near Chowpatty beach and sang prayers—always miserably out of tune.

The singers were a congregation of bored or lonely people who found solace in this morning service, a time that took them away from nasty spouses and indifferent children, haughty bosses and insufferable colleagues. In a city which is populated by people who wake up one morning to suddenly find themselves feeling alone, dispensable specks in the crowd, it was hardly surprising that places like Shraddhashram were sprouting up everywhere. People would pass by, or hear about it, and stop to join.

Among the old-timers was a middle-aged woman whose husband had chosen to be with a secretary half his age. A family of four—the parents and their two teenaged sons—came only on Sundays when they didn't have school. A woman came with her mentally challenged granddaughter who would wail plaintively in the middle of the singing. There were several older couples who came in with their own histories and heartaches. One pair would be dropped off in a battered Fiat every time by their devoted son. Others walked, and found in Shraddhashram a way to get out of the way until their children left for work and school. They didn't know one another, yet there was a quiet camaraderie and a comfort of being among strangers. When they sang of god and love, their worlds came back into an equilibrium that nourished them until the next morning.

One of the old-timers was a man called Gurnath Advani. The sixty-year-old had opted for early retirement from his job as senior human resource manager at a biscuit manufacturing company. After spending a few mornings singing bhajans with the rest, he took it on himself to organize the group.

He began by naming it the Dharma Biradari. Next, he started a newsletter with the help of his daughter-in-law who had taken a course in graphic design, and sent one out to each of the people in the group. The newsletter featured a 'thought for the day', a pithy fortune cookie type message, like 'Let Go, Let God!' After a few months, Gurnath Advani started including small news items about the members of the singing group, such as 'Please congratulate Pishu Mahtani for passing his SSC successfully' or 'We extend our condolences to Gayatri bhabhi, who lost her father last week'. With the help of his daughter-in-law, he learned how to decorate the newsletter with little swirling aums, swastikas, and lotus flowers. On Sundays, the music session was followed by a hearty breakfast of puri-aloo which was cooked in a kitchen at the back of the hall. The group got a new life. More people were joining and feeling like they were part of something distinctive, a private club. Soon, the Dharma Biradari had organized itself into a full-fledged body, with sixty-odd members, a president, and a vice president.

No one in the group realized, or particularly cared, that Gurnath Advani was maniacally committed to the notion that Hinduism was a superior religion and that, while others his age played golf or minded their grandchildren, his post-retirement goal was to convert the entire world to this view.

Rajan Papa met Gurnath Advani that morning, while he was on his morning walk on the Walkeshwar Road promenade. Rajan Papa was sitting on a bench facing the sea, feeling faintly misanthropic; attempting to prevent his mind from wandering off into turbulent waters and settle instead on the calm horizon, when a sheet of pink paper flew into his lap. He picked it and vaguely perused its contents. He first noticed the pretty flowery patterns along the sides and then started reading a passage titled, 'Memo to God'.

'Sir, what do you think of our newsletter?' The voice came from behind him.

Rajan Papa turned around to see a tall man with a shock of puffy snow-white hair that looked like sutarfeni, and a chin that extended like badly kneaded dough into his neck. He came around and sat down beside him and pulled out a pad. 'Hari Om. Let me introduce myself. I am Gurnath Advani, vice president of the Dharma Biradari.'

'Oh! Very nice to meet you,' Rajan Papa said, cordially, pleased just to have someone to talk to.

'What a wonderful morning. I feel even better because I have just come from singing songs in praise of the lord. Such a sense of peace one gets, I tell you.' He looked contemplatively at the ocean, shook his head and declaimed, 'Ours is a truly great religion. We just haven't tapped its potential.'

Rajan Papa, mired in his own misery, was intrigued by this man who had chosen to talk to him. Something told him that he would be making a difference in his life. Gurnath Advani reached into his pocket and threw some puffed rice on the ground next to the bench, prompting a flurry of pigeons to focus their guttural gurgling around the two men's feet. They watched the birds nibble at their feast and then Gurnath Advani turned to Rajan Papa.

'What do you do, sir?'

'Well, I am semi-retired. Now I just manage my investments. My investments, you know.' Rajan Papa had this habit of repeating himself, the second refrain always spoken softly, almost to himself.

'Oh. You must come and join our group. We could definitely use the expertise of someone who understands money matters. In fact, we would be honoured if you could become our honorary treasurer. Let me tell you a little bit about the Biradari...'

And that was how the Dharma Biradari fell into Rajan Papa's lap—literally.

The fit was perfect. Gurnath Advani was recruiting new members for his Hindu club. Rajan Papa was a dissatisfied, lonely man with a lot of time on his hands. He was now being offered the position of honorary treasurer at a respectable organization. He would even get his name on the letterhead. He felt flattered and pleased, a sensation that he had not experienced in a very long time, and didn't really care to find out too much about the Biradari. They sang bhajans every morning, and had breakfast together on Sundays, which was pleasant enough. They did social work and were planning to adopt a village just outside Bombay. Rajan Papa generally believed in god—yes, Hindu gods, though he'd never really viewed them quite that way.

He agreed to attend the morning session at Shraddhashram the following Sunday. When he got up to leave, he reached out to shake Gurnath Advani's hand, but Mr Advani shook his head. Instead, he folded his hands and said, with a big smile, 'Jai Hind.' That, Rajan Papa would understand, was the mandatory greeting. He had been initiated.

Rajan Papa left his bench and crossed the road. The sun was already up and the school buses parked along the sea were being washed down by men wearing checkered loincloths, before they chugged out to pick up their little passengers. It was getting late and Bhatija was going to come home. Rajan Papa was seized by the familiar melancholy when he thought of dealing with the oily money broker with white shoes who picked dandruff from his hair with the back of his pen and then scrutinized it, before wiping it on his trousers. Not because he was revolted by the man's personal hygiene, but because he knew that he would have to enter into yet another prolonged, hopeless negotiation with him to get his money back.

When Rajan Papa entered his house, Manju was sitting at the breakfast table, nibbling at her makkai paratha, her homemade face pack cracking like an arid corn field. She looked at him and informed him, irritably, that Bhatija had phoned to say he wouldn't be able to make it as his mother was not well.

'That rascal,' said Rajan Papa, peeling off his socks and wiggling his toes.

'He must be lying,' said Manju. 'Listen, why don't you go and visit him at his office today. I'm certain you'll find him there, entertaining more desperate clients. We should really work on getting at least some amount organized so that we can pay my father back.'

On a typical day, Rajan Papa would have revolted at his wife's suggestion—because it highlighted his incompetencies. Because he knew his wife was struggling to be kind about it. Because it made him feel more small.

Because even his mother was not able to pull him out of this. Because it was too early for him to reach for a glass of Directors Special. But today, there was none of that resentment billowing inside him. On the contrary, and to her surprise, Rajan Papa agreed with his wife instantly.

'I think that's a good idea, dear. A good idea. I'll find him there today—no, tomorrow is Dhan Teras, so maybe the day after that, and catch him. Come, let's have tea together on the balcony.'

Manju bustled into the kitchen and told the cook to get her husband's breakfast of parathas ready, a little suspicious, though not entirely unhappy, about her husband's unusual burst of positive energy.

***

Bhatija was a banker for the cash community—this widespread network of people included businessmen, landlords, traders, housewives, retirees, and anyone who preferred not to use an official channel for their money transactions. They did not declare their earnings to the government and never used banks so that they did not have to pay tax, a leftover of the days when the rates were so high, it was inevitable that people would dodge the system. If someone wanted to transfer money from Bombay to Delhi, he would have to hand over the cash to the broker in Bombay, then call the receiving 'party' in Delhi and give him the last three digits on the topmost note he had submitted. The recipient would then go to the broker's associate in Delhi, give the three code numbers, and take his money.

The cash community relied on an extraordinary and intangible asset—trust. Once you were in the network, the money flowed seamlessly back and forth because it ran on the same principles as a regular bank—goodwill and customer service. There were enormous loopholes and no guarantees, but default rarely took place because there was no reason to break the business. Besides, most people within the network were from the same community and there were compelling honour issues at stake. So, the brokers borrowed and lent and lent and borrowed and pulled out their malai cream layer and everyone was happy.

The parallel economy of unaccounted wealth in the country grew and grew, creating an underworld of business and money dealings that would make any banker's eyes pop. Bhatija was one such seedy but useful element in all this. He took their wads of cash and paid them a whopping rate of interest, much higher than what the State Bank of India offered. In turn, he lent out money at an even higher interest. But if he had an offer document, the fine print would include an important statutory warning: Invest at your own risk, for you may never get your principal back.

And, every once in a while, that happened, and this time, the lightning struck Rajan Papa. For the last two years, Rajan Papa had lived off the interest of this money, which Bhatija's younger brother had religiously delivered to his house on the second of every month. But six months ago, the excuses began. The markets were down. A big client was not returning cash. Everyone was suffering including Bhatija... In between, some money came in, but it stopped again. And in the world of parallel finance, where cash and trust went hand in hand, and both went down together, there was not much recourse. There was nothing personal here, but in the hierarchy of lenders, Rajan Papa came fairly low—lower, at least than Mummyji, who continued getting her dues.

Mummyji was aware of this discrepancy but there was nothing she could do. She had to protect herself and the business. She was still angry about that terrible day when her two sons had lashed out at each other, leading to this mess.

After lunch, Rajan Papa settled into his favourite easy chair in front of the television and stared at the Doordarshan symbol that was rotating on the screen. He started fantasizing about Mummyji's suji halwa, and the whistling rockets that went up into the night, echoing the children's screams, and the long, cosy nights where everyone sat around and played cards. Even if they didn't see much of one another during the year, Diwali was the one time when they met and pretended to be one big happy family while the skies lit up and crackled to commemorate many other such fake family reunions. Sometimes, the children would complain about not being able to go away during their Diwali holidays, but when they did meet, the excitement of bonding with cousins and sharing new secrets, made up for everything.

It was Mummyji's unwritten rule. The family had to be together for the festival, despite differences and enmities. Last year, some people had been missing—Rajan Papa's son Rahul was at a school camp, and Sunny's wife

Jasmeen was in Delhi because her grandfather had died. Otherwise it was the same, year after year. The brothers would meet at Mummyji's house in the morning, then buy new ledger books and accompany her to the old family shop at Kalbadevi. She would sit on a big white armchair while her two sons sat on either side, cross-legged on the floor. Opposite her would be the rotund family priest Purshottamdas, leaning over his belly which resembled a big white drum with just a thin black line of hair winding its way down from his belly button and disappearing under his billowy dhoti.

He would begin the pooja by rendering a large swastika the colour of blood on top of the book of accounts, their object of worship. Money was their means as well as their end, and the goddess of wealth had to be bribed, with imploring chants, faith-tinted incense sticks, sandalwood, and gross, empty promises of charity. That meant praying to an utterly quotidian object—an account book, covered in red, bound with a white string, and bearing in it thousands of little numbers which wound around and bound up the Todarmal family, inexorably, without remorse.

Every year, the goddess sighed, but the priest's loud and nasal chanting drowned her out.

***

The money seed may have been planted that afternoon in 1960 when Daddyji came home to Cozy Villa the day after Diwali, took his cap off slowly, placed it in its usual cubbyhole in the hallway next to the pooja room and said, 'Everything is over.'

Rajan Papa was about fifteen, Suman a year younger and Saroj, an unusually quiet eight-year-old. Sunny was still a toddler. They were sitting around the dining table, eating cut fruit sprinkled with chaat masala, while Sunny was lying with his head on Mummyji's lap, his feet on another chair, sucking at her breast, a bit too old for this indulgence, although no one seemed to care. Milk was the family legacy. As long as she lactated, the children had the privilege of unbuttoning her blouse.

Daddyji walked past them slowly, without saying anything. He took off his shirt and lay down in the Fairy Room, frowning at the smiling cherubs embossed on the pale pink peeling plaster ceiling which was how the room got its name: 'Pariyan da Kamra'.

Mummyji and Sunny followed him into the room. She switched on the fan to try and dispel the oppressive gloom that her husband had brought with him. Sunny climbed on to the bed to perch on his father's stomach and twirl his little fingers around his chest hairs, but Daddyji shoved him off. The frightened little fellow ran off and hid behind his mother's sari.

Mummyji looked at her husband and, in an instant, knew what he was thinking. At that moment, more than anything else, Kulbhushan Moolchand Todarmal wanted his mother next to him. But his mother had gone off on a long pilgrimage to Badrinath and then to her other son in Delhi, and would not be back until next year.

Mummyji came and sat on the bed next to him, with Sunny on her lap, rocking him slightly, not allowing her fear to show. Finally, Daddyji spoke.

'Phoolchand has defaulted,' he said hoarsely. She let him pause, while she organized the alarming finality of this information in her head. Her husband had been tense and distracted for several weeks now, and Mummyji knew that something was awry in the business, but everyone had been clinging like polyps to those two devilish life support mechanisms—faith and denial. Now, it was really over and the wall of delusions was crumbling.

'The mountain will fall on us because we are his guarantors. We may have to move out of here. I have no idea what we will do,' he growled, almost threatening his wife as if it was all her fault.

Bimla was used to her husband's high drama and his inability to deal with anything that went beyond the regular ambit of tolerance. If he nicked himself while shaving, he would holler as if he'd been grievously injured; if he had a slight fever, he would want his entire family by his side. But this sounded serious. She started pressing his calves, and mumbling, 'It's okay…it's okay…'

'It's not okay. Why can't you understand? We may be wiped out. Who would have thought that this could happen?' Daddyji was now shouting.

The two older children came into the room and hovered around the door, pretending to read their school books but, in fact, they were intently paying attention to the conversation and trying to make sense of what they knew was a crisis. Rajan Papa had just started sprouting his first moustache and his first insecurities, which manifested in a stammer, where he started repeating everything twice over while twirling a lock of hair in his hand. He had also started chewing on the cuticles of his nails, leaving bits of skin hanging off his fingers like laundry on a clothesline. The lanky teenager's heart sank with fright at what was being discussed, for matters only half understood can be more terrifying.

Saroj remained on the dining table, alone. As she heard her father's voice rise inside the room, a tiny stream of pee came out of her and she clamped her pelvis. Various unwelcome thoughts that had been safely stored deep down bubbled to the surface incoherently—she was dark, she was the second daughter, she was not Suman, she was no one. They all turned into an amorphous tangle, making her first a bit scared, then despondent. She tried to weakly fence off the feeling, but gave up and continued to vaguely pick at her apple, peeling off the edges of the skin with her teeth.

Inside the Fairy Room, Mummyji had already made the miraculous switch from wife to maternal figure. It was an instinctive transformation, one that came from years of watching mothers and aunts and grandmothers morph at the drop of a hat by tapping into some all-powerful mother goddess energy that lies dormant within them.

'Let us see what we can do, ji,' said Mummyji gently, her mind racing to think of suitable words of solace. To herself she said, the most important thing was that no one should get to know that they were in rough times. That was even worse than being poor. It was like walking naked on the streets. The children's marriage prospects should not get affected; they must all be suitably placed. That was her mission. Suman was beautiful, but still...

Her thoughts went round and round in her head, as if they were being churned inside a vat of buttermilk.

'Nothing. There is nothing we can do. The house of cards is collapsing...' muttered Daddyji. 'I should have known this would happen.'

But how could he? Money has a mind of its own, which is what a clever businessman should realize, though most do not. Like a river, it takes its own course. If you try and control it, at some point the bunds break and the water flows where it wants to. But if you let it flow naturally, alongside your existence, it will heap its wellness upon you. By the time this understanding starts drizzling down on people, tup tup tup, it is too late in the game.

Above all, money despises arrogance. And that was the price Daddyji was paying for his vanity. In a flamboyant, impulsive move made one Diwali, during a heady card-playing evening at his friend Phoolchand's house, where every man present thought he was the master of the universe, Daddyji had offered to back his friend's growing business and become his guarantor. The statement was made with a hidden motive—to flash his net worth. Blinded by his vanity, Daddyji did not think through the consequences.

Phoolchand—a dwarfish man who had long drooping moustaches and looked like a walrus—was Mummyji's distant cousin and Daddyji's close friend. They shared an office in Kalbadevi, a long room between a wholesale cloth merchant and a shop that sold musical instruments. The room was lined wall to wall with a thick mattress covered with clean white sheets with a border of bolsters, also covered in white. This arrangement lent itself to quick snoozes in between customers and account-keeping.

Their families belonged to the trader community—the baniyas—known for their formidable business acumen, where the boys were taught their multiplication tables in quarters. At some point they may or may not have come from Marwar in Rajasthan but, over the years, they had dispersed all over the country, following the smell of money. The Todarmals had long adopted the language, food, and dress of their adopted home in Punjab. Yet, their identity was baniya first and they continued to intermarry within this diasporic business community. One of Daddyji's favourite jokes was about a Marwari who was visiting his old college friend, the sheikh of Dera Arabia. After a heavy evening of food and drink, the sheikh suddenly complained of severe heartburn and was rushed in his car to the hospital. He needed blood and the Marwari offered his. The sheikh got well and rewarded his friend with a new Rolls-Royce. The Marwari said it was not necessary etcetera, but accepted the gift. About a year later, the Marwari was visiting his friend and, again, after a heavy evening, the sheikh had to be rushed to the hospital. Marwari blood was transfused again. When the sheikh recovered he sent his friend a box of chocolates with a note saying, 'Most grateful for your timely help. Can't offer more than chocolates as I now have Marwari blood in me!'

Both Phoolchand and Daddyji were moneylenders, though Daddyji also used to speculate in grains and pulses. Daddyji was a simple man whose taste revolved around money, food, and dirty jokes. Phoolchand had a poetic side, unusual for someone from his background, and used to spend hours writing and reading verse or wandering off in the middle of the day to listen to great musicians in the nearby Girgaum area. His favourite was a young singer called Ameer Khan whose music he found particularly enchanting. Phoolchand said his music felt like the undulating waves of the ocean, one washed over you before the previous one had receded. He introduced Daddyji to Ghalib, Rumi, and Kabir, and helped his friend appreciate the existence of a world beyond the one he knew.

Daddyji lent only to the grain traders he knew and worked with. Phoolchand's moneylending business had a unique clientele—wealthy Punjabis and Sindhis who had moved to India after Partition. These were families who, through their well-placed contacts and influence, were given homes almost comparable to the ones they had to leave behind. They settled in housing colonies built especially for them, enrolled their children into decent schools, and gradually recreated their private bubbles of affluence, by setting up trade—shops, warehouses and small factories that made buttons or tap fittings.

Phoolchand helped get them the money to do this. By the mid-1950s, his business was so successful that he went to the banks and borrowed from them to lend to others—with Daddyji as his guarantor. The two young men revelled in the headiness of easily begotten wealth and bought generous gifts for themselves and their families. Daddyji first moved from a crowded chawl in Bhuleshwar to a two-bedroom flat in Cozy Villa, just off Marine Drive, a few minutes away from Churchgate station, next to a nightclub where pretty Anglo-Indian singers crooned until late into the night. Then, he bought himself a navy blue Plymouth with plush leather interiors. He also splurged on new furniture which he took great pride in sourcing, including a stylish and extremely expensive dining table which he had custom-designed, getting his inspiration from a Hindi movie that had featured a similar table in the villain's den. The table was an aquarium—a thick glass slab placed on top of a water tank. The walls of the aquarium were made of toughened glass. The two short sides had a double layer, fitted with tubelights inside so that you could see the fish swirling about under the food even at night. When he first bought it, Mummyji and the children were thrilled and would take great pains to count the fish, drop food inside, and call friends over to see it. But it didn't take long for the novelty to wear off, and it soon became the fulcrum point for arguments in the house, with Mummyji having to clean it every two weeks.

Then one day, as it happens when the going gets too good to be true, two big Sindhi borrowers, both in the real estate business, defaulted. One case ended in suicide, the other in jail. The business was over and the banks were at Phoolchand's door. And they would soon be knocking on Daddyji's doors. He was finished. His material existence was at stake. Above all, he felt like a failure, which was far worse than the actual loss of money.

Inside the Fairy Room, Daddyji had fallen asleep or at least his eyes were shut. Sunny had also nodded off after taking a few last loud sips from his mother's breast. Mummyji quietly put an Anacin tablet and a tumbler of water on the table next to the bed and watched her husband's body twitch periodically with tiny spasms of tension, those invisible currents that constantly run up and down our bodies that dictate so much of what goes on in our lives without us even knowing it. Then, she folded her hands, shut her eyes tight and started muttering the Hanuman Chalisa, imploring the monkey god to fly through the house and drop his blessings on her family.

Gloom has a way of afflicting all those around as much as the depressed person. It leaves a lingering aura that seeps into the furniture, settles on the food grains, and shadows all the people in its immediate circle. It disguises itself and reappears in the form of fear or anger. It perpetuates an ongoing sense of loss, sometimes even worse than the outrightness of death. This is what gradually took over the Todarmal home, despite Mummyji's efforts to keep things light.

Daddyji stopped going out. He met no one. He stopped shaving and each passing day added to his beard of protest until he could hide under a thick unkempt salt and pepper mane. He would sit at home most of the day, either sleeping or listlessly lying on his back, listening to his Murphy radio. After breakfast, he would go back and lie down in the Fairy Room, fiddle around with the tuning on his radio to catch Binaca Geetmala, which played an endless stream of popular film songs. For a while, he stopped communicating with his family and the mahogany-veneered music box became his soulmate. The soft-spoken host kept airing songs by a fresh new singer from Bengal called Geeta Dutt. Her jazzy rendition of '*Babuji dheere chalna*', which had rocked the entire nation, could have alleviated his melancholy but he seemed to want to wallow. He wallowed and growled and wallowed and growled, finding things to blame and criticize—from the heat to the food—circumventing the real problem of his own misjudgements with the typical hubris of a man raised to believe he was perfect.

Mummyji tried desperately to please him by cooking his favourite halwa. As an occasional treat, she would send for vermicelli feni from Parsi Dairy Farm and serve the scraggly sugar-coated strands to him with warm milk, with diced pistachio swimming inside, just the way he liked it. She made raspberry-flavoured Rex jelly for the children. She ensured that they didn't bother their father as he lay for hours in the Fairy Room. She didn't let her anxiety come near him, protecting him further from reality just like his mother may have done.

But she was secretly terrified as she bustled about the house organizing the children and the food. She knew that soon there would really be a famine in Cozy Villa. She was dipping into the secret stash of money she had collected over the years in anticipation of such a calamity, and the pile was getting thinner and thinner. Every time she thought about money, she would involuntarily start fidgeting with the gold chain around her neck nervously, because she knew that it would be the first thing she would have to sell. But she never dared to bring up the topic of money with her husband. She didn't want to confront his denial, or highlight his shame. For, she knew that she would end up bearing the brunt of his frustration. And just so that no one outside could have even an inkling of what was going on with their financial crisis, Mummyji ensured that her daughters always wore round-round gold balis in their ears and two gold bangles each on their wrists.

One day flowed into another but nothing changed for the family. Newspapers carried monumental news about China accusing India of supporting Tibet and the city of Bombay being split into two states, Maharashtra and Gujarat. But for most people, there was very little interest in such distant issues. The only thing that mattered for families such as the Todarmals was the ebb and flow of money.

Cozy Villa continued to live in this bubble, its inhabitants myopically attached to their miserable lives. One Monday morning, Daddyji surprisingly managed to pull himself out of bed, have a bath and get ready to go out. He even dabbed a bit of Tata eau de cologne behind his ears. As he picked up his cap the way he used to every morning on his way to work, Mummyji asked him where he was going. He grunted, 'To Kalbadevi.'

When he returned, the family realized where he had been, for he announced, 'I am going to sell the car back to the sethji from whom I had bought it. And driver Shantaram will have to go.'

'Noooooo!' Suman wailed. It came out before she could stop herself and Mummyji looked at her and felt a jab of pain at not being able to fulfil her little princess's expectations.

The rest of the family didn't say anything but they were enormously disappointed. They had got used to this luxury and, more than the car, they loved the attention it attracted from friends and strangers. Suman was particularly angry and ashamed at the thought of having to take a bus or tram to school and deal with the sweating pushy men who would touch her and then pretend to look away.

Then the worst happened. Rajan Papa had just come home from school and was loosening the knot on his tie when Mummyji said, 'Beta, I need to talk to you. You know, Daddyji and I were thinking that maybe you could learn something a little useful.'

Her son looked at her quizzically. 'What do you mean?'

'Just for a short while, why don't you stop school and learn a bit of accounting from Phoolchand mama. You can always go back to school...'

She said it matter-of-factly, with a calm that made Rajan Papa feel a little more secure. He let the idea sink in. His middle finger went automatically to his mouth and he started chewing on his cuticle. He knew about the fee hike that had been announced to pay for the new school extension. He realized that his family could no longer afford his education. The girls were luckier because their year's tuition had been paid in advance, so they continued going to school. But Rajan Papa, the eldest son, had to bear the brunt of the family's misfortune. That was the year his repetitive stammer settled into his voice box and stayed with him for the rest of his life.

One morning, Suman complained of a toothache and stayed home from school. Mummyji made her lie down with her head on her lap and pressed her temple. A few minutes later, she pushed her mother away and entered the room where her father was lying down, still unbathed, the Murphy radio gurgling away softly on the table next to him.

'Daddyji...' She paused. He looked at his beloved daughter with a faint smile. 'Can I get that gold kundan necklace you had promised? Like the one Sarita has... I want to wear it to the Baisakhi di Raat dinner-cum-musical programme.'

Her elder brother stared at her, almost awestruck by her self-absorbed and insensitive request that was completely out of place given the family's current situation. Daddyji did not answer. He turned on his side as if she had never spoken and closed his eyes, shutting out the world.

Suman simply wanted to confirm her suspicions that she was being rejected so that she could justify the anger that was beginning to well up inside her. The adored princess felt as if she had been slapped on the face and her cheeks turned hot. She turned around and went to the dining table, where she put her head down on the cool glass and, from the corner of her eye, watched two goldfish glide in the misty water. They were the only fish left in there.

The days that followed catalysed a peculiar alchemy in her brain chemistry, leading to a lifetime of irrational tight-fistedness. She became obsessed about never having enough, always wanting what she couldn't have. It didn't matter that her father's fortunes turned within a couple of years, in keeping with the usual ebb and flow that stalks business families. The damage had been done.

Rajan Papa left behind an unfinished boyhood and forced himself to grow up. He couldn't bear to see his mother suffer. He became serious and withdrawn but went regularly to Phoolchand to learn a bit about business and start wearing the topi in the house.

By April, the gulmohar buds started appearing on the trees around Cozy Villa and the bird calls became more audible, signalling hope and renewal, but nothing seemed to change for the Todarmal family. They struggled to survive the longest, most discontented winter of their lives. Ironically, Geeta Dutt's chirpy songs would forever remind them of those miserable days.

It was Mummyji's maddeningly delicious melt-in-your-mouth khoya barfi that saved the Todarmal family from complete collapse.

A few months after the bad news, the general manager of the Bank of Ludhiana came to meet Daddyji for tea. Now, he could have easily come to the Kalbadevi office, but he chose to come to Cozy Villa for two reasons. First, he wanted to gauge Kulbhushan Todarmal's lifestyle himself. He also wanted to gently point out that the financial crisis had reached the family's doorstep, and that the wife should be warned. That was only fair to the family. Business dealings must be driven by honour—much in the way maharajas went to war; while they killed one another during the day, they strictly followed the rules of the game and the minute the sun set, warring cousins would dine with one another before getting ready to battle the next day.

The bank manager, a six-foot-tall Sikh from Lahore called Kartar Singh, arrived at Cozy Villa on a Monday morning. Rajan Papa was at Phoolchand's office trying to learn how to maintain a ledger and the girls were at school. Only Sunny was home, trailing his mother from room to room. Mummyji had just cut up a tray of khoya barfi into neat little squares, and was sprinkling crushed almond on them, judiciously, so that they covered the entire tray. She had also fried kachoris stuffed with the last peas of the season. To go with this sweet and savoury fare were glasses of chilled lassi made from yogurt she had gently churned. In a bright yellow Banarasi sari, Mummyji looked like a spring canary poised to mate. Despite giving birth to four children, the constant workload had prevented her figure from dissipating into a pile of fleshy lard. Her skin had a natural olive tan and her bushy eyebrows were almost sexy. Kartar Singh stood up, folded his hands, and greeted her with the warmth you wouldn't expect from a man who was about to gently unload her husband of all his worldly possessions.

Mummyji lay the tray of sweets on a table in front of the guest. She picked up two pieces, put them on a plate and handed them to him. He accepted with both hands and smiled. No one spoke for a few minutes.

The minute the khoya barfi entered his mouth, Kartar shrank from master to slave. He was seized by a strange sensation that he couldn't quite understand. His taste buds unlocked an ancient room where he was an infant sucking on his mother's breast. The creamy crumbling sweetmeat melted on his tongue. The aroma of gulabjal and saffron made him smile as threads of almond tickled his palate. He let the feeling trickle into his oesophagus and then seep into his entire being. He gulped down the lassi, still in a daze, and then produced a long loud burp, the ultimate sign of satisfaction.

Later, while he sipped his tea, he said, without even realizing what had just been triggered inside him, 'Sethji, why don't you just take your time and figure out how to get back the money from the customers. We are willing to wait.'

As he was leaving, he said softly to the yellow canary, 'Parjaiji, who made this?'

'I did, sardarji,' she said, coquettishly.

Daddyji thought he saw her wink lightly at him and was seized by a sudden surge of pride towards his enterprising wife.

'Gazab di. Would you be so kind to send some more of your handmade mithai for me to the office some time? By God, this is the best khoya barfi I have had since I boarded the train from Lahore to Amritsar almost thirteen years ago before landing up in this city, where people have no respect for...you know...food...no time to savour the most delectable things in life. This has brought back happy memories.'

Nostalgia has a wonderful way of lightening the load of the present. It can be like a patterned bamboo blind that lets in selective triangles of light and makes reality appear prettier than it is. And if that light lands in the right place at the right time, in a moment, a family's destiny can change forever.

It was then that Bimla Kulbhushan Todarmal had the brainwave.

It came to her while she was staring at a goldfish darting back and forth belligerently under her cup of tea. The summer holidays were just about to begin. The family was sitting around their aquarium dining table. Daddyji was complaining about the water inside looking murky. Your mood is murkier, was the sentiment that ran through his elder son's mind, though he couldn't really articulate it—even to himself.

Daddyji was muttering on, about the fish and the family and the heat, his comments saturated with sleep-deprived irritability, when Mummyji declared, 'We will make mithai.'

Rajan Papa looked at her with aching worry, anticipating another burst of rage from his father. Daddyji stared at her in disbelief.

'Yes, we will make and sell mithai,' she continued softly, in a stream of consciousness. 'We have to organize the milk. We will need…yes…buffaloes…no…cows. Wait, both buffaloes and cows. We have to tell Lochan to get working on this in the farm. And we have to think about where we can store it and how to sell it.'

By now she was nodding to herself and had a maniacal gleam in her eye. As Mummyji spoke and grew more and more excited about her idea, her enthusiasm became infectious. Rajan Papa giggled nervously, happy that his father had not reacted adversely. Saroj smiled shyly into her lap. Even little Sunny started jumping up and down, sensing something good happening in the family. Kulbhushan stared at his wife, incredulous but relieved. And that thickening sickening vapour of gloom that had settled on this family over the past six months began dissipating. Everyone suddenly saw a thin thread of hope dangling precariously above the aquarium dining table.

That night, after a long time, young Rajan Papa slipped into a satiated sleep and dreamed of being surrounded by mithai in all the colours of the rainbow, streaked with silver, sparkling in the sunlight. In the middle of all that, his lovely cousin Sarita was walking naked and feeding him mithai, putting her long fingers in his mouth and allowing him to bite them, laughing softly. He woke up to the squishy sticky feeling of rasgolla syrup streaming down his legs.

As for Daddyji, he reached out and made long and loud love to his wife in the translucent light of a cool moonbeam, breaking six months of silent angry celibacy.

Slowly, very slowly, Daddyji and Mummyji began setting up their sweet business.

In the morning, Daddyji continued to go to the room he shared with Phoolchand in Kalbadevi. They had a lot of things to sort out, even if the bank had given them some time. The defaulting client's property, which was under lien with them, had to be liquidated, their lenders had to be paid back.

In the afternoon, he would go and buy the various things he needed to start shop—to start with, two large cooking utensils, a thinner one for the khoya, one thicker for the chhenna so that the milk didn't burn while being cooked. He also got the big spoons they would need to stir the milk and condense it. He bought ten steel trays on which the mithai would be laid out to cool overnight. He picked up a large weighing scale and different weights and measures. Finally, he bought one more table fan for the kitchen, for he realized how hot it was going to be for his wife who would now be spending hours stirring milk.

Their farm was suddenly activated as the main supplier of milk. It was a small chunk of arid land in the middle of nowhere, a couple of hours south of Bombay, in what used to be a Portuguese settlement dotted with temples and an ancient synagogue. Daddyji had bought the plot on a whim when there was extra money lying around. Sometime in the next few months, a dozen cows and buffaloes were bought, with the help of some money from a sudden spurt in the price of bajra on which Daddyji made a speculative trade. They needed cow's milk for the paneer and buffalo milk for khoya. Milk, sugar, and ghee were the three staples required for their new business. That, and a long contact list of potential customers. With the help of Phoolchand and his friends in the grain trading business, Daddyji started getting in touch with various wholesale spice traders—cardamom, cinnamon, and cloves came from Cochin; saffron and rose water from Kashmir; almonds, pistachio, and walnuts from Amritsar, having made their way across the border; and mustard from Uttar Pradesh and Punjab.

Phoolchand, who was overwhelmed with guilt for financially destroying two families—his own and that of his friend—took an active interest in this new venture. He knew someone who worked as a court clerk in the Small Causes Court and suggested that Daddyji start by getting in touch with the courthouses that had just started small canteens, to see if they could supply sweets and savouries.

Daddyji brought home an old Remington typewriter with round metal keys, and instructed Rajan Papa to start writing letters to various court officials, listing the food and the prices. It was set up on a desk near the window in the Fairy Room. Rajan Papa did not go back to school, for there was now too much work to be done at home.

When Ma returned from Delhi later that summer, she was astonished to find that her daughter-in-law had suddenly acquired a new power over her household. The kitchen was too busy to entertain her special food needs. Now, even her beloved first-born, Kulbhushan, seemed too distracted to care about her complaints. She quietly retreated to her prayer beads, muttering curses between the mantras, and decided to leave again soon afterwards for her other son's home in Ludhiana.

While the men were handling the business side of things, Mummyji worked out the logistics of the food chart: Since rasgollas were the most perishable, they would be made in lesser quantities and perhaps twice a day; barfi and son-papadi lasted longer so could be made and kept. She went and met her cousin Paro to find out what it was that made her chhole taste the way they did, telling her that she was helping someone make it for a child's birthday party.

Daddyji never expressed it but he was overwhelmed with both astonishment and admiration for his wife's business skills and this changed their equation for the rest of their lives. It was the birth of his emasculation and her machismo, but they both continued to play the required roles of dominating husband and subservient wife, only faintly aware that they were pretending.

They got their first order to supply barfi, kachori, and aloo parathas to the canteen of the Sessions Court in Dhobi Talao. After a few months, word got around that their food was delicious, and they managed to bag another court canteen, and then another.

By the end of the year, the house in Cozy Villa had been converted into a sweet factory. The manufacturing shop floor was the kitchen or chauki. The Fairy Room was cleared out, the beds were pushed against the wall, and it became the storeroom and the place where the mushy mithai would be laid out to cool and harden every evening. The drawing room became the place where the book-keeping was done. It would be a year before they could make enough money to move the business to a small kitchen in Kalbadevi, near the old office, and hire two muscular men to spend their day stirring enormous vats of milk.

A few months after they started the business, the consumptive Lochan, who looked after the farm, went to his village in Darbhanga and brought back his nephew, Ratansingh, a skinny lad who was deputed with the sole job of carrying milk from the farm to Bombay every morning and returning with the empty containers in the evening—a task he performed for the next twenty years, numbed by local hooch, unfazed by the stunning monotony of his existence.

The mithai business grew at an astonishing pace, leaving no time to burp. After servicing two canteens, Daddyji decided to rent a shop even though he had to pay the high rate of two hundred and fifty rupees per month. It was a small space next to a travel agency that specialized in sea passage, across the street from where he used to sit and conduct his grain trading business in Kalbadevi. The shop opened into an open courtyard at the back, which was perfect to set up the cooking operation.

It was at this point that Daddyji finally rewarded his wife with a move that would subtly change all their lives forever. He was lying next to her on his side while she massaged apricot oil into his back. Months of taking liberties as the official taster in his business had made him too fat to lie on his stomach.

'What do you think, Bimmo,' he said, in between gentle grunts, yielding his body to the magic with which she kneaded his tensions away. 'Let's call the shop Bimmo di Barfi. After all, it was your luck that has made it happen.' He sat up, suddenly excited about his epiphany.

He realized that the name he had just come up with was not just a tribute to his wife, but also had a lovely homey ring to it. It conjured up the alluring image of an eternally obliging Punjabi woman slaving away, tiny dew drops of sweat dotting her upper lip as she kneaded and pressed and moved her fingers dexterously, her crimson georgette dupatta gliding off one bosom to reveal a deep welcoming valley. Bimmo was an amalgamation of seductress, mithai-maker, and mother goddess all in one. It didn't matter which, because she could make a man orgasm with her virginal virtuosity, merely by stirring up a heady alchemy of aroma, texture, and taste all conjoined with pure ghee.

Mummyji could not believe what she was hearing. Bimmo di Barfi? Oh Khuba, I love you for that, she said to herself. The first thought that came into her head was that her mother-in-law would be ridiculously envious, and that made her even more pleased. She didn't say anything, but stopped rubbing oil and hugged her husband, though she noticed, with a hint of dismay, that her arms did not manage to entirely envelop his protruding stomach.

Kulbhushan sat in the shop most of the day. Rajan Papa's designated job was to look after the canteens. Mummyji took care of the occasional catering jobs that came in every once in a while, especially during the wedding season, when people liked to show off through food.

One day, when Mummyji visited the shop, she found that while the customers were waiting for their sweets to be weighed and packed up, they couldn't help succumbing to the sparkling foods on display and inevitably asked for a bite of something to eat. So she suggested that the shop should start serving snacks in little disposable plates made of dried banana leaves. She was right. At any given point, there would be a cluster of people standing outside the shop, guzzling gulab jamuns or devouring a crumbling kachori filled with hot fresh ground masala, while gossiping about the cloth markets or commiserating over the recent death of Jawaharlal Nehru.

A year later, Kulbhushan rented the travel agency next door and squeezed in as many tables and chairs as would fit comfortably into the small space. And that is how Bimmo di Barfi, or BDB as the children liked to call it, grew from being a small canteen supplier to a popular eatery, servicing a steady supply of hungry regulars who had been touched by Mummyji's food wand.

Kalbadevi was the central business district of Bombay. It grew around a temple complex dedicated to the presiding goddess of the city. It was essentially a long busy street which went from the Christian neighbourhood of Dhobi Talao to the Muslim area of Pydhonie, with numerous Hindu and Jain temples dotting the way so that businessmen could pop in and out and ask for better prospects. Most of the business was conducted on gaddis, thick mattresses, where the proprietor would sit upright every time a customer walked in. The rest of the time he lolled around daydreaming about future earnings or about Nargis in her latest movie, or about that tasty mithai available down the road. This is where Bimmo di Barfi found its happy corner.

Every time one of these businessmen wanted to celebrate a small victory—a good deal struck or a customer cuckolded —he would run to Bimmo di Barfi. Here, he would reward himself with a sweet or savoury delicacy. If it was the elevenses, he would ask for hot jalebi, followed by crisp phaphda with slices of raw papaya and tea. At lunchtime, they would ask for pitthi puris and drippy rasse wale aloo; the four o'clock pangs would be serviced by kachori and tea. And when hunger hit these businessmen at seven in the evening, just after shutting shop, you could count on the array of fresh barfis that lay under the glass. It was meant for those who had had a good day as well as those who were making up for not having had a good day. It was just nice that it was there.

Late morning visitors included women who would have been out sari shopping or on their way home after buying vegetables wholesale from nearby Crawford Market. Children stopped by on their way to or from school and were given sweets at half the price, plus a little hanky with a cross-stitch flower as a gift on special occasions—Mummyji's idea.

In the afternoon, between two and four, when business slowed down, and even the flies went to sleep, Daddyji would get into his car and go home for a short nap, then leave again after a tall glass of milk. At first, he used to do the half-hour brisk walk from Churchgate to Kalbadevi, to get some exercise but as his stomach grew in size he would get breathless and finally gave up and drove. During that time, Rajan Papa took over, for the court canteen would have closed. Later, Phoolchand offered to send his younger son to help manage the shop and give the family some respite.

Ever so often, Daddyji opened a drawer under the cash register and pulled out a red accounting book. The first page carried the customary swastika inscribed with wet kumkum during one of their Diwali poojas. But he did not use this particular book for number crunching. He used it, instead, to write down his thoughts on business, money, greed, and life, remembering what his grandfather had taught him when he would take him on his walks around the lake in Ludhiana, or from his own life experiences or the chats with Phoolchand in the days when they worked together and lazed around on the gaddis, exchanging philosophical thoughts on profit and loss.

On the first page, he wrote a verse he had once read in a book of Kabir's poetry.

Khaye pakaye lutaye ke
Kar le apna naam
Chalti biriya re nara
Sang na chale chhadaam

(You can make good while you are alive and can eat well, earn well, live well. But when you are lying dead in your funeral procession, nothing goes with you.)

Every few days, he made a diary entry about some mundane fact. Today Rajan worked so hard I rewarded him with a gold chain, or today, on our first Diwali, we made the highest profit we have ever made. He jotted these points in immaculate handwriting, his alphabet running like a string of well-formed pearls across the page.

Sometimes, he wrote down nuggets of wisdom. His father had once told him of the two rules of running a business successfully—regardless of whether one manufactured lead pipes or made mouth-watering sweets. First, your second in command must always be either from within the family or a close friend, but only from the baniya business community. Only then can he understand your ways and be trusted with the cash. Second, loss in business is inevitable and must be borne with fortitude, even if it means having to completely start over.

One day, Phoolchand came into the shop and said, 'Khuba, listen to this one. I heard it at a mushaira where they had a poetry competition, and knew you would love it, so I jotted it down for you.'

Makhhi baithe shahad par
Leene par liptaye
Haath male sir kar dhune
Laalach buri balaye

'Did you get it?'

'Not really. Please explain, Bhai sahib.'

'When the fly sits greedily on honey, wrapping its body in it, its own greed eventually kills it.'

'Fantastic! Fantastic! Give me that piece of paper, Phoolo. I have to put it down in my diary. We are all bloody flies getting stuck to the honey and killing ourselves. At least you are a smart fly who loves poetry! Teach me how to be clever too. I don't want to get stuck to the honey! Ho ho ho!'

After he was done he pulled the white string around it and tucked it back into the drawer below his cash register, where it stayed and grew heavier with both information and wisdom as the years went by.

Once again the family had more money than it knew what to do with. Jewellers regularly came around to the house and Mummyji built up enviable trousseaus for both her daughters in gold and exquisite kundan. Each piece of jewellery represented a raised notch in the marriage market. Kulbhushan started thinking about sending Rajan Papa to Switzerland to a catering college for a few months. Sunny was enrolled at a good Jesuit school. When the going is good, jewellery and property are the two places families park their money. Without telling anyone, Kulbhushan bought ten acres of land next to the farm and sent the papers to a place that he thought was the safest.

By the time she was eighteen, the beauteous Suman was awash with a monsoon flood of proposals from the most well-to-do baniya families all over the country. Mothers and aunts of eligible young men had already seen, at family weddings or festivals, the fair girl with the pretty button nose and fleshy lips and long hair entwined into a lovely thick plait, with the teasing pompon dangles at the end, and had nodded approvingly.

The phenomenal success of Bimmo di Barfi meant that the girl would be accompanied by a generous dowry, which always helped. Kulbhushan and Bimla finally selected Shyam Gupta, the only son of his parents, and the scion of a successful typewriter and telephone dealership. It was the first wedding in the family and both sides went all out to show that they had done well for themselves. The wedding took place in the rented garden of a private club in Colaba. The guests included the top-billing actresses of the time, who came looking like Chinese dolls in sleeveless blouses with thick kajal extending upward from their eyes and beehive bouffants on their head. His Highness the Maharaja of Patiala and His Excellency the Governor of Bombay also attended the wedding. They used gold varak instead of the usual silver to embellish the sweets. The wedding was announced, along with a photograph, of the handsome couple in the centre pages of *The Illustrated Weekly of India*.

The night of the wedding, Saroj was driving back home in the car when her grandmother said, 'Your turn will come soon, too, little Saroj. We will get you a palanquin even more beautiful than the one your sister sat in.' Then she playfully pinched her. 'But you are dark and may not find such a handsome husband.' She laughed at her joke. Saroj did not respond. She felt a lightning flash of envy course through her. She stared out of the window as the twinkling lights from the wedding venue grew more and more distant.

A year later, in the middle of his catering course, Daddyji sent his elder son a TWA ticket and made him fly down for a week to meet a prospective bride, Manju. Rajan Papa went to see her in her house in Santacruz along with his sister Suman, now considered a mature married woman and therefore counted among the 'elders'.

Manju was a pleasant-featured woman who had studied up to the eighth standard and had an affinity for paan masala which gave her smile a colourful twist. She was wearing a tight crimson kurta with a salwar and a chiffon chunni. She had a long loose plait which ended at her nicely shaped bottom. Rajan Papa wasn't quite sure what he felt, but he liked the sparkle in her eye. Besides, he thought about all the nights of passion that he could look forward to without the frustration of recreating stale fantasies in his head.

On their second meeting, he was allowed to be alone with her for a few hours. He took her to the Juhu Sun n Sand hotel for a coffee and vegetarian sandwich. They sat on the parapet overlooking the beach and watched the balloon sellers as the sun went down, while he told her about the sweet business and about the loneliness he felt in Switzerland where everyone was whiteskinned and everything was frozen. She was a good listener.

Somewhere in the course of the evening, he was seized by a fit of romance and, copying a scene in one of the many movies shot at Sun n Sand, he kissed the girl's hand.

She whispered, 'Listen...'

And he said 'yes'—to her and later to his family, before going back to complete his course. From that day on, Manju called her husband 'Listen' because she was too old-fashioned to say his name, at least in public.

Rajan Papa didn't know it, but their marriage was a business alliance. Manju's father, Banwarilal Khandwala, ran sugar mills in western Maharashtra, and used to supply the second most important ingredient for Bimmo di Barfi. The families had been introduced by their common friend Phoolchand. He knew Banwarilal from the time they were both boys in striped shorts flying kites together in pre-Partition Lahore.

But the matrimonial alliance was really Mummyji's suggestion. It was a masterstroke to ensure that the price of sugar remained stable as far as the business was concerned, despite the impending prospect of war. Kulbhushan had voiced his hesitation on the match. He wanted Rajan Papa to remain abroad longer, to see the world, to be free of responsibilities. He was also concerned about the poor educational qualifications of his future daughter-in-law compared with that of his son, but Mummyji insisted that this discrepancy was one of the prerequisites of a happy marriage.

So, these two youngsters were married in the same rented garden used for Suman and Shyam, amidst the most extraordinary display of sweets in all colours and textures. The inanimate mithais silently witnessed the ceremony in which people were bartered like perishables. The groom came on a white horse, with his little brother Sunny sitting in front of him, and the sugar heiress giggled like a little girl when she saw them, uncomfortably perched and somewhat terrified. The horse was even more nervous than his riders because of the fireworks that took off around him.

When Rajan Papa's friends lifted him to make it difficult for her to throw the garland of pink roses around his neck, she whispered, 'listen', and he instantly jumped down. After a short holiday in Kulu-Manali, they moved into the smaller room next to the Fairy Room and stumbled into some form of love.

One night, as Daddyji sat in the Fairy Room, counting wads of crisp cash with the dexterity of a superfast note-counting machine, his wife looked at him and said, 'I am worried, ji.'

Daddyji didn't reply immediately. His fingers moved faster than a man on the verge of giving himself a climax, periodically darting to his tongue to wet the tips. He waited until he finished the bundle on hand, put a rubber band around it, scribbled a number on the topmost note, and then looked at his wife quizzically.

'It is about your weight, ji,' she said, gently.

Daddyji grunted and reached for another bundle of notes from the enormous tin trunk filled with cash that he would bring home from the shop on the last day of the month. The final bundle he kept out and said, 'For this month's kharchi.'

The cause for Mummyji's worry was an unexpected outcome of the business. Over the years, there seemed to be a correlation between the company's growing fortunes and its proprietor's belly size. Daddyji, who was already on the short side for a Punjabi man, had developed a rather enormous paunch in direct proportion to his greedy tongue. Ten years after he had founded his mithai business, he bore not the look of a 'healthy' man but rather that of an obese man. It had been taking its toll on his daily routine. He could no longer walk to work. He found himself easily tiring. His breath was shorter. He was not able to have sex with his wife with the ease and vigour that he used to. And he dealt with his problem in a rather peculiar manner—eating in vast quantities, loathing himself for it, and then eating more to make himself feel better.

'Arre, leave it. Listen to this joke, my dear.' He pulled his wife to the bed and made her sit next to him. 'There is this sardar who runs a dhaba. He has just made firni and it is lying cooling on a huge dish near the cash counter. There is an interesting collage of black and green specks against the white surface. But as you get closer, you realize that the green is crushed pistachio and the black is...' Kulbhushan stopped his joke, threw back his head and guffawed. 'It is...it is...hundreds of flies who are having their siesta after gorging on the fresh firni. A customer who has just walked in says, with some irritation, "Sardarji, why aren't you shooing the flies away?" And the sardar replies, "See, these flies are like politicians. This lot has had its fill and are now comfortably resting. If I shoo them away, a fresh bunch will arrive. Better they only stay."'

Kulbhushan continued to laugh at his own joke, almost choking. Mummyji smiled and got up to put the piles of cash in the secret chorkhana in the cupboard. The safe clicked shut and she put the bunch of keys under her pillow.

'Come here,' he said.

She went and lay down next to her husband. He reached into his pocket and pulled out a little navy blue velvet pouch and pulled the drawstring.

'Here is the second one,' he said. 'I was finally able to get it. Now your pair is complete.' She remembered that day, almost thirty years ago, when he had bought her the first stone. She was even more excited than when she saw the gigantic sparkler the first time, because she had scarcely understood its value then. Now she did. And two is always greater than one.

Daddyji told her that she should keep the diamond in the same secret place where she had hidden the other one. They both giggled like children over their little secret. An aura of deep contentment took over and undid the earlier unease that Mummyji had felt. They lay there, without talking, feeling the quiet restorative pleasure of success.

A month later, Daddyji celebrated his forty-ninth birthday surrounded by pethe di barfi and milk cake and beautifully patterned imartis and friends and children and grandchildren. After a stately burp, he said he had some quick business to attend to and disappeared. Mummyji found him flat on his back in the Fairy Room under the cherubs, his hands on his side, fingers curled and frozen, with the beatific smile of a satiated man on his pale blue fleshy lips.

***

After Daddyji died, Rajan Papa ran Bimmo di Barfi.

The business now had three divisions—it was a shop, an eatery, and it also did some catering. Each had its own character—the shop was a friendly space which had a regular supply of customers. The enormously popular eatery had a welcoming sign on a column which said, 'Enjoy your burp', and next to it hung a garlanded photograph of Daddyji, grinning behind a triangular mound of motichoor boondi laddoos. The catering business specialized in making a mouth-watering visual spectacle of cooking, especially displaying the heavy use of fresh white butter.

Sunny was still in college. By his third year, he stopped going for his pointless commerce classes and started helping out with the purchase business, loving the lively interaction with the vendors and wholesalers from all over the country.

Rajan Papa, who now had a little boy Rahul and had moved to a small sea-facing flat on Walkeshwar road, sat every day on the seat that used to be occupied by his father. He handled the cash counter, spending all day placing the different denominations of notes meticulously in each compartment. He even began to resemble his father and a small paunch had started sneaking its way out from under the cash register, making it difficult for him to open the cash tray fully without pushing his chair back.

But the chairperson of the business remained its founder and namesake, Bimla Todarmal, and she continued to run it by remote control. She was the major shareholder and the bulk of the dividends still went to her. She was a compulsive businesswoman and loved the scent of money. She sat at home and played good housewife, screaming at the servants and haggling over fruit prices until the vendors either succumbed or ran away, but her most exciting times were the ones she spent with her cousin Phoolchand, discussing the details of the sweet business or the twists and turns in the money market. Every once in a while she came up with a brilliant idea like her massively popular Bournvita Barfi.

The other masterstroke was her suggestion that they make theme sweets. So, during Holi, there would be multi-coloured barfis, and on Independence Day, the mithais would be fashioned saffron, green, and white with a toothpick stuck in to look like a flagpole.

After these specialized theme-based mithais started taking off, and the kitchen hands also got the hang of crafting unusual shapes and colour combinations, she came up with another clever suggestion which catapulted the company's fortunes to yet another level.

The boys were sitting with their mother one evening, when she said, while spooning sugar into the tea, 'Beta, I was thinking, why not custom-make boxes of sweets for offices in such a way that the sweets resemble their company logos. This could be sent out on festive occasions?'

Rajan Papa burst out laughing at the sheer reach of his mother's imagination. 'Ma, you are incredible. All the baniya genes of this family went and lodged themselves in you. You should have been born a boy.' He laughed at his own joke.

'Oh ho. Why do I have to be a boy when I am blessed with the best boys in the world on either side of me?'

Sunny stared at her, astonished at her acumen and said, 'Great idea, Ma!'

The Marwari shopowners of Kalbadevi, always hungry for innovation and one-upmanship, lapped up the idea and the orders started flowing. Soon Bimmo di Barfi was churning out mithais shaped like bunny rabbits (with almonds for ears) for the local ladies hosiery shop called Lovable Bunny Bras, and big round laddoos decorated with edible colouring to look like footballs which went to a wholesale sports shop. The only one that went a little off was when they attempted to make brown pedas shaped like tanpuras for the music instrument shop next door, and the first instalment looked like a box of miniature phalluses.

And so the business grew and grew until it became a household name associated with Diwali and good eating.

Mummyji's involvement in the business had its own repercussions and with the growing fortunes came the diminishing returns—nature gives with one hand, takes with the other. There was no doubt that both sons loved their mother but, there is a small possibility that, without realizing it, they resented her indispensability in the business. With Rajan Papa, content with sitting in his father's place manning the store, Mummyji's constant need to grow the business made him feel mildly inadequate. For Sunny, it was the opposite. He wanted to prove himself as the key man in the enterprise but silently endured the hierarchical role-playing of being the younger, obedient brother. He didn't agree with the way Rajan Papa was running the company, but did not have any say. But he knew he had to bide his time. His life was taking a different turn. He had fallen in love with, and was engaged to Jasmeen, a Sikh girl from Delhi whom he had met during a college festival. They were soon going to get married and fly off to America, where he had been admitted to a medium-grade business school in upstate New York.

Sunny never finished his degree. He found it terribly difficult to handle the killer combination of the workload, the cold winter, and a miserable wife who could not cope with the lonely life of a student with a very limited dollar budget. He asked Rajan Papa for more money, but no matter how much they had in India, it was not easy to convert rupees into dollars. The foreign exchange laws were very strict. There was only so much that could be sent through Bhatija's havala contacts without attracting the attention of the government. Getting caught could mean landing up in jail.

One freezing winter day, when the car got stuck in the driveway and Jassu was throwing a massive tantrum about having to cook daal every day, Sunny made an impulsive decision to return to Bombay. The day before they were leaving, they discovered they were going to have a baby.

When Rajan Papa went to pick up Sunny and his pregnant wife at the airport at an unearthly hour, he could see the tension on his younger brother's face. Rajan Papa gave him a tight hug and whispered, 'Do not worry, puttar,' just as his father would have done. 'Come and work in the shop. We need you there. Chalo, at least you had a nice taste of America and learned some new things.'

Sunny settled back into Cozy Villa and soon became involved with the sweet shop, especially the catering side which was teetering slightly and needed attention. Jassu took off for Delhi and spent most of her pregnant months going back and forth between the two cities.

From very early on, Sunny revealed a natural flair for business. While supervising a catering assignment at a wedding in the Santacruz Gymkhana, he formed a theory which he confirmed at another wedding at Khar Gymkhana the next night. He was strolling up and down the long buffet table, watching the guests greedily pile up their plates, when he noticed an emerging pattern. The sight of all that free food unleashed a monster of gluttony among the guests which blinded them to the nuances of taste. By the time the guest reached halfway down the table, two things were happening. Firstly, his plate had become already quite full and secondly, he would begin to suffer from an element of food fatigue. As a result, the amounts he picked up from the latter half of the table were much less. Sunny made it a point to watch the next wedding and found the same thing happening. So, he instructed his staff to keep the most expensive items, such as prawns or almond kofta, on the second half of the table and got away with making them in lesser quantities.

He also observed that customers would try and stinge on their cost by reusing the plate, for the caterers charged per plate. So, if the groom's father had finished eating, the mother would take the same plate and help herself to dinner on it. It was a case of one shrewd baniya versus another and, in this case, Sunny couldn't really do anything about the trickery. He merely told his staff to be aware of this and to whisk off a plate as soon as it seemed like the person had finished.

This once led to an ungainly plate tussle between an aggressive waiter and a woman of rather bulbous proportions. With both making a grab for the plate and trying to pull it from the other's clutches, some very brown curry ended up on the lady's strawberry pink georgette sari, which eventually cost Bimmo di Barfi one thousand rupees. Rajan Papa was not pleased by this. He called Sunny aside and told him that a few plates here or there would make no difference, but it was more important for there to be goodwill among customers. Sunny heard him out but decided that he would get his own way. He quietly started overinvoicing the number of plates. Some families got wind of this and started placing one of their own people at the head of the buffet to count the plates and ensure that there was no hanky-panky.

Rajan Papa learned of these new developments through Phoolchand's son who was now one of his senior managers. When it was brought to his attention, his forehead corrugated into that familiar frown. But he did not dwell on the issue. His brother was still young and he would give him time to understand that trust was the most important ingredient in the food business and that the greatest pleasure lay in customer satisfaction. Instead, he spoke about it to Mummyji, who nodded sagely and said, without taking sides, 'Kakka, he is learning. You must guide him. But it is something to think about, at least. After all, money is money and every plate adds up.'

Bimmo di Barfi remained closed on Mondays, the day most of the market was closed. Every Tuesday, around eleven, just after the shop opened, one of the first people to walk in was Daddyji's old friend, Kevalram, after he had spent an hour doing pooja at the Mumbadevi shrine down the road. Kevalram ran Melody Wholesalers, a shop that sold harmoniums, tablas, flutes, and banjos. Its proprieter Kevalram Khurana used to import old, slightly damaged formica sheets from Germany. His biggest clients were harmonium makers. Gradually, as Bombay grew more and more attached to the world of melody, his business flourished and he started manufacturing the harmoniums himself and then moved into making other instruments.

'Bauji. Welcome, welcome. What news from Punjab? I hope things are settling down a little.'

Kevalram nodded at Sunny who was sitting at a corner table and came and slapped Rajan Papa's arm.

'Not at all, Rajan. The families are really suffering. Last week, my uncle was sitting at his shop in Trunka di Gali, and he got summoned to the Golden Temple. He knew he had to go. There, on the first floor, one of the Sant's men told him, just like that, that he must give them half his farm plot. One full acre. Ancestral property. What is all this? Something needs to change. They are thinking of moving to Bombay, but I don't know where they will stay. The house in Wadala is too small, really. Okay, will you please get me a plate of jalebi?'

'This is very disturbing news, Bauji. No, no, I'm not going to give you jalebi. You know your diabetes problem. Mausiji will come after me with a rolling pin. Here, have some chhole instead; it's the best chhole in Bombay. And okay, you can have one jalebi, just for taste! Ho ho. Here, ji.'

'Punjab is in a mess. We had to cancel our trip because there had been a bandh in Ludhiana called by the Congress party in response to some Akali leaders showing disrespect to the Indian flag. And then there is that whole issue of whether Chandigarh should become a part of Punjab. Bad news everywhere...'

The customers were now filing in and the place was getting a bit noisier.

'Namaste, Thakur sahib. Please come, please come. Will you have your usual? Arre, kaun hai. Get Thakur sahib jalebi and gathiya and chai made with extra ginger and elaichi.' The withered Sindhi owner of the oldest wholesale cloth shop in the neighbourhood sat down with his head in his hands and lit up a cigarette.

'What is the matter? All well?'

'Yes, Rajan beta. Just that my daughter has decided to become an air hostess and her mother wants to get her married to one of her bhai-bandh relatives. They are constantly fighting at home. And I am caught between these two crazy girls.'

Thakur Bhojani always seemed to run into some problem or the other and the shop was like his refuge. A few years ago, a member of a local Hindu political party had shown up at his shop doorstep and made his life miserable, forcing him to change the name of his shop from Karachi Cloth Mart to Bombay Cloth Mart, which was painted over the old name in big orange letters. He had protested and told them that his brothers had mutilated several members of the minority community before leaving Karachi to come to Bombay, but it didn't work.

Sunny was reading the newspaper in a corner, and quietly watching his elder brother handle this stream of customers. Rajan Papa seemed so at ease here, just the way Daddyji had been. He knew everyone who came in, their tastes, their problems, even their insulin levels. He felt a pang of envy and a slight impatience. If his elder brother had his way, the business would remain exactly as it had been since Daddyji's days. He missed that cup of coffee and the muffin he had got used to having in the morning on campus on his way to class. Here, he could only get sugary milky tea. Maybe it was a mistake for him to have left America. He didn't fit in here. He had very different ideas about what business should be, ideas that involved bankers and expansion.

Sunny's eyes ran over an article titled 'Ravana spearheads revolt along with Hanuman and Sita'. It piqued his interest momentarily. 'Two hours before the main Dussehra show, while effigies across the city were being burned, the actor who played the role of Ravana produced his charter of demands against the show management. This included a forty per cent increase in wages, payment of overtime in accordance with the law, and dearness allowance. He was supported by both demons and gods...'

He went back to the front page because he remembered something that had caught his attention. It was the steep rise in the price of silver. 'Despite the ban on exporting silver since 1979, clandestine smuggling has been going on merrily, causing the price of silver to rise to Rs 3,500 per kg.' He mulled over it and then decided to bring it up with his brother after Bauji, Banwarilal, and the others had left.

But Rajan Papa was now chatting with someone else, passing on the information that he had just gathered and learning something new in turn. And this was how everyone got to know everything about everyone. Discussing any news at Bimmo di Barfi was like sending out a mass mailer into the community.

***

One of the best-kept secrets about the mithai business is that the delicate sheet of silver that is used to embellish mithai is made by Muslim men who expertly beat little pieces of the precious metal inside the soft folds of a sheep's intestine, until they are thinner than the finest tissue paper.

Once a day, their old-time supplier Javedbhai Varakwala would drive down with a big stainless steel box strapped on the back seat of his two-wheeler. The box contained layer upon layer of the delicate glistening silver sheets called varak, separated by butter paper. These would then be gently slapped on to the naked mithai, which lay like a beautiful bride awaiting her final jewels.

Although the price of silver had gone up, and therefore their costs, Bimmo di Barfi had not raised their sweet prices. There was an unwritten rule that price lists would be revised no more than once a year and that had already taken place.

Sunny thought that this method of making varak was not only disgustingly unhygienic, but led to wastage. Besides, it was patently non-vegetarian and it puzzled him that most customers were either unaware or chose to be in denial about the fact that the sweets they were eating, offering to gods, and serving at their weddings and poojas, was steeped in the juices of the filthy innards of an animal. He figured that there had to be a way out so that business did not suffer. He got in touch with an old friend who had been to engineering college and learned that one of his classmates had just imported a German technology that machine-made this varak. It was the first of its kind in India. He had just set up a small operation in Thane. Sunny went to meet his friend and got a sense of what it would cost as well as how it worked.

The brainwave came to him the morning his wife delivered their baby daughter in Delhi, while he sat smoking a cigarette in the bathroom in Cozy Villa. He chuckled silently to himself as the idea took shape. Ha! They would turn the sweet shop into a chain and advertise the outlets as the only hygienic vegetarian mithai shop. That would be their unique selling point, the differentiating factor, which is what all businesses need to survive and grow. He had written a paper on that in business school. Yes, and they would change the name. He saw an advertisement for Nirma detergent in the paper, a product that had given all the big multinational companies a run for their money. What an excellent, short, catchy name, he thought. They needed something like that. Something that was modern and scalable. He took the last drag and dropped the cigarette stub into the toilet bowl—even though he knew it irritated his mother when it didn't flush down.

Bimz—that's what they would call the chain.

Sunny suddenly felt heady from the two newborns in his life—his baby girl and his business plan. After his bath, he went and lay down on his bed, his towel still wrapped around him, and let it fall to the side. His mind was in a whirl. Should he talk to Mummyji first or to Rajan Papa about his idea? He also had to fly to Delhi to be with his wife and the baby. Oh god! He had a baby. How on earth did that happen? How could he be a father when he wasn't even sure about being a husband? They were so much better off as girlfriend and boyfriend. He felt a sense of panic. Sunny did what he found most reassuring when he was stressed. He braced his body for release, while thinking of a hazy, squirming Jassu the way he remembered her that night they spent in a wood cabin in the Catskill Mountains. He then lay on the bed, feeling lighter, debating whether he should have another cigarette, when he heard the door open. Mummyji walked in and he jumped up, clutching his towel.

'Mummy, how many times have I told you to knock before coming into my room?'

'What is the problem, Sunny? Don't forget I have seen you naked a thousand times! Just because you have become a father, don't think you can throw your weight around.' She giggled. 'Any way, come and have some hot hot parathas. I am ordering six boxes of mithai for you to take to your inlaws.'

As Sunny munched on his breakfast on the aquarium dining table, he suddenly felt sad. The excitement he had earlier felt over his business plan had gone away. Instead, he was irritated with his mother, frustrated with work, and fearful about the future. Then he remembered what his mother-in-law had said on the phone earlier that morning—that the baby had his eyes—and he managed to smile.

Sunny returned from Delhi within a week. Jassu was even more hormonal and bad-tempered than she had been during her pregnancy and he thought it best to leave her with her parents for some more time. Although he was elated to hold her, Sunny could barely connect with the infant who stared blankly at him and seemed to only want her mother's breast which is what he also wanted, but was not getting.

He went straight from the airport to Cozy Villa, and found his mother sitting in her armchair, with an enormous vat of boiled milk in front of her cooling under a whirring fan.

'Come come, kakka! Who does she look like? Is she fair or dark?' said Mummyji, ringing the bell for the servant. 'First tell me, would you like tea or lassi?'

'She looks just like you. Achha, Mummy, I wanted to talk to you about this idea I had for the business,' said Sunny, grinning as he pulled off his shoes with each foot.

'Tell me.' She shooed Ratansingh away and sat back, delighted to talk shop with her son, for she often felt alienated from the operations.

'But I don't know if Rajan Papa would agree.'

'You don't worry about that,' she said, with a hint of impatience.

And so Sunny laid out the idea meticulously, describing the technology that made varak and the advantage of rebranding the business. His mother listened carefully, her mind carefully absorbing the information, stopping only to dip her little finger into the milk to see if it had cooled. She asked how much the technology would cost. He told her that even though it was expensive, it would pay off in the long run.

'Let's do it,' she said and Sunny spontaneously touched her feet as if he had already struck a great business deal.

Armed with renewed confidence, Sunny decided to speak to Rajan Papa about his proposal. But it was Tuesday morning, and five minutes into the discussion, Rajan Papa became distracted by a group of old associates who came into the shop. Rajan Papa cut him short and got up to greet them in his usual good-humoured way and said to everyone present, 'My little brother now wants to teach me about business. About business, ho ho ho!'

Rajan had no idea that his innocent playful comment would have such an impact. Sunny felt belittled. The anger inside him started welling up. It was that same feeling of frustration he used to feel when his wife would pick arguments with him and he had no control over the situation. He left the office early that evening and went to an old bachelor friend's house for a party, where he had such a good time that he felt even more unhappy about his current situation.

Sunny tried to talk to Rajan Papa again the next day. This time, he brought with him his friend who had imported the technology and asked him to explain the details to Rajan Papa.

But even before he could listen to what Sunny had to say about the machinery, Rajan Papa said, 'But why, Sunny puttar? Javedbhai is our oldest supplier. His father was our father's friend.'

'What do you mean, Papaji?' growled Sunny. 'Business is business. There should be no friendship or emotions when it comes to work.'

'Okay. Look there are too many customers asking for me and one of the cooks has sprained his ankle. Can we please talk about this some other time?' He turned to Sunny's friend who looked uncomfortably at the floor. 'Hope you don't mind, Chetan? Please do have some tea.'

Sunny was livid. He walked outside with his friend and they sat in Sunny's car, smoking cigarettes. That was when he saw Javedbhai parking his two-wheeler outside the shop. Sunny narrowed his eyes like a wild beast that has just seen his prey and stepped out of his car. Javed went, as usual, into the courtyard at the back of the shop where the mithai was being made and stored.

Sunny followed him there and said, loud enough for all the cooks and their helpers to hear him, 'So, Javedbhai, I wonder if people really know how you make the varak.'

Javedbhai looked at him quizzically.

Hearing the commotion, Rajan Papa came into the kitchen area. 'What are you doing, Sunny puttar,' he said softly. 'Show some respect.'

'What respect? Why don't you show respect to me.' His voice was rising.

'Sunny…?' Rajan Papa had not heard this tone of voice coming from his brother. 'Calm down, brother…'

'I don't want to calm down. Stop treating me like a child.'

Rajan Papa looked helplessly at Javedbhai and then his forehead corrugated. He didn't know how to handle what was happening around him. He went back inside, sat down on one of the chairs in the eatery, and held his head with his hands. The happy space where people generally came to feel good suddenly smelt of hatred.

Just then, Sunny started shouting. 'We don't want your filthy stuff. We don't want to bring in disease.'

'Don't talk to me like that, please, Sunny sahib.'

'What do you mean don't talk to me like that? This is my shop.'

Then, in one indiscriminate, impulsive move, he did something that surprised even himself. He pushed Javedbhai. He didn't push very hard, it was more a shove, but the shock of it made the man fall backwards on to a pile of syrupy gulab jamun that started spreading into a sticky swamp on the floor. His hand landed on a tray of jalebi and his foot on a mound of flour, sending up a cloud of white dust. It was a terrible moment. He could barely lift himself off the floor of sticky sweetness and continued sitting in it for a few minutes, trying hopelessly to pick at bits of mithai stuck to his clothes.

Sunny and Rajan Papa stood in the middle of the debris, neither of them able to speak. Finally, Rajan Papa helped Javedbhai up and told one of the cooks to start cleaning up the mess.

Anger is usually a disguise for fear. And the intense fear that Sunny suddenly felt over what he had done gave vent to another burst of rage.

'How can you be so incompetent about everything, Rajan? You know nothing about how to make a business grow. This shop has remained the same for the last fifteen years. I can't bear to be here. I should have just stayed on and finished my degree. I don't know what came over me and brought me back to this dump.'

It was the first time in his life that he had called his brother by his name, without the added term of respect. Neither of them was aware of this, but terminology can entirely change the tenor of a relationship.

He then walked out of the kitchen, past the picture of Daddyji and his laminated laddoos that hung behind the cash register, out of the shop, and got into his car. Daddyji looked forlorn inside the photo frame. He knew that the fight between the two brothers was a karmic thing that they had no control over. They were playing out the battle that would have some day taken place between him and his wife. Sunny raced home to Cozy Villa, seething, barely able to see ahead of him, almost running over a stray cat.

It was not who was right or wrong in this pointless argument, but the fact that the staff of Bimmo di Barfi had witnessed this scene. They had seen it all—Sunny's disrespect, Rajan Papa's shock. That was the real horror of the situation. Rajan Papa would never be able to command the same respect after his younger brother—who was like his son—had spoken to him in this manner. In business, if anyone broke the protocol of hierarchy, everything became messy. Businesses and families thrived on strict lines of control, otherwise there would be anarchy.

As Rajan Papa helped Javedbhai clean the mess off his body with a cloth duster, with the help of one of the assistant cooks, his entire body trembled with humiliation. He then quietly walked past his staff, who looked down uncomfortably, and sat behind the register, his eyes smarting with tears.

Rajan Papa walked home that day, crossing over to Marine Drive. As he walked along the ocean, a stray dog bounded up and sniffed at his kurta, trying to lick the remainders of the gulab jamun syrup that was still stuck on him.

Later that night, as Rajan Papa sat alone in the dark in his living room, with only his glass of whiskey for company, he wept. What had happened? This was his younger brother, the one whom he had taught to wash his bottom, to tie his laces, to hold a cricket bat. He had speed-posted his college application to make sure it made the deadline, and used his contacts to break the queue so that he could get a brand new Premier Padmini before anyone else.

He remembered the long trunk call made to America in which he had counselled Sunny. Neither of them had vocalized what the troubles were, because men didn't discuss such things, but both knew the problems, and Rajan Papa had only offered reassurance and then made the big mistake of advising him to come home. He felt regret and confusion. Had he done the wrong thing? But he would never know that Sunny's rage was not really directed at him. It had merely found an easy target because rage is like that. It is senseless and volcanic and hits anything that comes in its way.

Fuelled by the alcohol, Rajan Papa became nostalgic. Life could play such cruel tricks. How strange that the flaky silver decoration on the sweets that had flung them apart had once brought them so close. It had been a most peculiar moment of bonding, involving a case of bad rabri and an Indian-style squatting toilet shaped like an elongated eight, one hot summer in Ludhiana.

They were at Mummyji's parents' old house in Wadiyanwalla Bazaar, deep inside the old city, where houses kissed each other across the street and where women didn't have phones but shouted from trellised windows, *'Bimla de munde bambaiyon ayen e!'* so that within hours, the entire community would get news that the boys from Bombay were visiting and they would somehow find an excuse to show up at the old house to see their fancy clothes and hear their accents and listen to their stories about their Anglo-Indian maid and their Parsi friends. Sunny must have been five and Rajan Papa almost seventeen.

The old house was near a gurdwara which had an imposing clock tower. There was no need for anyone in the house to wear a watch because if you looked out of any window you could see the clock. Everyone's timetable revolved around the call for prayers. In the afternoon, when aunts and grandmothers were snoring in darkened rooms, the cousins would run out to the neighbourhood murabba shop where they would get candied fruits in 200 gram pouches and guzzle them down. One day, as they were sitting in the shade under the porch awning, falling asleep to the sound of the gentle mooing from the buffaloes in the room behind them, they heard the sound that makes all children sit up like little dogs who have heard something no one else has—the jingle of Chachu, the ice-cream man. Chachu brought with him a lovely array of sweets made from the richest, creamiest milk. Sunny looked at the little pots filled with rabri, the silver varak on them glittering in the sun.

'Please can I have that, Rajan Papa?'

'You sure you don't want the kheer, Sunny? What about you, Surinder?' Surinder was their cousin who was exactly halfway in age between Sunny and Rajan Papa.

But Surinder was snoring, his mouth open, revealing teeth like little irregular pieces of stained marble.

'I want to eat that shiny silver,' said Sunny, jumping up and down.

'Can we have three, please, Chachu,' Rajan Papa handed him three rupees, and sat down to eat the yummy rabri. The one for Surinder was also soon devoured between the two brothers.

It was a rather enormous punishment for their small act of gluttony but later that night, the boys from Bombay faced the worst attack of crummy tummy. It started at around nine, as they were lying down on their charpoys on the terrace of the house, discussing whether magic was real or not after listening to a new spell that Surinder had made up to turn his father into a giant boondi laddoo which they could all nibble at. It was then that a light gurgling, like the sound of a distant brook, emanated from Rajan Papa's belly. He didn't pay it much attention until it came again, this time the brook giving way to a waterfall sensation in his bowels which made him shoot like an arrow to the bathroom on the corner of the terrace. He returned clutching his stomach and groaning. And that was when Sunny shouted, 'Rajan Papa! It's coming!'

Rajan Papa grabbed Sunny and took him to the bathroom where he held him as he squatted, howling at the pain in his stomach as firecrackers swooshed out of his tender baby buttocks.

The two brothers spent the rest of the night, back to back, their bottoms almost touching, on either side of the toilet, while their bodies churned out everything they had consumed in the past week. They finally lay down to rest when the granthi called out the dawn prayers, completely washed out and desperate to be back home where they could take toilet flushes for granted. Sunny clutched his elder brother the way he would his mother and fell asleep. The next day, their grandmother nursed them back to health, and Rajan Papa applied the healing ointment on Sunny's sore anus. By the following day, they were back at the murabba shop, bargaining for more of their favourite aam-papad.

The story had become part of family legend, just like Mummyji's seduction of the young sardar banker from Lahore with her khoya barfis. When she had first heard the story about the two brothers, Manju had laughed so hard that her blouse buttons almost burst.

The shop remained closed the next day. Sunny left for Delhi to be with his wife and newborn and, on Manju's insistence, Rajan Papa went on a long overdue holiday with his family and in-laws to the hills of Himachal. They went to the gurdwara in Manikaran along the Parvati river. There, he bathed in the hot springs that bubbled miraculously out of the icy waters and ate rice that had been cooked in it. He felt rejuvenated. During the drive back to Delhi, he snuggled up to his wife in the back seat of the Ambassador and felt grateful for her enduring support.

They had originally planned to visit the family in Ludhiana but changed their plans and stayed on in the tranquil hills. Visiting Punjab in the present climate was not a wise idea. The security of the region had deteriorated to a level not seen after Partition. Innocent villagers were being pulled off buses and gunned down. Young girls, pregnant women, even the elderly were being brutally raped and killed by the extremists. There was a sense of madness and desperation in the air and families lived in a constant state of terror.

Sometime during the month that Rajan Papa was away, Sunny invited Mummyji to a meeting with three investors at the Taj Mahal Hotel. She arrived with her big leather purse slung on her arm, wearing large black sunglasses. She liked the way they all stood up for her and kept addressing her as if her approval mattered. She was, after all, still chairman of the company. She didn't understand their language for they were using words like 'scalable' and 'franchise' but she got a sense that something new and exciting was about to happen.

'What do you think of a new name, madam?' the one with the funny American accent said, turning towards her suddenly. 'We were thinking of Mithais R Us—something different for India, something that will catch people's attention. But your son here wants to keep your name, although a short form of it, for good luck.'

'Mithai da Rus? It doesn't sound right.' She chuckled.

'Ma, you are so silly,' said Sunny warmly. 'No, we are going to call it Bimz, after you.'

When the cheque arrived, Mummyji liked the way they all fought to pay it and, especially, that eventually the one with the American accent did.

When Rajan Papa finally came back to Kalbadevi a month later, he noticed that his old wickerwork chair had been replaced by a new rexine one. That was the first of the changes that slowly crept up on him. He began to realize that while he had been away, Sunny had been working on Mummyji, convincing her that it was time to evolve into something more than a cosy little shop, that this kind of business would soon become outdated, and that with mechanization, they could cash in on the vegetarian model.

And then the worst happened. The two brothers were sitting with Mummyji in her living room. She chatted animatedly while her hands darted through a tray of basmati rice, picking out the gravel.

'Rajan beta, I think Sunny's idea for expansion is not bad, you know.' Her hands continued to move on autopilot, picking out grits and stones and setting them aside in a bowl.

Rajan Papa knew what was coming. He did not bother protesting. He drank his tea, chomped down two samosas, gave his mother a hug, and left.

Within a year, the shop had a new signboard outside with the name. 'BIMZ: the only vegetarian mithai shop in Bombay'. Gradually, two more small outlets sprouted—one in Colaba, the other in Dadar. They were all painted the same colour—pink with yellow stripes to create uniformity. A room next to the Kalbadevi shop was turned into a small corporate office. Rajan Papa continued to sit behind the cash register in the old shop but he knew he was getting more and more dispensable. Sunny became the main force behind the business, while Mummyji carried on contributing her ideas and recipes.

Sunny was secretly mortified over what he had done to his brother, but he had no idea how to handle it. Shame and ego came in the way of any reconciliation and the result was a complete breakdown in communication between them. They did not speak much, except for shop talk and superficial family matters which was usually monosyllabic. He felt embarrassed every time he came home and bumped into Phoolchand mama or Manju bhabhi. He would retreat to his room and soon found himself disconnecting more and more from the family.

That was when Sunny and Jassu decided to move out of Cozy Villa into their own home. They bought a small flat in Worli. Her father sent her some money to contribute to the purchase and also sent Premsingh, an old beloved servant who had been with her family for many years.

For a while, Manju's visits to Cozy Villa became less frequent. She was upset to see her husband hurt by his beloved mother. When she met Jassu, they would greet each other but then avoid eye contact and somehow breathe through the fog of hatred that enveloped them until one of them found an excuse to escape. The only thing that remained consistent was Mummyji's relationship with her beloved grandson Rahul. In her eyes, he was the only real Todarmal grandchild—for he was a son's son. She could not see beyond him and the feeling was mutual.

Mummyji could see her family disintegrating before her eyes but also chose to ignore it. Besides, her first child was the mithai business, and the money that came with it, and that took precedence over even her sons. If she had money, she would have her children around her, for money has a way of turning into a ball and chain that can invisibly shackle people to one another. If that went, there would be nothing.

There was one other little piece of history which no one knew about. While she was still breast-feeding baby Sunny many years ago, her husband had lost everything. Although she had put up a brave front, all her anxiety over money seeped into her body fluids and was sucked up by her unknowing son, who sent his hungry juices back to his mother. That intense bond remained with them for life and the same milk flowed into, and corrupted, the sweet business of life.

Food and money thus became this family's soulmates, one gorging on the other. Both settled inside them like gradually sedimenting fatty fixed deposits. They helped the family to eventually disintegrate. But Mummyji kept them together like a stick of Fevicol that was slowly drying up. She reminded them of childhood holidays spent in a house outside Ludhiana and of long train journeys on which four children shared little packets of aloo and puri and scared each other with torches when the lights went out. She bribed them with food from heaven and an endless supply of jewels and trinkets, which kept them coming for more.

The boys continued to come to her for solace from their lives, for she reminded them of how great they really were, how badly misunderstood. Despite his feelings of betrayal, Rajan Papa gradually fell back into a comfortably numb relationship with his mother. On his way back from or to the shop, he would spend an hour with her a couple of times a week, and Mummyji ensured that his visits never clashed with those of her other son. She would lay before him his favourite oily scrumptious snacks, the ones she claimed his wife never bothered to make for him. Monday was usually malpuas, syrupy and dreamy, soft in the centre and lightly crisp around the edges. Saturday, the day Mummyji visited the wholesale vegetable market, there would be fresh samosas, flaky on the outside and well-padded inside with the potatoes and peas that had been bought at that soul-satisfying ten per cent discount. This was the food that had brought them fame and wealth. Each plate came laden with many burps of satisfaction.

They discussed nothing in particular and everything under the sun, listening to each other's daily miseries—the price of potatoes going up, or how Rahul was growing more and more secretive—and gossiped about cousins and aunts, even the ones who were their friends. For them, mean banter was merely a harmless exercise in filling up a bored mind, there was no malice. They rarely argued. Mummyji continued to be his first love, someone who would always be forgiven.

Gradually, the women also fell back into their routine visits and she indulged them equally. When Manju came to Cozy Villa, she was told how uncouth her sister-in-law Jassu was. When Jassu was over, she was lavished with news about Manju's uncultured family. Daughters-in-law were pitted against each other and sisters were thrown into the ring as well. Suman was told that she was the favourite, and Saroj was made to believe that the most beautiful diamond bangles had been reserved for her.

She divided. She ruled.

Over the years, on Diwali, they continued to do the morning prayer in the shop, followed by the evening prayers in Mummyji's house, and then the two biggest rituals—dinner and presents. It was during this time, after the meal, and before the card session began, that Mummyji staked her place with the family. She gave out little boxes to each person and inside, there were not merely jewels, but well-thought-out strategies.

She wielded her family like little puppets and they happily danced along, year upon year upon year—until that last Diwali when India fell apart.

Three days before Diwali…

UPSTAIRS, MANJU WAS TWEEZING HER moustache hair and getting ready to leave for her card game at the Gymkhana. When Rajan Papa walked in, she handed him the phone and said, 'It's Mummyji. She wants to talk about the Diwali plans, and to make sure that you are picking up the fireworks from Mohammad Ali Road.'

He held the receiver to his ear and lay down on the bed.

'Jai Ram ji ki, Mummyji. Everything has been organized. You just take care of your yummy food, and I will bring the rest. And tell Ratansingh that he can't go on leave until after the pooja…after the pooja. I've also arranged for the little Laxmi statues and Manju will pick them up on Dhan Teras tomorrow. Oh yes, and Mummyji, I wanted to talk to you about something, so when I come over, we will discuss it…no, I'll tell you when I see you tomorrow.' Money was not something he wanted to talk about over the phone.

As Manju's taxi drew into the driveway of the Gymkhana, her hand reached into her purse and fingered the bundle of notes inside. Oh god, would there be enough to last through the month? Her brother was not very pleased about her father dishing out money to her periodically. His view was uncompromising. Girls are girls and boys are boys, and fathers must relinquish their responsibility once their daughters sat teary-eyed in the palanquin. Manju gently flicked off the fear that had been climbing over her, not realizing that fear doesn't like being summarily banished. So, it would seep its way into her skin, prompting purplish-brown rough patches to erupt on her body, especially near her elbows. She smiled slightly insanely to herself, opened a value pack of sweet betel powder and emptied half of it into the side of her month.

As she reached the entrance to the clubhouse, she saw her son Rahul standing at the gate with his tennis racket. What a lovely strapping young fellow he is, she thought. She blew him a kiss and he waved back. Rahul's attention was directed at a well-built man who had just emerged from the badminton courts, dripping with sweat and body heat. He stared at the muscular figure, then hastily turned away and unconsciously stroked the hard base of his racket with fervent finger movements.

By the time Manju got home, she was pleasantly mellow after finishing the betel powder and several rounds of mah-jong followed by rummy. She entered her living room and found her husband equally numb from his second peg. This was the time they liked each other most, which is what carried them through the reality of the next day. It was perfect—reality interspersed with delusion.

'Listen, shall I have dinner laid?' she asked, screwing off her earrings and sighing with relief. She was home, where there was no need to jab mini-chandeliers into her earlobes. 'By god, my ears are not in good shape at all.'

Rahul had stopped eating with them, preferring to have his tray of food sent into his room. The two of them sat on the dining table and Manju prattled on, dishing out details about some person they both barely knew, while Rajan Papa wiped the chicken gravy off his shiny white melamine plate with his roti. Dinner was followed by an hour of news on television—today, there was a section dedicated to terrorism and plane hijacks, revolving around a series of threats that Air India had been getting in their Canada office from an unnamed extremist Sikh group.

Manju nodded off. After Rajan Papa woke her up, they both headed to the bedroom they had occupied for the last twenty years.

As he passed his son's room, Rajan Papa heard the muffled music emanating from it, causing the walls and floor to thud silently. At his parents' insistence, fifteen-year-old Rahul had stuffed his mother's old saris under the door to make it more soundproof. He had readily agreed because it also made it smellproof. Now, without worrying, he could walk out on to his little balcony and smoke his green herbs to ease his terrifying confusion. Only the gulmohar tree outside knew what he was doing, and her crimson blossoms nodded sadly, with understanding.

All three of them had their substance of choice to help them deal with reality, making it more bearable, even fun.

Rajan Papa woke up an hour later to hear sounds coming from Rahul's bedroom. They sounded like grunts. He tried to believe it came from the television, which Rahul watched endlessly, but he knew that there could be other possibilities. He felt embarrassed that his son was now on the cusp of adulthood. He would no longer be the little boy of the family, who played on Mummyji's lap and pretended to drive on the tractor in the farm, just like in the album photographs. Rajan Papa recollected the picture of his bald two-year-old baby, the day after his head-shaving ceremony, sitting on a tractor with a much younger Mummyji holding him tight. He had a passing worrisome thought about how he never found him talking about girls—but then let it go.

Rajan Papa got up, stealthily walked into the kitchen and opened the round stainless steel box which contained the scrumptious crumbly laddoos that his mother had sent earlier that week. He popped one into his mouth and allowed it to melt on his tongue, savouring the crunchy almonds that had been seamlessly kneaded into the chickpea flour and jaggery, creating different textures for his senses. He ate another and felt his mother's love seep into his bloodstream and generate a sense of well-being. He closed the lid, running his index finger over the letters that had been crudely etched on the edge of the box so that it would always find its way back home. T-O-D-A-R-M-A-L.

He went into the bedroom where Manju lay snoring on her back with her mouth open, wearing a frilly blue nightie that had a bib of white lace smocking around her bust. It had climbed up to her knees, revealing fat white legs streaked with thin black hair. Feeling vaguely satisfied about the future, Rajan Papa went to bed, nestling under the armpit of his wife.

Rajan Papa was sitting on a white sheet, surrounded by a feast of his favourite foods, which an unidentifiable woman fed him, bit by bit. His mind suddenly switched to another channel. Now, a couple of men wearing masks like the ones in the movie he had just been watching barged into Bhatija's office. They started beating him to a pulp. Bhatija's secretary just sat there, staring at her nails. Rajan Papa was shaking her, asking her to do something.

He was woken with a start. Manju was shaking him. 'Listen, wake up, wake up.' He opened his eyes to see his wife's large face, covered with a yellow paste of egg and chickpea flour, on top of his. A small wet blob fell on his forehead. It took him a mini-second to register that it wasn't some awful apparition but, rather, his loving wife. She thrust a cordless telephone at him. 'Listen, it's Rajni. Mummyji has collapsed.'

SUMAN

Four days before Diwali...

OCTOBER IN MUMBAI, JUST BEFORE Diwali, can get unbearable. Most people escape from the burning concrete to their villages. By the end of October, just before the cooler winds from the north drift in, the air is so pregnant with humidity that even the pigeons don't have the energy to gurgle.

To cool themselves, Suman and Saroj sat on delicate wrought iron chairs on the veranda of Suman's spacious flat overlooking the Oval Maidan, and sipped salty lemonade which they had to make themselves because the cook had allegedly gone to meet a sick relative a few buildings down. The maid had quit the previous day. Servants did not last very long in her home because Suman insisted on paying the same salaries for the past ten years. More than her tight-fisted behaviour, servants became irked by the way she would scrutinize how much rice and daal they ate and constantly accuse them of eating her homemade pickles.

Suman plucked a couple of mint leaves from the potted plant in her veranda and popped them into the lemonade to add flavour. They sipped and gazed in silence. The green maidan gave relief and cooled the eyes. And one couldn't tire of gazing at the magnificent Gothic buildings looming on the other side. They evoked the glory days of a past that so many people craved. The good old days, when life was simple, servants did not answer back and wealth was a birthright.

Suman was in her black-and-white batik kaftan. She held a hand-painted paper fan in her hand and periodically flicked it to set off a whiff of warm wind. With the ludicrous fan, her kohl-lined eyes, pasty face, fleshy lips, and her pointed pink nails, Suman resembled an ageing geisha madam who was gradually losing control over her world.

The phone rang. Suman picked up the brand new cordless that her husband had brought back from Singapore. It was her mother's routine call after lunch. Mummyji prattled on about how she was preparing for the Diwali dinner next week. She asked her what she and Saroj were doing. She told her she was thinking of raising Rajni's salary and giving her a pair of bangles, but was concerned that the price of gold had crossed two thousand rupees. 'Not just that, beta, but the price of ghee has suddenly shot up to more than forty-six rupees a kilo.' That was Aarey. The higher-end Saurashtra ghee was more than sixty rupees.

Suman murmured her 'yes Mummyji, absolutely Mummyji', but her thoughts were somewhere else. She wanted to go to her mother's house and check the jewellery boxes to see who would get what before they were handed out on Diwali later that week. She switched back to her mother's favourite subject—ghee. 'Mummyji, the price rise was probably because the milk supply was being diverted these days to make things like cheese and butter. People's taste buds are changing.' Before putting the phone receiver down, she said she would see her later in the evening at Cozy, after her chanters meeting.

Suman shifted her weight on to one side of her body, lifted her buttock a little above the seat and let out a long noisy jet of hot air that had gathered in her belly after a hearty meal of rajma and rice. Her sister did not blink, for gasification had always been the normal, even welcome, outcome of a successful dining experience.

Although Suman had moved into loftier spiritual realms, and was now rapidly moving up the nirvana ladder to become one of the chosen leaders in her spiritual group, she had not been able to forgo elements of her former, more earthly existence. For instance, even though she generally wore white, she continued to wear her sly, see-through blouses which highlighted the seductive, lace trellises within. She knew Shyam liked this. Her nails were always perfectly manicured and painted in bright lustrous shades that set off the daunting sparkles which squatted smugly a few inches away. Her fingers bulged out of the rings like erectile penises, because the rings were always just a bit too tight. Vestiges of her old beauty still peeked out of the puffy body that had overwhelmed and disguised her looks. But inner beauty? The topic for numerous discourses she gave at people's homes? That was debatable.

'God is great. Everything will be all right. But if Daddyji were alive, things would be so different.'

'So true, behenji.'

Suman was not referring to anyone in particular, but voicing her general resentment at the world. Her younger sister, who had grown up in her shadow and continued to find shelter in it, generally agreed with everything she said.

'Baap re, did you see what Purnima's daughter-in-law was wearing the other day at the dinner?' Suman's voice lit up with enthusiasm at the prospect of demolishing a fellow citizen. 'I couldn't believe it. She was walking around in a low-cut kameez and had no chunni to cover her modesty. People have no decorum. I wonder how Purnima tolerates it.'

'The mother-in-law is no better. She plays cards all day. No one is in the house to say anything. What do you expect?'

The doorbell rang. A dog barked. Suman's daughter, Smriti, bounded in with her retriever, Toffee, behind her, both their tongues hanging out from heat. She pulled her walkman headphones off and gently massaged her ears where the plastic had clamped the flesh.

'Hi Saroj masi! What's new?' Smriti picked up her mother's drink and gulped it down.

'Hello beta. How are you? Where have you been? We never see you these days.'

Smriti dragged in a stool from the living room into the balcony and perched herself on it, petting Toffee, who continued to pant with his tongue hanging out, looking longingly at the drinks in front of him. Smriti had touches of her mother in her face—the fleshy lips and the creamy complexion—but there was a charming sparkle in her eyes which could only have come from her father.

'I was at the club. There was great commotion because they're debating whether they should let women become voting members. About time. Purnima aunty and her friends are behind this. It's totally cool.'

'Purnima should be taking care of things inside her home before worrying about outsiders and clubs and women's rights,' her mother retorted. 'That daughter-in-law of hers is completely out of control. She doesn't bother about what to wear and how to behave. In fact, that whole family is like that. Purnima goes out at night with her friends, while her husband stays home. Asking for trouble, if you ask me.'

'What do you expect, Ma? He is the most boring man on the face of this planet. At least the women have a life,' said Smriti, with a look of exaggerated disgust. She added, in a baby voice, 'Toffee, don't you agree, my baby?' She stroked her dog, momentarily distracted.

'I don't even like how they dress. There is no sense of modesty. They are always bounding around in loud costume jewellery. People would think they have no money. And Smriti, darling, why do you have to wear such short shorts?'

Smriti stared hard at her mother. 'You know, you people are hopeless. You have nothing better to do than sit around gossiping mindlessly about people who have no connection to your life. Just live and let live. I really don't know why I bother coming home. I always, always get depressed. Toffee, let's get out of here before we kill someone.' She jumped up from her seat, tossed her ponytail like a playful colt, and strode into the house, calling back, 'I won't be home for dinner. In fact, I am going out for a movie with Purnima aunty's daughter-in-law.'

Suman pursed her lips and stared blankly into the distance. Then, with practised condescension, she mumbled, 'Young blood. These days there is fire in everyone's home. It is the kalyug...' She sighed. 'Everything will be all right. God is great.'

Saroj mumbled in agreement. Pretty soon, they were both lying on the big couches in the darkened living room, flat on their backs, snoring loudly.

As they lay there, the afternoon shadows darkened and the ghosts began to tiptoe into Suman's dreams. She thought she heard the door open and her son Sumit entering. Or maybe it was her husband Shyam, after a long business trip. She recognized his step and wondered whether he was going to walk into the bedroom or back out again. She heard the door open and shut for the hundredth time in her life.

It didn't matter whether she was awake or asleep for the dream had always been the same—her husband went and came back and went again with his hanky and air ticket always flopping out of the jacket front pocket and a big smile on his face. The clock tower across the maidan chimed four times and the ghosts slipped away. She woke up, her back tense from unresolved dreaming, and rubbed her hands across her face in a few rapid strokes. She walked into her bedroom in a soporific daze. A portrait of her spiritual guru—a striking man with a long white beard and a white turban—stared down at her, smiling, patronizing; perhaps berating her for still feeling insecure about worldly matters.

In the bathroom, she stared at her reflection in the mirror. She turned her face this way and that way, preening like a contender in a beauty pageant, then slipped on the well-worn mask of placidity that made her face look like an alabaster statue, expressionless, almost other-worldly, with a faint Mona Lisa smile playing on the lips. She changed into her crisp white Kota sari embroidered with giant white butterflies, put on pink lipstick, rubbing her lips together to even out the colour, sprayed perfume under her armpits and left, in a cloud of cloying sickly sweetness, for her prayer meeting—while her sister continued to find solace in her very own dream world.

Suman entered the musty Baroque-style living room in a Cuffe Parade high-rise. The room was embellished with sculptures—a heavy-bosomed Greek goddess holding a robe to cover herself and a Chola-style bronze of Ganesha. She sat on a high-backed chair under a giant chandelier, with another senior chanter next to her and the audience in front. Her story today was about the elephants and the rope that bound them. 'There was a group of magnificent elephants who stood shifting their weight from one leg to another, as their legs were bound by rope. When someone asked their trainer why couldn't they just break free, he explained that when they were very young, they were tied to these ropes and then the ropes were strong enough to hold them. As they grew older, they became conditioned to believe that they would never be able to break the ropes even though they easily could. These powerful giants were stuck because of their past. We are all bound by our mindset and find it very difficult to break our conditioning. We hold on to a belief that we can't do something simply because we once failed. We must learn to break free,' she said.

There was a tea break and the group dispersed around the dining table where chai, coffee and bhajias had been laid out by a bearer clad in white. A beautiful woman came up to Suman. 'Behenji, I have brought five kilos of wheat and rice from our farm. Should I tell the driver to transfer them into your car?'

'Oh thank you! Tell me how much I owe you.' Suman beamed, reaching into her purse.

'Arre, nothing. Please do not embarrass me, behenji. You have changed our lives. Please consider it my Diwali present.'

Suman protested for a few seconds and then, with an exaggerated look of grudging acceptance, agreed to accept the generous gifts. She went back to her high chair and this time, the other leader took over. Her subject was the fine art of detachment. Suman wore a patronizing smile on her face while listening to the other woman's more earnest lecture.

'Do not allow yourselves to have ties to the world—even to your children, husbands, parents,' the woman declaimed. They sat around her, nodding like sages, murmuring their appreciation, goading her on.

'The bigger goal is more important. We have seen the truth. We have a direct link to the higher power.' More nods. They then chanted together, in high-pitched nasal tones.

After the prayer meeting, Suman instructed her driver to take her to Mummyji's house. They drove on Marine Drive under the strawberry pink sunset that emerged out of the leftover monsoon clouds. But Suman did not notice the colours. Nor did she see the calm ocean which licked the seafront wall. Her mind was still crowded with the murmurs of Teflon-coated women discussing their personal gods and their demons; she thought about the one who asked her whether it was all right for her not to attend her daughter's housewarming pooja, because she did not believe in such rituals. 'Do what you have to do, but with complete detachment,' Suman had replied, while the flock nodded sagely.

The previous week, she had told them the story of the farmer who went to a sadhu to learn the secret for eternal happiness. The sadhu had told him to find someone who was always happy and to bring back one of his shirts. The farmer went from house to house, but found that everyone was suffering from one thing or another—a wife who was a terrible cook, or a husband who was attracted to men, or too much debt, or a disobedient child. Finally, as he turned around dejected, he passed a stream and saw a man lying in the water, blissfully humming to himself. This man looks like he doesn't have a worry in the world, he thought. He went to him and asked him if he was always happy. The man replied, 'Of course!' Thrilled, the farmer asked him if he could take his shirt. The man laughed and said, 'I don't have one!'

Suman had puffed up like a white pigeon when she saw the warm murmur of gratitude that surged towards her after she told her story. Everyone could relate to the man who sought happiness and everyone felt relieved that it was not really accessible.

The car turned into the road where Mummyji lived. At one end was a famous hosiery shop, one of the first to stock foreign-made bras and underwear. Across that was Cozy Villa. At the corner of the gate sat a wizened old man with a basket in front of him, the centre of it filled with peanuts, gram and puffed rice, and the circumference mottled with a medley of coloured sweets. This sight always made Suman sigh with comfort, for the peanut and sweet vendor had been there since the time she was a child. This was home. She waved at him like a little girl when she passed him. He raised his hand to his forehead slowly, for although she had grown up and become a memsahib, he had remained where he was. The equation had changed.

She walked into the building, lifting the end of her sari pallu to her nose to keep out the sudden stench that emanated from the staff bathroom on the other side of the lift, next to Babu's ironing room. The lift wasn't working, as usual. She cursed under her breath and walked slowly up the long wooden stairs, breathing heavily. She felt dizzy by the time she reached the middle landing. As she looked up, her vision mildly blurred from the exertion, she saw her sister-in-law Manju shutting the front door behind her.

'Arre! Jai Ram ji ki, behenji,' said Manju chirpily, grinning to reveal a set of white pillars highlighted with brown. She was holding her sari pleats up slightly, which is what she always did to enable ease of movement.

Suman frowned and raised her hand slightly, too breathless to respond.

'Saroj has just come. Rajni has made hot-hot kachoris today. Okay, bye. I must run. I am late for rummy. See you next week, at the Diwali dinner.'

Suman broke into her sweet-and-low smile, where only her mouth curled up but the eyes did not flicker. They remained stone cold. She didn't trust either of her sisters-in-law, but that was also because she didn't trust most people. She remembered the time she and Rajan Papa went to see Manju when she was a prospective bride. Her brother was handsome and eligible, like freshly baked brown bread from the catering college in Switzerland.

Suman had accompanied him to his future in-laws' home, and watched intently as Manju sat there, pouring tea out of the family's best silver-plated set, her hand trembling slightly, but not for the naked eye to see. At twenty-one, she was a pleasant-looking girl, with a broad forehead, large brown eyes, and a nicely shaped nose. Suman looked at Manju's mother. She was well preserved, which meant that Manju too would grow into something palatable. Good stock, Suman had thought, as if she had just examined a cow. It was later that Suman and the rest of the family learned that their dusky daughter-in-law was terribly myopic, and she and her parents had hidden this throughout the couple's three-week mating period.

For some odd reason, Suman viewed that as a terrible betrayal and the venom stayed embedded in Suman's mind overriding anything else she may have felt about her brother's wife. She always held it against her. She also resented Manju's perpetually chirpy state. But what Suman hated the most was that she had no control over this sister-in-law because her father was so wealthy and anything she breathed for, she got. A daughter-in-law of the house was not supposed to be so independent. She just did not like it. Definitely not this simple creature with brandy-coloured eyes and thick glasses.

They crossed each other on the landing outside. The constant stream of visitors to Marine Drive was like a never-ending family relay—one person handed over the baton to another. They were collaborators but also competitors, which is how large families function. And the judge who gave out the trophies sat inside, sifting through her gigantic thali of rice, crunching the bad elements between her fingertips and casting them into a little katori, not entirely aware of her own crushing powers.

The minute Suman entered her mother's house, she felt at ease. Rajni and Ratansingh were standing at the two ends of the corridor, pulling the ends of a pale blue sari that had just been soaked in a starch solution to make it crisp like a papad, almost as if they were engaged in a martial art form. Suman found much comfort in this old practice. In the living room, Mummyji was sitting in her faded paisley-covered throne, next to the empty chair where Daddyji used to sit when they both held court together. Suman sat down heavily in her father's place.

Saroj was already there. After Suman had left, she had woken up and left for her mother's house. Ever since the terrible tragedy in her life, she spent her time floating silently, like a cloud no one pays attention to, between her mother's and her sister's homes and that third place that no one knew about.

On the other end of the room, under the statue of Mirabai hugging her slender one-string instrument, sat Bhatija, wearing a polyester white shirt, white pants and white socks. His moulding white shoes lay outside the room. If anyone bothered to look down, his left sock had a hole on the side of the left toe. He had a startlingly beaked nose and, under it, thin untrustworthy lips. His hair was lavishly oiled and slicked back. He sat with his feet pointing at each other, a flat black briefcase on his lap.

When Suman walked into the living room, Bhatija had finished his business and was snapping his briefcase shut. He then noisily slurped down the dregs from his teacup and got up to leave. As he slipped on his white leather shoes at the door, he said, 'Okay, till next month then, Mummyji. And I promise I will try and pay back Rajan babu soon…'

Mummyji lifted her hand in a gesture of saying bye and pretended not to hear the last comment. It was very complicated. They were all drinking from the same well. If Rajan got his money, she and the shop may get compromised. The business had also lent some money to

Bhatija and relied on the regular disbursements of interest income to run. That would not work. Someone had to pay the price. She had to take a call. Her elder son would have to bear the brunt, there was no other way. When Bhatija had laid the facts before her, she had given her answer and, later that evening, deftly deflected her guilt by making a special preparation of suji halwa to send her son, stirring into it her love and affection and commitment—but on her terms. It worked. Rajan Papa continued to come to Cozy Villa and sit, sometimes with his head tucked into her lap while she massaged his forehead after feeding him one of his favourite snacks.

Mummyji gently put the quandary of her eldest son's money problem out of her head and tugged at the ball of beige wool that sat near her feet. Clickety-clack, clickety-clack. The rhythm of the knitting needles lulled her into her Mummyji world. Her V-necked sweater for her darling Rahul was almost finished.

The four bundles of securely stapled notes lay on the coffee table next to her. Mummyji pulled out a hanky from her left sleeve where she usually stashed it, and placed it protectively on the money. After Bhatija had left, she pulled out two bundles and handed them to Saroj to lock away, keeping two aside. One would go into her purse, the other to her daughters Saroj and Suman, who would divide it equally between themselves, greedily, guiltlessly.

Saroj went into the Fairy Room, pulled the keys out from under the top right corner of the mattress, and opened the steel almirah. The door groaned, perhaps with the weight of all the silver that sat heavily inside.

She looked for another key from the bunch, the one which had the blackened graze on its surface which was its defining marker, and she twisted open the secret chamber.

This space was like Mummyji's external uterus—dark, cosy, comfortable, and mysterious. Saroj quietly put the two bundles inside and shut the door, too scared to let her fingers probe within the folds of the vault. This is why Mummyji trusted her.

Back in the living room, Suman was sucking her index finger in pain and rocking back and forth. Mummyji giggled conspiratorially as Saroj entered. 'Your sister broke her nail because she was in such a hurry to break open the staple on the bundle.'

'Oh no, behenji, show.' Saroj nursed her sister's torn crimson nail between her fingers gingerly. 'You should have let me do it.'

She went into the kitchen and returned with a knife and a pair of scissors. She took the bundle and then shook her head. There were two staples securing one side, and one on the other. But they were not regular staples; they were monstrous industrial staples that went right through the bundle. It was impossible to break this open with anything other than a set of pliers. Bhatija had secured the notes. He knew their importance. He had to make people sweat a little before they felt the crisp papery pleasure crackle in their fingers. Mummyji had made one small condition with Bhatija, which he indulged because she was one of his oldest customers. She always wanted her notes to be new, fresh off the mint.

Suman left after three cups of sugary tea and hot flaky mathris, with her pocket money tucked inside the inner pocket of her fake Louis Vuitton bag. Because of the little accident and her injured finger, she had forgotten to check on the jewel boxes. She clutched her bag as she swayed slightly down the stairs. What would she do without Mummyji? This was her comfort zone, where she broke her diet rules and gave vent to her basest thoughts and emotions, unfettered, often encouraged. Once she entered her own home, she would again slip on the mask that she wore for the rest of the world—for the god-flock, for her husband, for her son and daughter. And the only person who saw her move in and out of these incarnations, like a blithely oblivious schizophrenic, was her sister Saroj.

Suman had absolutely no idea that this would be the last handout she would get from her dear mother. From next week, there would be full-blown war. And she would have to bring out her trick dice. She had to play to win.

As her car sped down Marine Drive towards Churchgate, Suman thought of Shyam. Around this time of the day, at sundown, she sometimes missed him—actually, not so much him, but the idea of him. He was always away, either on some business trip abroad or spending months with his guru in the ashram near Haridwar. She hated entering an empty house with just the servants skulking around. Her daughter and son were never home and even if they were, she could hardly count on them for companionship. That is why she liked having her younger sister around, just for the company. Although she harboured an enduring disdain towards her, hated her weakness, her successive failures, at least she was an adult presence and not a servant waiting for his benefactor's back to turn so that he could get on the phone or watch his Bhojpuri porn.

Suman remembered the previous week, when she and Shyam sat on the dining table, not speaking much, but comfortable. She had ordered the servant to get him the black salt he loved to sprinkle on to his yogurt. She had read in a magazine that this particular condiment suppressed sexual desire and was fed to prison inmates. Later that night, Shyam had started kissing her neck and then climbed on top of her and she had actually enjoyed it. It had been a while.

***

Shyam had always been a courteous if distant husband, although their early years had been rocky. When they got married, they were like two teenagers who had been pulled out of the comfort zones of innocence and discovery, and thrust together in a grand ceremony meant more for the world than for them. Nothing changed inside them except that they were now living together in a big house. Shyam continued to live in the world of bachelorhood that he had just about entered with his mates, and Suman continued to be the vain, spoilt daughter of her parents, discontented by her husband's distance towards her.

She remembered her first Diwali with him. It had been a week before the festival, not even a year into her marriage. After dinner, he had gone into their room and shut the door. She had followed him in and stood by the window, looking into the courtyard below, braiding and rebraiding the end of her plait nervously.

'Suno ji, I would like some money to get Diwali gifts for the family. This year I also wish to get something small for everyone, especially for Sunny.'

Shyam did not say anything. He was silently clipping his toenails on a sheet of newspaper on the floor. He looked up at his beautiful wife, frowned, and continued to drop his nails on to a picture of the Prime Minister Indira Gandhi visiting a tribal community in Assam, wearing their traditional headgear of feathers. When he was done, he picked up the newspaper carefully, flushed the nails down the toilet and dropped the paper in the bin. He came back into the room, slipped off his clothes down to his underpants and, without saying a word, went off to sleep. That was when they still lived in the big white house in Girgaum, walking distance from the twinkling lights of Kennedy Bridge, where nights never ended.

In those days, her father-in-law Babaji was still alive, limping around and plotting chaos in the courtyard below. Babaji's world revolved around money. Every time he was displeased about something, he would transfer his expectations on to his son so that Shyam would become even more unsure about his ability to make money and therefore even more insecure about parting with it.

Suman was convinced of it. He was the ventriloquist and Shyam was his dummy. She was told by one of Shyam's outspoken relatives that it was because Babaji was so short and his late wife had been taller than him—their marriage had been clinched when they were both ten and no one knew that they would grow into disparate heights. He had transferred all his insecurities about his physical appearance into making money and holding it back, and that was the culture the entire family inherited.

From very early on, Suman learned to become a survivor, constantly fearful of her husband's irrational miserliness. She quietly launched a private investment scheme which trickled down from the household budget. She would, from the bundle of crisp cash that she got on the first of every month, count out one thousand rupees, sticking her fleshy index finger on her tongue to count the notes like she had seen her father and father-in-law do. She counted out hundred after hundred, releasing the pungent malafide odour of old notes—notes that had been touched by garlic sweat, incense, saliva, piss, perfume, as they went from hand to hand and imbibed all the daily detritus of the material world. The notes would then be stashed into her private locker. Later it would be sent to a small bank down the road where the cashier with a badly dyed moustache would re-count them and send them into one of thousands of little accounts. This was part of her survival scheme.

The two of them lived with all the trappings of a marriage, like the double bed and shared toothpaste and dispassionate sex, but the marriage itself had not yet set root. It was like an empty vessel. Neither had started dropping their coins into it—the little investments of thoughtfulness and care that eventually add up to a rewarding future together. But there is nothing consistent in a marriage. This curious befuddling relationship has a mind and momentum of its own quite separate from the two people involved. It ebbs and flows like a hungry tide, sometimes swathing the two people with unexpected and breathless love, other times evaporating to leave behind two desperate, bewildered, parched individuals. For Suman and Shyam, things started to change slowly, perhaps because of the chubby little boy who suddenly came into their lives.

When Sunny was nine years old, he was pulled out of school for bad behaviour. His parents could no longer handle him because of the pressures of the growing mithai business and he was sent to stay with his sister for a short while. Suman had been married a couple of years and they had not yet conceived. So, little Sunny entered an adult-heavy household that was thrilled to suddenly have a child in their midst. He was enveloped into it with ease and turned into the plaything that young girls—who were expected to turn into mature women too soon—still craved.

Suman spent her mornings dressing her little brother up as little Krishna, in a yellow dhoti, while her sister-in-law Sweety put on the lipstick and kohl. His curly lashes and fair skin made him a favourite with the whole family. Babaji arranged to bring in Masterji, a professor from Allahabad, who had sat patiently with Shyam as he ploughed through Premchand and Kabir, to come and do the same with Sunny.

Every alternate morning, when Masterji was not expected, Sunny would drive out with his Shyam jeeju to the typewriter showroom in Marine Lines in the big car. There, he would fool around on one of the machines, banging away at the keys and writing short letters to his mother, interspersing the red letters with black, or he would sit with the phone operator, Maria, and twist around the wires and plugs that crossed each other on the large switchboard. He would then be given either a sheet of carbon paper or tracing paper to play with and doodle on, and sent back home in time for lunch. These were perhaps among the happiest times in his life—and also in Suman's.

Every weekend, Suman took her little brother back home to their parents. On one such visit, Mummyji was sitting in her usual place, with an enormous vessel of milk in front of her and the fan on full speed. The milk had just arrived from the farm, had been quickly boiled and was cooling under the fan, after which it would be stored and transformed into some delectable mithai.

Rajni, Mummyji's new maid, was sitting on her haunches staring into the milk, while Mummyji was gossiping about her nephew Kundan who had just got engaged to a rich girl from a jeweller's family. Kundan's mother had boasted relentlessly about the wealth in the girl's family until she actually saw the bride for the first time and got the shock of her life. The girl was jet black. She came home and scolded Kundan's father saying that the girl was no match for her white-as-a-foreigner son, but he had laughed it off saying that it was too late to change anything; the wedding was the following month. Mummyji chuckled. Rajni smiled.

Sunny bounded into the room, gave his mother a quick

hug, and then went down to play cricket with his old friends on the street outside Cozy Villa. Suman sat down next to Mummyji, looking lovely in a pale blue shaded French chiffon sari with pearls around her neck, her hair tied into a low bun twisted out of two braids. When Mummyji saw her daughter, she winced. At twenty, the girl was gorgeous, and yet she had the cold sad eyes of a prize horse that knows it is loved only because of the fortunes it brings in. She told Rajni to bring tea and halwa for her and asked her to take the milk away.

Suman didn't have to say it, but Mummyji knew that she wasn't happy. But neither of them talked about it. It is too terrifying to acknowledge the pain of an adult child, especially the favoured spoilt daughter of the house. The mother could feel it, perhaps more strongly than her own afflictions, but she preferred to let life work itself out; she had faith in the process of life, in the inevitability of change. Instead of talking to her daughter, Mummyji started doing the only thing she knew to make up for sadness. She started giving her money.

A few months after Sunny had come to stay with them, and summer descended, Shyam and Suman took him on a long vacation to Srinagar, where they stayed on a houseboat on Dal Lake, in the days before blood started spilling into it. It was there, just before dawn broke and the day's first azaan drifted across the rippling waters that Shyam and Suman really connected as lovers, not just married people, and she conceived twins. It was almost like a belated long-awaited honeymoon. He kissed her longingly and hungrily for the first time. It could have been the purity of the air, the still mirror on the water, the absence of Babaji, the happy child curled up on the floor next to them, the scent of rose attar that filled their houseboat or just a change in the planetary configuration high above, but something changed and Shyam and Suman's marriage began amidst the chinar trees.

On their way back, the three of them went to Vaishno Devi, climbing up the rocky hill to the shrine with little red and gold bands fluttering on their heads and chanting, 'Jai Mata di'. While the two of them walked, Sunny went up on a pony, wearing a woollen cap and chanting the loudest of them all. His favourite part of the climb was crawling into the garbh jun, the rock cave which was supposed to symbolize a womb where the goddess had hidden for nine months. He loved the sensation of sliding through the cold rock as if he were in a Disneyland tunnel and then emerging into sunshine again.

Suman prayed for a son and for her husband's well-being and Shyam prayed for peace in the country and the success of his new electronic typewriter dealership. Sunny went back home to Cozy Villa and his reluctant parents soon after that, but like a musical chair that did not go empty, the twins Sumit and Smriti came into their lives.

As life went on, the magic of the chinars faded out and gave way to the more mundane motions of daily living. Bearing the burden of his father's ambitions, Shyam became more and more involved with his work and was away from home at least half the month. At some point, he found a guru in Haridwar which took him away from home even more. Suman was bored. She was too intelligent to be satisfied with kitty parties and beauty salons, so she too found a different spiritual group, which she cultivated with the same drive and zeal as if she were an ambitious executive in a corporate job, gradually climbing up the hierarchy of the order.

It was only years later, when Sumit and Smriti were older, that Suman realized how much she missed having her husband around. Yes, she had her children, but Sumit was away at boarding school, and she knew that Smriti would go away some day. Girls were only half yours and they always ended up belonging to someone else. Gender discrimination was embedded in their family. Babaji openly adored Sumit more than Smriti. While they were still living in the big house, he would tell the maid to pick out the choicest pieces of chicken from the curry for him before serving everyone else. Sumit always got new clothes and Smriti had to make do with hand-me-downs from her cousins.

Suman felt horribly alone most of the time. She woke up late one morning, well rested after a pill-induced sleep and remembered that it was her thirtieth birthday. Shyam was away in Germany and there was no news from him. The children were at school. She came outside and found a box of her favourite moong dal barfi sitting in a thali, along with a sealed envelope with her name written in her mother's familiar back-slanting handwriting: 'Suman rani'.

She looked over the balcony and saw Babaji downstairs, sitting on his bed in his white dhoti and kurta, fingering his prayer beads, probably plotting more ways in which he could control his son's movements and balance sheets. A man was pressing his feet. Some relatives and business associates were sitting around sipping tea next to him. She could hear Sweety didi, Shyam's sister, shouting at a servant over the water not being hot enough. She sighed and sat down at the long oval dining table. The room was in disarray, with carpets rolled up and everything lying in half-filled open boxes. A tiny cockroach scrambled out of a stack of records of Manna Dey and Madan Mohan, her husband's favourites. They were in the process of moving from the crumbling old house to their new flat overlooking the Oval Maidan where they would be on their own, with no Babaji and no Sweety didi, who had continued to live in the haveli with her ineffectual husband long after she got married.

Suman went into the bathroom, shut the door and turned on all the taps. That was the first time in her life that Suman cried plaintively to an ancient brass bucket, in a watery mingling of pain and prayer. She had to ensure that the gushing water drowned out her noise. That was how they used to live in those days—finding maddeningly short, desperate getaways in the midst of a chaotic household, where people creeped out of every corner and even the seemingly neutral furniture had eyes and ears.

That was almost ten years ago. Since then, they had moved out. Babaji died. But the irrational obsessions and patterns had already seeped into their flesh like chemical waste in soil whose effects last long afterwards and keep revealing themselves in ugly ways.

***

The Oval Maidan loomed large, dark and empty when Suman reached home after spending the evening at her mother's house. The commuters had slowly emptied out of the streets and it was too early for the night prowlers to start staggering in with their stained foil and soiled matchboxes. Suman listlessly walked into her building. As usual, her servants had not put the balcony lights on and the house felt gloomy, lonely. Shyam was away on one of his extended trips to Japan, negotiating a deal with a computer company, for word processing had now graduated to these new machines that beeped and blinked and made correcting the written word so much easier. More and more offices wanted them.

Saroj had decided to stay on at Mummyji's house to help her reorganize her cupboards in the Fairy Room and take out the dishes that would be needed for the Diwali dinner. She loved the familiarity of this task. In her childhood it had made her feel like a grown-up, and now it took her back to those days, when she would sit on a criss-crossed straw stool, with her frilly frock tucked between her knees, surrounded by inanimate objects, which she felt more comfortable being around.

Suman went straight to her bedroom, threw off her butterfly sari, blouse and petticoat and slipped on her black-and-white kaftan. She then popped two little white tablets into her mouth, poured a glass of water from the Eagle thermos flask left on her dresser, guzzled it down in one shot, and flopped on to her bed. Within minutes, the pain subsided and she entered the lovely forgiving space between her pink embroidered sheets.

She slept till noon the next day, waking up hungry and disoriented, only to be told by her servant that Rajan Papa had called six times. Something had happened. She didn't want to be told what it was, she already knew. She felt a sickening sensation in her gut. She picked up the phone and called the number that had stayed the same since she was a child. Rajni picked up the phone. Yes, she had collapsed. Yes, she is lying down now. Rajan Papa has gone home. The doctor has been there.

Suman went into the bathroom, sat on her steel bath stool, looked up at the faint cobwebs that dangled from the shower curtain, and wailed loudly like a deeply disturbed cat. It was the second time in her life that she had cried like this.

Suddenly, she stopped. Oh my god! What about the jewels and the land papers! She had better rush there to take care of business before someone else got to it. She gathered herself and put her mask back on like a reverse peel.

SUNNY

Three days before Diwali…

IT WAS A GOOD THING that Rajni did not call Sunny and Jassu that morning when she found Mummyji, for the young couple was, at that very moment, engaged in killing each other. In fact, around the time that Mummyji fell unconscious, her younger son was being lunged at with a sharply serrated bread knife by his wife. He, meanwhile, was fending her off with a golf club, and in the process managed to lacerate her left eyebrow.

Their daughter Diya woke up to the screaming. She had no idea what they were fighting about, but kept hearing 'that bitch, Lolita' and knew that this accursed person, who had become the faceless monster that invaded her dreams almost every night, had something to do with her parents' behaviour.

She had seen similar scenes between them before, and every time they transpired, the little girl would be sick in her stomach and shut herself in the toilet for hours until someone found her there. Her parents were not at all discreet and Diya was convinced that all the neighbours in their Worli high-rise had front-row seats for their reality show. Every time she went into the building elevator, she felt like people were looking at her with contempt or sympathy. She felt the same about the drivers and watchmen downstairs. It was awful and unfair. It didn't stop in the building. Gradually, she began to believe that even strangers on the road knew that there was something wrong with her and her family.

Diya lay in bed and heard her mother crying in loud honking shrieks. She went into the bathroom, shut the door so that she could no longer hear anything, and sat on the floor. There, on a furry pink bathmat, in bewildered hurt solitude, she lay silently, shedding dry tears.

Diya had fallen asleep on the pink rug when Premsingh, the cook, gently lifted her up and took her to the breakfast table. 'Baby, eat your eggs. You will be late for school.'

Diya pushed the plate away and put her head down sideways on the table. From this angle, in between strands of wet hair, she got a direct view of a photograph on the sideboard. It featured her parents bundled up in winter jackets standing in a forest of flaming orange somewhere in America. Their happy faces instantly reinforced the misery of the moment and she started crying, this time with real tears streaming down. Standing behind her, Premsingh looked even more miserable.

There had been no noise from the bedroom for a few minutes. Then her mother stormed out, holding her hand against her bleeding temple. 'Premsingh, give me the car keys. I have to get to the hospital to get this damn thing stitched up.'

'Memsahib, the driver will be here any minute. Please wait.'

Sunny came out and snatched the keys from his wife. 'You don't need stitches. But come on, I'll take you, if you insist on making a scene about it.' Then, under his breath, but not soft enough for it to pass his daughter he said, 'Bitch.'

He absent-mindedly kissed his daughter on her forehead.

'It's all right, I can manage,' said Jassu. 'God knows I can't rely on you for anything.'

She swished into the kitchen in her white satin robe and groped around for an ice cube, which she thrust on her left temple, but it slipped from her hand and fell on the floor. She left it there, cursed, and went back to the bedroom.

In the dining room, Sunny sat on a faux leather chair, his head in his hands, a furrow screaming across his forehead. Across him, a six-year-old was shooting him down with a stare which a child psychologist may have interpreted as, 'Why are you doing this to me? I will show you people. Just give me time.'

Diya was perhaps oblivious to the demons that were slowly lodging themselves inside her. She slipped off her chair and went inside to change into her school uniform. As she walked out of her room in her blue-and-white pin-striped pinafore, like a little princess prisoner, she glanced into her parents' room and saw her mother lying on the bed, holding an icepack to her forehead, staring at the ceiling, tears rolling down the sides of her head. Her father was still at the dining table and was now growling for a cup of tea. Without saying bye, she left the house, with Premsingh running after her.

'Diya baby. You've forgotten your tiffin. I made your favourite cheese and chutney sandwiches today.'

The old man, who had seen her since she was born, slipped the plastic box with Minnie Mouse on the cover into her satchel and gave her a gentle pat on the head, a gesture which contained unconditional love and yet held back on account of position, and historic justification, and the fact that even though she was younger than his granddaughters back home, she had the right to call him Prem, and that she was in shiny patent leather shoes, but he would always be barefooted with visibly worn and cracked heels, minding his place in the world.

He loved this little girl, this vulnerable offspring of a spoilt useless man and a hysterical woman. They were going to be late for the school bus. He carefully shut the door behind him, in a vain effort to protect his sahib and memsahib from the prying eyes of the world outside.

When Diya had left, and Jassu had stormed into the bedroom, the house felt anticlimactic and quiet. Sunny picked up the newspaper and scanned the headlines. Bhindranwale's supporters had been thrown out of the Golden Temple for shouting pro-Khalistan slogans inside. He frowned and thought to himself, at the rate things were going, someone was going to gun madam down. Mrs Gandhi was too aggressive for her own good. But then, things *had* got completely out of control. He remembered how, last year, one of his supplier's cousin's neighbours had randomly been gunned down by militants while travelling in a bus to Vaishno Devi. All of them...men and women and two young children...in a moment of ruthless anarchy.

Sunny's eyes moved further down the page and he saw the news item about the price of both sugar and ghee skyrocketing because of Diwali and his mind clicked into action. He started planning his day, remembering that he had to call back the investors and give them updates on the Diwali numbers.

Sunny had one extraordinary skill. No matter what was happening in his personal life, he was able to switch off and focus on business matters with the clarity of an eagle swooping on its prey. His thinking room was the toilet and he usually went through his mental memos while smoking his first morning cigarette snugly comfortable on the toilet seat. It was a daily ritual. He went inside and shut the door. As he lit up his Gold Flake, the first bullet point popped up in his head.

* He had to tick off Radheshyam in the main shop for cutting the barfis too small. It brought down the weight and therefore revenue. (People ordered by number of pieces, and he charged them by weight.)
* Four kilos of jalebi had to get to the state revenue minister Ramesh Sinha by eleven tomorrow in time for his daughter's roka ceremony.
* He had to return ten thousand to Bhatija. Actually, that could be done after Diwali. No hurry.
* Set up a meeting with Citibank to discuss business expansion loan.

* Finally, the tough stuff—human resources. This was his weakest link. He knew he should turn to Rajan Papa to handle such things but his pride prevented him from doing so. He was also insecure about his brother's special relationship with the staff. They seemed to connect much better with him. The issue on hand was that one of the assistant cooks, Pooran, had been creating problems at work, picking fights, and getting high in the middle of the working day. But he couldn't throw him out because no one else could make jalebis the way he did. He had somehow mastered the fine art of controlling the speed with which he twirled the muslin cloth over the griddle of hot oil and knowing just how much to squeeze it so that the resulting circles were neither too thick, nor too thin. He was the maestro of the perfect crunchy oozing golden-orange jalebi. Sunny made a quick decision. He would keep him. It was good for business.

Now that business was over, he thought about what he would do that day with his mistress, Lolita. He suddenly felt his groin tingle and he sensed a little movement in his tight VIP underwear. Maybe take her to one of those new video parlours in Bandra that had just opened. Lolita had a peculiar daytime passion. She loved speeding in a virtual Benz down unnaturally clean roads, passing tiny virtual towns with a McDonald's shack and a Shell petrol pump. Sunny, who drove a real car, didn't find these video games fun, but occasionally went along with her to Magicworld, her favourite parlour, picked up a softie ice cream and sat around while she played and laughed and whooped. In that moment, she was almost as innocent as Diya.

It was only at this time, when he saw the young people around him banging away at the video games, possibly bunking school, that he would remember his daughter, and feel a creepy sadness emerging from behind his navel. He would give in to the feeling and let it climb up through him and pulsate to '*Moongda moongda*' that shrieked all around on the speaker system. Then, it would settle into his being and maybe re-emerge, unannounced, in a fit of random rage.

Sunny remembered the last time they had gone together and Lolita had asked him for ten rupees worth of tokens and Sunny had slunk off mindlessly to the counter where a man looked leeringly at her, counted out his change and gave it to him.

Sunny came out of the bathroom, looked at his wife lying on the bed, her forearm over her eyes, and felt a jumbled up feeling of sadness and anger. He was confounded. Their marriage had begun with so much passion and in less than six years it had declined so rapidly.

***

Jasmeen Kaur Dhingra had fallen in love with her husband the day she saw him taking part in a motorcycle race in Bandra ten years ago. She had come from Delhi to participate in a Bombay college festival. He fell in love with her when he drove the same motorcycle to her grandparents' farmhouse in Jalandhar to meet her and ask her family if he could marry her.

She was Sikh, so neither family encouraged the relationship which, for a while was a heady buzz of letters and expensive telephone calls, but they went ahead and got married. It fitted nicely into his serial acts of mini-rebellion. And slowly, while they continued to love each other, it got shadowed over by the process of life.

Most marriage photographs have an invisible third person in the picture—sitting cross-legged on the man's head or peeping out from behind the woman, or smirking in between. It could be a manipulative parent, a distracting lover or a demanding business partner. They come in and out of the picture and the relationship changes, like a kaleidoscope over which there is no control. And so it goes, back and forth, back and forth, until you die.

The problems between Sunny and Jassu were really a battle between Sunny's mother and Jassu's father—the personalities that had played out through their children and unwittingly tutored them on the fundamentals of marriage destruction. Sunny had been raised to believe that he was the king of the world—his chubbiness had won him the Farex baby contest trophy and his mother never let him lose even at a game of carom—and then suddenly rejected because his parents got too busy. That combustible combination of too much and then too little attention made its impact.

Jasmeen, an only daughter and her father's pet, could match his history of pampering. Her father saw in her all the things he could never feel towards his wife. She was his girl. And he lavished her with the best of everything: school, clothes, holidays. In most of her childhood pictures, she stood posing in a tiara, her head tilted, a fake smile on her face.

The marriage started unravelling within the first year, in the unforgiving American winter when Sunny was in business school. The change was too dramatic all at once. Marriage, a new country. Neither of them could cope with suddenly being taken out of their sheltered worlds. They also shared some very intimate times, with only each other to rely on, on an idyllic campus, but it was Jassu who caved in. She hated the simple student life, the sudden isolation, and her demands on him grew and grew until finally, in sheer exasperation, they came back home to what they thought would make it better. But it didn't. Sunny's frustrations only got worse at home, and having a baby too soon when they both were still like children, only exacerbated their tensions. The tipping point came after the big fight with his brother whom he actually loved more than a parent.

For a marriage to work, either one of the two persons involved must give in to love. The problem arises when both expect the other to bend, and neither obliges. Instead of being grateful for the good moments, Jassu would pick on the bad ones with the immaturity of an only child who had never learned to share her toys. Like most people who don't understand love or are too scared to admit their vulnerability, what came across was the opposite of what they really felt. There were no translators to help them. So what was love led to fear and, in turn, violence.

Their fight that morning had been triggered because Jassu had asked him for some money to pay grocery bills and Diwali bonuses to the various wallahs that came to the door, and he had growled at her. Why couldn't she stick to the household budget? It was only the twentieth of the month. She then accused him of having an affair which she had perpetually begun to fling at his face ever since she had discovered the two incriminating Indian Airlines boarding cards in his briefcase.

Sunny knew that his home had become a lodging where he ate and slept, that he was living a parallel life in a pleasure dome. He had a mistress. But he wanted to have his family around too. He enjoyed the Sundays he spent at Pizza Corner with his wife and daughter. He admired her when she dressed up and accompanied him to his school friends' homes. But he was also growing tired of her hysterical demands and constant criticism of him.

In contrast to Jassu, Lolita never wanted anything from Sunny. She didn't even harbour illusions of marriage. She just wanted to nestle in that comfort of knowing that there was someone who cared about her, even if it was part time. It was life in shifts. The rest was darkness anyway. She thrived on that blank uncomplicated bliss that they both experienced after they had fucked—that space of high-octane release and exhilaration, where it didn't even matter who you were with or whether or not he was going to pull up his pants and go back home. That is why she always held him. Those five minutes sustained her until the next time.

Lolita's real name was not Lolita. She was Lalita. It was when she started working as a film extra that they rechristened her and, along with her, Malini became Melanie, and Bindu became Brendy (as distinct from Brandy). She worked for Lovely Ladys, which was in the business of providing the women that filled up the screen with thighs and cleavages and long black hair, like a pulsating background score.

Her boss, Pramod Kumar, the manager of Lovely Ladys, knew very little about films. But he had the single most important ingredient that guaranteed success in this profession—the right contacts. His brother-in-law was an assistant producer and, through him, Pramod managed to get business with film units that needed a steady supply of young women. Pramod supplied girls to films, where they had to dance or lounge around by a pool or lie back in shorts and sip coloured water in a villain's den. For swimming pool scenes, he charged extra.

Like most people in the fringes of the movie industry, Pramod had aspirations to eventually expand to Hollywood films, so he created an atmosphere that he thought was international. Not only did he rename the girls that worked for him with western names, but he encouraged them to dress in tight miniskirts or shorts, not the usual shimmery cholis and tight kurtas which most extras wore. This peculiar feature distinguished his girls from the rest.

Lalita was introduced to Pramod Kumar by her friend and roommate. Meena knew that Lalita had been looking for a secretary's job for six months and that she was not getting very far. The companies wanted someone with fast typing skills, at the very least, and she couldn't afford another class. She had already spent six months at Davar's to learn the basics but she always fell back into single-finger typing. There was one opening at a faucets company, but Lalita would have to commute more than two hours each way. Meena suggested that, in the meantime, she take advantage of her youth and figure, and apply for a job as a movie extra. It was a decent upmarket job, she coaxed—her sister (Shelley, née Sheela) worked as one—and it merely meant learning how to wear certain kinds of clothes, keep her body hairless, and learn a few dance steps. Lalita was twenty-five and knew that she had to make her own dowry—and future. She wanted to earn her own living, not depend on her parents and the pension of a postmaster general, when she said goodbye to Jabalpur and moved to the tiny flat in Borivli, on the border of Bombay. She did not harbour delusions of a moral high ground. Wearing tight shorts and lying languidly on a leopard-skin bedcover in a room next to the room where a villain was being bashed up? She could handle it. She had faced worse humiliation and assault merely making her way through Borivli station's crowded platforms in the morning, where fingers reached out, elbows shoved, and eyes constantly undressed her. A combination of pride and practical wisdom prompted her to put on her tightest pink kurta—the one which pushed her breasts out to create an inviting semi-hidden valley of pleasure—and take Bus no. 81 to a lane off Goregaon, at around the time that Pramod Kumar was getting ready to interview his crew of potential thighs.

He was doing his evening arti in front of a large portrait of Hanuman tearing his heart open with Ram and Sita coyly nestled inside, like the hero and heroine in a Hindi film poster, when she walked in. His eyes were shut. She waited respectfully behind him. Suddenly, he jumped on to the ground, lay flat, as if he were doing a push-up, touched his forehead to the floor, and then got up, with a loud 'Jai Shri Ram!' It was then that his attention shifted to the mortal Sita in pink who had been standing behind him. He looked her up and down and asked her to turn around once. He pulled out a measuring tape and wound it around her bosom with the dispassionate asexual professionalism of a blouse tailor. He then lit his incense sticks and continued his pooja. A few minutes after he had tinkled his little silver bell and chanted a verse from the Ram Charit Manas in a loud nasal voice, the deal was struck. She would earn a fixed amount of three hundred rupees every shift, plus a little extra for certain kinds of shots depending on the level of flesh exposed. Swimming pool scenes meant an extra hundred rupees and a V-necked shot with a bit of oozing breast may get her a little more. After three months, she would get a small allowance to buy clothes—they must be Indo-Western. They wanted to see a composite of Neetu Singh and Marilyn, women who were coquettish, yet vampish, a bit of wife, a bit of mistress. To start with, she would get roles on railway stations and gardens, while the hero and heroine pranced in the foreground. Once she got used to the atmosphere and the arc lights, and picked up a few things from the other girls, she would move on to the more important parts, where she would learn to sway and pirouette. A final word of reassurance, while he took an incense stick and rotated it around his safety vault, spreading the monkey god's good fortunes on the place where it most mattered. 'Sister, don't worry, the men are not allowed to touch the girls,' he said solemnly. 'Hanuman ki jai ho. Sankat mochan ki jai ho.' Lalita stared at him in disbelief and then thanked him by touching his feet.

The slit-eyed, honey-complexioned Lalita transformed herself into Lolita with seamless, strapless ease. She was a natural and soon she became an A-class extra, who was used in the five-star hotel scenes, and was always called upon when they needed a shot taken at the swimming pool of Sun n Sand hotel. She also learned how to twist and turn and made it to the front row of the dancing girls.

This was around the time that the enterprising Pramod Kumar decided to start a new enterprise, a dance bar. He went into partnership with a man whom everyone called Shetty and created a haven for the many men who had left their villages and towns and come to the city to join the film industry but found themselves languishing in a world filled with dreams and loneliness and stale make-up and alcohol breath. It was called Las Vegas Bar and Restaurant and it was an extension of the fantasy world in the neighbouring Film City.

Many of the employees of Lovely Ladys ended up working at the dance bar. They were exhilarated with their newfound financial independence. They revelled in the extra money and bought clothes from boutiques along Colaba Causeway or Hill Road, went to the movies, and sent some home to parents or siblings. Some of them were married and had babies. Shelley started buying imported cigarettes; she even started smoking ganja, which Topi, one of the spot boys, happily procured for a small cut.

What happened after the bar closed at two in the morning was up to the girls. About half of them, including Shelley, had experimented with the next level of seduction and had one or two regulars. But it was on their terms. They got to pick the ones they wanted, and discard the stale spent ones who exuded garlic sweat.

As for Lolita, her biggest indulgence was that she no longer had to bother waiting for the early morning train to go home; no more lonely platforms where her only companions were the homeless who made the trains their dormitory, and the vegetable vendors who had to hit the wholesale market before the heat rotted their greens. Now, she would blithely jump into a taxi with four others and was even willing to pay the extra bit it took to cross the city boundary and get to Borivli.

Six months into her job, her eye had learned to catch the men who were old enough to be bored with their wives, but young enough to want to splurge for a good time. They were the ones with crisp bundles bulging out of their pockets, which they would generously sprinkle on the blurred girl-visions as if they were pleasure goddesses on whom offerings must be showered.

Nights in Las Vegas were the perfect antidote for the indifferent married man—a blurry respite from the hyper-reality of home and wife, a seductive haven in which temptresses drifted in, playing on senses, tickling latent fantasies.

Sunny first went to the Las Vegas ladies' bar with a group of old college friends. A classmate's younger brother was getting married and this was his bachelor night. It was innocuous, even if seedy, fun—a bunch of men, exchanging crude jokes about women and about sardarjis, feeling slightly guilty for letting their eyes and imaginations run amok in a ladies' bar, but finding justification in one another's drunkenness.

He decided to go back a few months later because it was such an unbelievably easy option. Las Vegas was the kind of place that had cleverly positioned itself on the cusp of the permissible and the illicit. It was not an indecent joint. In fact, it was acceptable for a bunch of young businessmen to drop in there for a spot of titillation after drinks at the Gymkhana. Some of the more adventurous, voyeuristic wives even came with them. But an unspoken class barrier was their safety net. These were women whom they would watch, even lust for, in those brief strobe-lit moments, but eventually they would stagger home to their respectable lives to play golf, take their children swimming, and send their wives to learn how to make baked casseroles.

But then some of them got hooked.

Sunny started enjoying his nocturnal entertainment. He would make excuses at home—he had to take a customer out for dinner and he would be late coming home, or his old school friend was visiting from out of town and he was going to take him out somewhere near the airport. Luckily for him, Jassu travelled to Delhi every few months to see her parents and he was not answerable for extended stretches. Deep down, Jassu had a sense that Sunny's eyes had begun to wander and rest on alien breasts, but she preferred to do what most women in her position had been programmed to do—live in denial. She started spending more and more time away with her parents, a safe refuge where everything was once again picture perfect and she was the adored baby girl. The minute Diya's holidays rolled around, Jassu would be on a plane with her to Delhi, giving her husband a season ticket to party.

So one night at Las Vegas, Lolita swished up in front of Sunny as he sat on a purple velvet-cushioned chair, his eyes glistening with whisky. She was dancing to her favourite song—'*Aap jaisa koi meri zindagi mein aaye*'—punctuated by a volley of staccato pelvic thrusts. It helped that there was an attentive, attractive, and fallible audience member right in front of her. Sunny was not bad looking. He was tall, had his mother's fleshy lips, which were sheltered by a luscious moustache, a brilliant touch which elevated his machismo for Sunny firmly believed that for a woman to kiss a man without a moustache was like eating a fried egg without salt and pepper. It was his pride and he carefully trimmed it once a week to make sure its trailing ends did not interfere with his other defining asset, his lips. He was paranoid about his first white moustache hair turning up and examined himself in front of the mirror every other morning to ascertain his youthfulness.

This was an extremely attractive woman, he thought, unabashedly picturing his hands on her twenty-five-year-old, pre-maternal and ah-so-perfect breasts. Lolita, by now an expert on the male psyche, which she found surprisingly uncomplicated to deconstruct, gyrated up to him and bent low, on the pretext of picking up his empty glass, so that his moustache was almost tickling her cleavage. She smiled and winked. They were now playing '*Mehbooba mehbooba*', from Sunny's favourite film and he had started melting. He reached out, but she swirled away with masterful precision, allowing her turquoise chiffon pallu to leave a diaphanous veil behind her, and shook her index finger in an exaggerated gesture of faux admonishment, as one would tell a little child that what he was doing was not allowed.

When the music stopped, the girls were encouraged to go and chat with the clients. This was an opportunity for them to 'get to know one another' so that the men did not feel they were mere bystanders to a show but rather, favoured participants. It also helped them bond with any one particular woman, which ensnared them into doling out more crisp notes.

'What's your name?' She giggled.

In his haze, Sunny knew he was merely a customer, like so many before and more to come. But that was hardly relevant. She was giving him the attention he loved to get and sorely missed.

'Sam,' he volunteered, unwittingly playing into the Lalita–Lolita syndrome. He took her hand.

'Mister, no touching allowed here. But we can meet later, if you like. I get off in half and hour. Give me fifteen minutes to change, and I'll meet you at Pleasure Palace hotel in Bandra. Just leave a message at the reception about your room number.'

Sam had never done this before. Some of his friends had joked about it, and he had read of it in foreign men's magazines in articles—cutely titled 'Anatomy of an Affair' or 'A Survival Guide to Infidelity'—but this was an exciting first. He had another drink, called for the cheque, and took off. As he drove his brand new Maruti 800 on the dark road down Juhu, it suddenly started pouring. It was as if nature had consented with the moment. Sunny threw his head back and experienced a burst of passion that left him elated and, to his surprise, overcome with sobriety.

Lolita became Sunny's 'good friend', which was how she described their relationship. She introduced him to marijuana-laced sex and red lace crotchless underwear. She made him feel young and desirable. Her price? She convinced him to employ her as his secretary, and said that she would continue to work as a film extra if they needed her for a special scene. Months into the affair, they became bolder and started going out to nightclubs together where they would dance in frenzied ecstacy, lost in the middle of thousands of similarly sweaty, lusty bodies. Millions of twenty-somethings from small towns in India were swarming into Bombay, aspiring to become dancers, models, pilots, movie extras, marketing 'gurus', even good old-fashioned secretaries. Along the way, they discovered the thrill of a big city which shrouds its millions with wonderful, powerful, intoxicating anonymity. There were no neighbours to pry, no aunts to tell-tale. Everyone was too busy trying to make the 8.33 local. During the day, they worked at ad agencies, offices, hotels, brokerages. And at night, they put on their masks, smoked some charas, and melted into dark, throbbing night spots, where they pulled off the stopper on all the repressed energies that had been bottled inside for generations. Clubs, ladies' bars, discos and brothels, sprouted up in what used to be Udipi eateries and vegetarian 'family' restaurants. The ones that survived learned to work the cops to stay open later than the rules permitted, others closed down a few months after starting. The conservative party bleated relentlessly about propriety, sobriety, fidelity, and modesty, but Bombay winked back and did exactly the opposite. It was bad and really really good.

Lolita took Sunny to bars and clubs in the western suburbs where he was less likely to run into anyone he knew. They would sometimes try hash, called 'Manali' by the locals because of its origins, which the Las Vegas bouncer also gladly provided, for a much higher cut. Sex was even more intensified. Life was great. And business was going well. The price he had to pay was merely a hysterical wife.

Sometimes, the two of them took off from work and spent a steamy afternoon with the curtains drawn on the third floor of a hotel in Marine Drive called Ocean Breeze, where you could book a room for half a day—or night—and the seasoned receptionist acted as if you were checking into Club Med with your wife and two children.

The office of Bimz had a sense of what was going on but no one dared to talk about it. Instead, the office boys began treating Lalita Madam with the kind of respect that they would accord the boss's wife. The marketing manager knew that when Sir was travelling to Delhi or Hyderabad, Lalita would be out of the office too. But Lalita never threw her weight around. She was smart enough to know where she stood, she knew she would never be the wife, and anyway she enjoyed interacting with her colleagues, sharing their lunch tiffins, or taking the evening train home together.

Then it got dangerous.

It happened a few months before Mummyji's last Diwali. Sunny decided to play high stakes in his lust caution game: He took Lolita for lunch to Cozy Villa. He called his mother up and said that he was at a meeting, and was missing her potato curry, fluffy puris, and mango milkshake. Could he come over, but his colleague was also with him. Mummyji was always thrilled to feed any of her children and said that she would get the mangoes cut right away. Alphonso season was over, but she had payri.

The minute her younger son walked in with the girl, Mummyji knew that they were sleeping together. She sensed it in Sunny's good mood. He was never this relaxed and jocular. And she sensed it in Lolita's coyness, in the deliberate manner with which she moved her lips when she spoke. She was bending over herself to be respectful to Mummyji, almost like a bride meeting her mother-in-law for the first time

Oh well, thought Mummyji, faintly amused, even gleeful. They all do it. And anyway, his wife was a bit too strong-headed for her own good. She remembered the time Jassu had answered her back in front of the other children, and gritted her teeth. The stupid girl deserved this. Who did she think she was? Just because her father was some government officer who was close to the home minister didn't give her the right to be haughty. They weren't even rich. Besides, didn't she give Jassu enough jewellery? She should be happy with that.

What mattered above all else was that her son Sunny be happy. She had always had that special little spot for him. He was after all...she quickly stopped the thought. Mummyji's head spun with all these thoughts before taking roost on Lolita's breasts.

'The mangoes are ripe and perfect for the milkshake,' said Mummyji, smiling at her own wickedness. 'Do you want to wash your hands, dear?'

Long after the aquarium dining table had been emptied of its fish, meals at Mummyji's house were served in the living room. It was the room where Mummyji spent most of her time during the day, gossiping on the phone, reprimanding the servants, and sitting with one or another family member, knitting sweaters for her grandchildren. It was a strange L-shaped room, with tiny frosted windows, which hardly let in any light. At one end of the room there was a life-sized portrait of Mahatma Gandhi with thousands of little people in white behind him, which had been commissioned by Mummyji's father-in-law. For some reason, there was a musty mouldy curtain that was drawn across it most of the time, as if it were shutting out an era of forced idealism.

After lunch Mummyji lay down on a sofa and started snoring gently. Sunny burped loudly, fetid and erotic, simultaneously flickering his tongue at Lolita. They went into the Fairy Room, locked the door and lit a joint. Sunny threw Mummyji's neatly folded saris to one corner of the bed and lay down, pulling Lolita on top of him. The familiarity of being in the room where he had lived as a child, and where he had played hide-and-seek with his siblings and cousins, made him feel more wholesome, less guilty, and breathed confidence into his lovemaking, his adult game of hide-and-seek.

Sunny woke up to the sound of something scraping against the balcony door. He nudged Lolita. Without bothering to find out what it was, he got up and went straight into the bathroom, without closing the door behind him. Lolita hastily got up, straightened her clothes, and looked around her. She glanced at a photograph of the family, taken at some wedding—Mummyji in the middle, wearing a white-and-gold silk Kanjeevaram sari, surrounded by her four children, their spouses, and the grandchildren—and she felt a short sharp pull in her stomach. She quickly looked away from it. What was she doing? She had no business being here. But the guilt was quickly crowded out by her own overwhelming misery. She had not had much of family life and because of that no one else had a right to one. Besides, Sunny and she were fond of each other, and didn't that matter? She sighed and stared at her shiny fuchsia toenail. Tomorrow she would try another shade. Her mind wandered off to the parlour and started fixating on the colours she could remember in the little silver tray. She smiled to herself. Maybe a soft cuddly baby pink.

They opened the door and the sour smell of sex floated out. Rajni was standing there, holding some freshly ironed clothes. She quickly looked at the floor, mute and expressionless. Sunny sauntered past the living room, where Mummyji still lay, now awake. 'I'm off, Ma,' he said, without stepping inside.

'Come again!' said Mummyji, to Sunny and, by default, also to Lolita. With those two words, she was condoning her son's parallel life of sin. Life was a lonely job. She wanted to see her children as much as possible, and if it meant that she had to cheat her way into fulfilling her desire, so be it. This disgusting girl would be her conduit to getting Sunny to spend more time with her.

The way he said 'I'm off, Ma' reminded her of the time he used to run downstairs to play cricket with the boys. She was always so distracted with housework and Daddyji's incessant demands and then the mithai business, that she hardly knew when he came in and when he left. He grew up virtually an orphan in a crowded joint family. There was nothing she could have done. Mummyji sighed, wiped the beads of perspiration from above her lip with the back of her sari, and slowly got up to go to the bathroom, remembering that sad time when she was forced to send Sunny away...

When Sunny was nine years old, he had been sent to stay with his elder sister Suman and her husband Shyam. Things were getting worse and worse until his parents could no longer handle him. Every week, his teachers at St Joseph's Boys' Academy would send an exasperated message home to say that he was a terrible influence on the other boys in his class. When they were doing their sums, he would make paper rockets and send them flying across the classroom, even at the risk of being caned. His exercise books were filled with doodles rather than the twelve times table or the Lord's Prayer. The only reason he didn't get thrown out was because he was so intelligent and that despite everything, he would manage to ace his tests. This is how he kept people at bay—by behaving obnoxiously and then coming out with flying colours.

But on a humid April evening Sunny hit the final wrong button. Mummyji had just finished supervising an order of suji halwa and dahi bhalla for a wedding party of more than one hundred people and was about to go and lie down. Her back ached with exhaustion and her head buzzed from the limited oxygen in the airless kitchen. She decided to go and stand in the balcony for a few seconds. As she pushed open the opaque green glass doors, she found that all the clothes hanging out to dry had holes burnt through them with incense sticks. It was not just their clothes but the saris from the floor above that flapped into their balcony, that had also been mutilated. Above all, the sight of seeing the beloved purple and green French chiffon sari she had just bought thus destroyed, made something in her snap. She walked back inside, as if in slow motion, delaying her responses, like a wounded tigress, and lay on the bed. When Sunny walked into the room, obliviously whistling to himself, she jumped up, held his left ear, and slapped him hard across the face.

'I didn't do it. I didn't do it,' he screamed, in between howls of pain.

She hadn't even accused him of the burned holes, but he knew what he was being reprimanded for. 'Saroj behenji did it. It was her idea. I promise. I'm sorry. I'm sorry.'

Mummyji's rage was fuelled by his lies and, as if making up for all the years of not correcting him, she continued to beat him with unexpected vengeance until he lay crouched and whimpering on the floor.

If someone had attempted to read a little overweight boy's mind as he lay there nursing his wounds, half asleep, one may have seen a sharp cry for attention, which his exhausted parents had not bothered to decode. All he wanted was a hug, a kiss of reassurance, a little more time and a little understanding. Instead, every time he turned to his mother, he would be given syrupy gulab jamun and told to go and play.

By the time Daddyji came home from the shop, Mummyji had made up her mind. She could no longer deal with the pressure of raising her last child, and also worry about getting the dark one married. The business was now so successful and they could not afford to lose momentum. Rajan Papa had been sent to Switzerland for a one-year course in catering so that they could move to the next level and make the shop more professional. She was maniacally obsessed about the business, even more than her husband, who was turning more and more to clairvoyants and astrologers for advice and growing more and more despondent.

Daddyji's index finger slowly rotated on the black telephone, dialling Gupta House. The old servant Bhimrao answered and Daddyji could hear the radio blaring a song from *Aradhana* in the background. Shyam and Suman were not home. No, the whole family was out. They had gone to a fund-raising event for the Bangladesh war veterans. Lata Mangeshkar was singing at Birla Matoshri hall. He left a message that Shyam should call back and lay down, absent-mindedly stroking the sleeping Sunny's head. He knew that his little son was in trouble, but he was too tired to move beyond that initial thought and respond to it. His acidity had already started creeping up towards his gullet, making him feel more wretched. He got up and reached out for the stainless steel glass next to the bed. Even the sprinkling of mint inside the water didn't help for his condition was now well beyond simple indigestion.

On the other side of Sunny lay Mummyji, half asleep and unable to shut out the buzzing inside her head. She was tired of her children. Just for a nanosecond, that moment when a thought is not fully formed, she wished them all dead.

Sunny and Lolita's visits to Mummyji's house became more and more frequent, mostly as a retreat into the Fairy Room. He had figured that none of the others showed up in the afternoon, so that was the time he came. Saroj behenji would be around but who cared about her. He could have easily taken Lolita to his own home, but that would risk the neighbours seeing him. Besides, Premsingh was there. And somehow, he didn't have the guts. Maybe there was too much of Diya's presence in that place. In any case, Mummyji's home was his marked territory. It was where he had been able to get away with much more than just a sexual transgression. He had lied, he had cheated, he had stolen...and no one had really cared. He couldn't exactly place why he was so comfortable taking his girlfriend to his childhood home, the home of parallel lives and deceit. When he entered the Fairy Room, it was almost as if he was in a space that reversed the judgements of the outside world. He was a king and the pink walls, the old bed, and the embossed cherubs on the ceiling cheered him and comforted him.

All Mummyji focused on was what she knew best—feeding Sunny. She regressed forty years and tried to make up for lost time. Miserably, manipulatively, she indulged him. He was the naughty toddler, and she was the mother, trying to get him to love her, to be next to her, to be her unconditional friend in a world that didn't seem to care.

The only day Sunny didn't come was Friday, the day that his wife usually came around for her duty-bound visit to her mother-in-law. Mummyji and Jassu mostly despised each other but, once a week, kept up a pretence of conversation—about the rising price of vegetables, the problems they had with servants, and other meaningless gossip. This is how women had been tutored, to create layer after layer of dishonesty within themselves that would calcify so that soon enough, the real feelings were trapped deep within, without oxygen to breathe and grow and die a natural death—or take the form of a child who would be trained to seek revenge.

Jassu had only one thing in her mind, like a bad mantra that kept repeating itself, when she came to see Mummyji. She had her eye on the crown jewels. The ones that she had seen only once—the day she got married, sparkling on Mummyji's ears like car headlights. They were the ones that had caused murmurs of wonder among lascivious relatives, who judged human beings entirely based on the baubles around their neck and on their lobes. She wanted desperately to get them for herself. She knew she would have to stay on her mother-in-law's good side—even if she couldn't stand the sight of her son.

***

When Rajan Papa called Sunny to tell him about Mummyji's collapse on the morning of their domestic fight, he had just emerged from his thinking room and lay down on the bed, his towel wrapped around his waist. Next to him lay his now subdued wife. Her eyes were shut, but she was not sleeping. She lay like a silent tigress, calculating her next move, figuring out a range of revenge possibilities. Premsingh answered the phone and knocked tentatively on the master bedroom door. 'Sahib...'

'What is it?' Sunny barked from inside.

'It's Rajan Papa. He says it's urgent.'

Sunny picked up the handset next to his bed and heard his elder brother's grave voice at the other end. He sat up and turned to his wife, his voice hoarse, subdued. 'Mummyji has had a stroke. We have to go there right away.'

Without flinching, Jassu said, 'You carry on. I'll come later.' It was a perfect jab. She wanted him to know that she didn't care about him, so she couldn't care less about his mother.

A momentary memory passed through her and she remembered the day she had been betrayed by Mummyji.

It was a couple of months ago, on Diya's fifth birthday, that Jassu had found two boarding cards inside her husband's briefcase. They were from Bombay to Goa, one for him and one for Lalita Chopra. He had told her he was going to Calcutta to meet the people who ran Bharat Sweets. Everything started falling into place and the deep denial that had surrounded her like a halo, gave way to reveal a terrible truth. Her husband was having an affair. She had gone numb and allowed it to sink in. It all started making sense. They had stopped having sex over the past year, except very occasionally; he had grown more and more distant and angry; he never wanted to accompany her and Diya to Delhi, even during the holidays...and then that evening when she had called the office and the watchman had said that sahib left long ago, but he had told her he was working late...Oh god! But when she confronted him, he had denied it, saying that she was paranoid and crazy. She had no reason to worry. He had had a one-night stand, and that was it. She had gone to Mummyji and talked about it, and complained and hoped for empathy and support. And Mummyji had said, 'Koi nahin. They all do it.'

Even that she could handle. Mummyji belonged to a different generation. She knew her mother would have probably said the same thing and dismissed her. But Jassu was still smarting from the remark made by her sister-in-law a few days ago, on Karva Chauth, the day they all fasted for their husbands' well-being.

Jassu was at Cozy Villa, getting mehendi put on her hands, her stomach aching with hunger and with anger at what she was putting herself through for a man who didn't care. Manju was pottering in and out of the room, and Saroj was scanning the newspaper to find out what time the moon was expected to show its silvery face to all the starving women of India.

Suman behenji walked in and said, 'Well, well, you look nice, Jassu. I love that crimson colour on you. Really offsets your skin! I hope that silly brother of mine realizes that only his wife can be the real woman in his life.'

Manju looked hastily at Jassu, a flicker of competitive triumph giving way to genuine sympathy, for a husband's transgressions tend to instantly become a collective female problem, and can foster bonding between the most unlikely women. But Jassu had caught the expression and, while she laughed off the remark, she smarted for days afterwards.

Later that morning, as she contemplated her murky future over an angry steaming cup of tea, Jassu decided that she didn't have a choice. She would stay with this man, but she would extract her pound of flesh. Her eyes glazed over the newspaper in front of her and she read the quote for the day: *Faith is the bird that feels the light and sings when the dawn is still dark*—Rabindranath Tagore. Her mind flickered into the time she and Sunny had gone together to the Golden Temple soon after they were married, and she had sat with him at the edge of the lake at night, staring at the shimmering golden reflection in the water, lulled by the calming sound of the shabad.

Suddenly, her eyes brimmed over as she was overcome with terror at what had happened to her, her sense of faith, her love, all lost. She didn't allow her true feelings to surface. Instead, she let the dark side take over. She pulled out a quiver filled with arrows of vindication. She said to herself that there was only one way to get back at him. She had to get her share of the pie and somehow get out with Diya. She had to win over Mummyji.

But now, what had happened to her cursed mother-in-law? She sipped her tea and stared at the curly purple design on the delicate Japanese-made porcelain cup, which was part of a larger set that lay inside a glass cabinet in Cozy Villa. It was one of many trophies Mummyji kept on display to keep her flock hungry. Jassu dipped her manicured index finger into the tea, pulled out a corrugated film of brown malai, and flicked it on to the saucer before licking her finger clean. She looked into the teacup. To her, it looked half empty.

SAROJ

Four days before Diwali...

SAROJ EMERGED FROM THE FAIRY Room wearing a faded salwar kameez, her hair uncombed. Mummyji was doing daily accounts with Rajni.

'We will do this later, Rajni. Get behenji's tea,' said Mummyji. 'Jai Ram ji ki. Chalo, Saroj. Let's go shopping to Bhuleshwar and get you some new suits for Diwali. We will get good discounts at Thakur's shop. I've called the tailor in the afternoon. We could go tomorrow, but it is Dhan Teras and it will be just too crowded.'

'No Ma, I'm not in the mood, really.'

Saroj sat on the dining table and stared sadly into the murky emptiness where fish had once glided. The water had long been drained out and there was now a long thin crack in one corner of the glass top. She found comfort in its shabbiness.

It had been several months since the tragedy that had turned Saroj into a corpse that walked. From where to where, thought Mummyji, every time she saw her daughter's empty ear lobes and naked fingers. A girl must always have a certain minimum amount of gold jangling on her—naked wrists are the ultimate display of penury.

This daughter of hers dressed like a widow, even though she wasn't one. In fact, compared with her other children, she had got the most amount of jewellery at the time of her wedding. That was only ten years ago but it seemed like an eternity.

***

When Saroj got married, the entire community was struck by the outrageous display of wealth. The groom arrived on a chariot, with two horses instead of one. They chartered an entire aeroplane to fly down their friends and family to Bombay for the wedding. Mahendra Mohan's family owned steel mills, electric cable mills, acres and acres of land, and even a small medieval fort in northern Haryana.

It was a major coup for Mummyji, who had conspired painstakingly to get her children married well. By the time it was her younger daughter's turn, Daddyji had gone and she had had to handle the alliance market on her own. She had waited several years before she found the right person. In fact, Saroj had crossed twenty-four when she was a bride and that was ancient for a girl.

Mummyji didn't stop boasting about her son-in-law for weeks after the wedding. She blathered on about how they used crushed pearls instead of rice to put on the teeka. She claimed they threw silver coins along with flowers at the time the couple garlanded each other. She described in riveting detail, especially to the eternally envious Swarno behenji, Daddyji's cousin, the jewels and clothes that had come for her and the rest of her family, elaborately gift-wrapped with noisy crimson cellophane and gold ribbon.

Soon after the wedding was over, she called Narottamdas, the marriage broker, with eyes the colour of shit. Within an hour, he was over at the house to collect the envelope which would carry his commission—a fixed percentage of the cost of the wedding. He had already collected his share from the other side, taking the train to the small dusty town outside Delhi where the family of Rai Sahib Daulatram Mohan lived.

Mahendra adored Saroj from the moment he embarked on the seventh round of the sacred matrimonial fire that bound them for life. He was painfully good-looking. His tall, muscular frame and honey-coloured skin made him the cynosure of many mothers' eyes—except for one thing. Over the years, his looks had been marred by a small feature: when he grinned, after telling one of his favourite jokes, he revealed a perfectly cast set of teeth outlined a reddish brown like marble slabs that had been inlaid with a sandstone border.

In fact, this dental decay bore a direct correlation to his mental decay, for the excessive consumption of betel nut and cigarettes had gradually dulled his critical faculties, and made him increasingly oblivious to the machinations of his family members who were slowly, surely, surreptitiously, plotting his end.

Carrying several packets of betel nut powder and Wills cigarettes in the inner pouch of their VIP suitcase, right next to the extra travellers' cheques, Mahendra and Saroj left for Europe. It was here that they would really meet for the first time, for they had only met three times before their wedding and the ceremony itself was a blur of squawking tailors, gawking aunts, food, and flowers. They left two days after the reception in Pitampur for a month-long honeymoon, arranged by Mahendra's brothers.

The first stop was Zurich, where they stayed in a hotel that belonged to one of the family's business associates, off the Bahnof Strasse. Their room overlooked an ancient stone steeple whose bells chimed gustily every hour, a counterpoint to the wind that howled through the steeple.

It was Saroj's first time out of India, and as she stepped gingerly on to the cobbled street, wearing her dark glasses and a beige camel-hair overcoat which was too warm for the spring air, she was exhilarated. She felt like Asha Parekh, but in a European film. She clutched her husband's hand unconsciously and pulled him along the wide pavement, almost skipping. She saw a café down the road and pushed open the glass door. Inside, she threw her head back and, with one flick, pulled open her bun, letting her long black hair come undone in a liberating wave.

Mahendra looked at his beautiful bride with delight, and ordered two large hot chocolates and a plate of doughnuts. As they both sat and munched the freshly baked goodness, their lives seemed perfect.

'You are very sweet, Sujjo rani,' he said, referring to her by the endearing name only her mother and her oldest school friend Rati used. He stroked her hair and pushed a strand behind her ear.

'And you are very handsome, Manu,' she replied, giggling.

Saroj reached out and quickly pecked his cheek. She glanced around instinctively to see if anyone had seen her.

Then she realized that she was no longer in the family prison. She remembered that awful moment while she was being dressed for the wedding reception. Her elder sister-in-law Anu bhabhi had draped the heavy red brocade sari around her head, lifted her chin and said, without any emotion, 'Just remember, keep your head covered always. That is the rule for the daughters-in-law of the house. And do not address your husband by his name around anyone in the family, especially not around Big Ma or Bauji or Munimji.' She hissed, 'They will kill you.'

But right now, her bow-shaped lips were lined with molten chocolate and she was calling her husband Manu, and she couldn't care less. She would deal with them when she had to.

They walked up to the lake and passed the Sprungli café that Manu had told her so much about. He told her to go back to the hotel lobby and read a magazine or relax in the room, because he had to visit a bank on some important work. She couldn't be bothered to ask what it was. Business was a male thing. As he walked down the road with a small suitcase, she looked at the back of his tall frame and hugged herself. She was the happiest bride in the world. A few minutes later, she was on the big sinking bed in the hotel room, fast asleep in a foetal curl, with her camel-hair trench coat still on.

The sky wore the lingering brightness of dusk when Saroj woke up, disoriented. Her armpits were damp and she was desperate for a cup of tea. She had been dreaming of her grandmother's loud prayer bells but they suddenly changed tones and became unfamiliar clanging church bells. She suddenly missed Mummyji, and all her cousins and the pooja room and the tsunami of smells that lunged out of their kitchen all day long. She got up and looked for her husband. He was not in the room or bathroom. Saroj's eyes filled up. She suddenly felt exhausted, emotional, and a little bit scared. As she sat on the bed, slipping on her shoes which were blurred by her tears, the door turned and Manu walked in. He sat beside her and gave her a long hug. His cold cheeks pressed against her warm skin as her tears fell and finished and she felt better. But a faint feather of fear continued to tickle her stomach and only went away when he moistly and gently kissed her lips and she lay in his arms on the bed.

Perhaps because Saroj was the second daughter, she had lived her whole life with a vague sense that she was not welcome. It afflicted her all the time, without her even knowing it, especially when she walked into a gathering of people—in school or, later, at a party or even among strangers in a bus. For an Indian woman, she was tall, but felt small. Most of all it happened around her own family, and often when her beloved, beautiful sister Suman was around.

There was always a lingering aftertaste of fear and loneliness that stalked her, following her movements, watching and waiting for the right moment to erupt into panic. When this happened, the bilious feeling would rise within, take over, and completely immobilize her.

She would then retreat like a tortoise, drawing herself in, so that she was no longer vulnerable. She hid her fragility by keeping a distance from the world. People mistook her for being an ice maiden, hideously snobbish, not understanding that she was actually mortifyingly, miserably shy.

As far as she could remember—she had cemented and irretrievably buried away most of her memories—the feeling first started settling into her those days in the Fairy Room. She may have been five, or seven, or maybe ten or eleven. Her parents had gone away, and taken Rajan Papa with them on some extended trip on a ship, perhaps to drop him off to Switzerland. All she remembered was that they were away and she was miserable. Only Suman was around, her elder sister, whom she both adored and hated, she was never sure. Their grandmother would come into the Fairy Room where their beds would be laid out, and as they lay there under the blankets, entering the dream world under the cherubs, she would pinch them and tell them stories about little girls in her village, and how they were married to old men, and how they were not wanted by either their parents or their husbands. She said girls had to learn to be slaves if they wanted to survive in the world, especially if they were dark like Saroj. She would then laugh and hug both the girls before turning off the light, leaving little Saroj to fight off the monsters which danced behind the curtain. By the time her parents got back, it was too late, and Saroj had already moved into a more shadowy world, where swaying tree branches became the flagellating arms of ghouls. And fear was her constant faithful companion.

Many years later, like a handsome magician waving his wand, Manu came in and the bile began disappearing.

For the first time, she forgot herself, her fright. It would come back every once in a while when she woke up, but then she would see her husband next to her, as a live reminder that she was no longer an unwelcome ghost. The volcano became dormant. It got better and better with every sunny day in Europe. After Zurich, they went to the sparkling snow-capped peaks of Interlaken, then drove through the dark woods of Germany where she tasted her first freshly brewed beer in a tiny village, until they finally ended up in France.

One beautiful pale grey morning in Paris, when the filtered sunlight made everything look even more beautiful than before, Saroj Mahendra Mohan went up to the very top of the Eiffel Tower with her husband, looked down at the world and, perhaps for the first time in her life, felt truly happy.

Rai Sahib's haveli in Pitampur was built around an open courtyard. In the centre was a fountain; the water emerged from an urn held by a buxom plaster-of-paris woman wearing a red sari and a green blouse, bending forward suggestively and balancing on one leg, with the other lifted up. In the summer months, grateful pigeons and garrulous sparrows would come to rest on the rim of the fountain and dip their little beaks in for a sip, bobbing their heads at the men and women who sat around gossiping or working. Even the sound of the water was cooling.

Life in the haveli moved along the courtyard and in the corridors that ran along the three sides. On one side was the kitchen, which spilled out into the open space around. There was always someone squatting outside, peeling or chopping or sifting or pounding.

On the other side of the courtyard sat the curmudgeonly family munim, cross-legged on a gaddi, in front of his little desk, his cap folded neatly next to him. He was the financial fulcrum of the house, the person who controlled every bit of the money that came in and out of the house on behalf of the Rai Sahib. Even the grown-up sons had to plead before him, 'Please, Munimji, mark hundred rupees against my name...' And they would either be met with a cold stare or a straight no or, if they were lucky, they would get the cash to buy their movie tickets or a new sari for their wife or mistress. When he was not sitting outside, the munim sat in a small room behind, where he met select visitors who came to borrow money at the high rate established by the Rai Sahib family.

Next to this room was the family pooja room, a pride of place, swept and swabbed three times a day, and presided over by two beautiful marble statues of Radha and Krishna. When Manu and Saroj got engaged, he told her that her eyes reminded him of the Radha in the pooja room. There was always a sprinkling of parijat flowers at the statues' feet, the orange stems perfectly matching Radha's sari. Every year, on Krishna's birthday, the family tailor would stitch a fresh baby blouse to her size and Big Ma would change her clothes—beautiful parrot greens offsetting bright rani pinks or sometimes a white-and-gold with a crimson blouse. The accountant's room and the pooja room were the two stops that every family member made to grab a blessing on his way out.

Saroj found her new home mildly amusing, though sometimes terrifying. She slipped into the role of a daughter-in-law like a young girl entering a new doll's house, excited to wear her new saris and the toe rings that marked her new status. What she most loved was to carefully slide on the crimson powder in the centre parting of her hair.

Like the others in the house, she slowly tuned in to the jingling sound of Big Ma's keys which hung at her waist, warning bells that she was approaching. On hearing them, she would either hide like a child behind her bed or, if outside, she would quickly pick up the nearest thali containing peas that had to be shelled or mustard leaves that had to be sorted, and pretend to be hard at work.

The younger maids and cook's helper indulged her subterfuge, for their sympathies lay with these young girls and not with their bossy senior madam. The older retainers were immune to Big Ma's ways because they had once seen her as the young victim when *her* mother-in-law had ruled over the house and treated her like a cockroach. Now, the wheel of life had turned. Ammaji was a widow and it was Big Ma's turn to take over, for widowhood took away your rights overnight and forced you to retire into a fragile ghostly dependent who was best off muttering prayers in a corner. Some day, Anu or Saroj would turn from victim to villain. It was a centuries-old tradition. While the men lorded over their business, the women were masters of this universe.

Dusk was a lovely time in the old haveli. Everything became quieter outside as the little people of Pitampur started winding down. Wherever you were in the house, you could hear the sound of the ancient Ammaji droning her evening prayers, followed by the tinkling of her little prayer bell. Then, the dhoop, made from all kinds of herbs and camphor, would be taken around every room to ward off mosquitoes, until its musky smell pervaded their curtains, clung to their clothes, their skin, not just in the evenings, but all the time. The servant carrying the dhoop would be followed around by another who would then drop the muslin curtains from all four sides of the bedpost, tucking them into the mattress so that no creature except its rightful inhabitants could then enter.

Every other evening there would be a vendor at the gate, asking to be let in with his wares. In the hot months, the sari man from Dhaka came with his young son, bringing yards and yards of the finest soft muslin as appealing as a baby's skin, or the Lucknawi vendor carrying cloth embellished with white thread as intricate as a spider's web. As winter approached the shawlwallah from Kashmir would inevitably descend, carrying beautifully embroidered shawls with paisleys shaped like the teardrops of the families that stitched them.

And every few months, the bed bug annihilator would show up to absorb any lurking vermin. He catered to all the Jain families in the town and Big Ma was Jain. Because they were averse to killing animals he performed a unique function. His job required him to sleep on the beds that had become infested with bed bugs and allow them to bite him until they were satiated and dropped dead. That way, they would not bother the next sleeper. The pace of the haveli was slow and followed the natural rhythms of the day and the season. It went down well with Saroj, even though she often missed the ocean and her mother.

One evening, Saroj was lying on the bed in her elder sister-in-law Anu's room, chatting with her and waiting for the toothless old kaku gardener to drop off the strings of aromatic flowers that he wound every day at twilight for the women of the house. It was an old family ritual. Just around the time the men came home from work, the women of the house washed up and dressed their hair with these jasmine strings, then hovered around in anticipation, hoping for an evening plan like a drive out to the haveli or, if they were lucky, a movie. The previous night, Manu and Saroj had gone out without permission, pushing two rupees into the chowkidar's hand to silence him. Instead of driving the old Dodge out of the gate, they had pushed it out in neutral gear, with Saroj at the steering wheel, giggling like teenagers, so that no one would wake up with the sound of the engine. They watched *Hum Dono* and Saroj fell deep in love with both Dev Anand and her husband.

Anu lay on the bed, humming to herself, moving her hands this way and that. Suddenly, she got up and opened the gigantic rosewood cupboard that stretched from floor to ceiling. Her husband's starched shirts hung on top. She unlocked a large drawer at the bottom. Inside, lay a harmonium. She picked it up carefully, with both hands, and placed it on the floor. She took the back of her sari and wiped a thin layer of dust off the top and in between the individual keys. She told Saroj to shut the door and windows. Big Ma was out at her sister's place and wouldn't be back for a while. The men were not yet home and Munimji had left early.

Anu sat in front of the instrument, cross-legged, shut her eyes and began singing, playing the accompanying keys without opening her eyes, as if she knew exactly where each note resided. As she sang, hitting higher and higher notes, she transformed from a boring housewife into a magnificent diva, filling up the room with her presence. She sang about a woman whose husband had gone to work in foreign lands while she lay there, restless and sleepless through the night, not knowing when he would return. Her mother-in-law and sister-in-law chided her. She missed her parents' home...

'Hai bhagwan, that is so beautiful, please don't stop,' said Saroj, when Anu finally stopped, opened her eyes, and smiled. 'Where did you learn to sing like that, bhabhi? Does anyone here know?'

'I used to learn music from one of the greatest singers. She was from Maharashtra but lived in Delhi for some time,' said Anu, a secretive smile playing on her face. 'Her name was Dhondutai. She came home to teach me and my parents would sit outside on the veranda and listen. They knew I was gifted. They started encouraging me to sing on the radio too, and I even sang in a concert at my father's partner's house.'

'What!' Saroj was astonished at this secret that was being unravelled. She stared at the intriguing instrument being played before her, focusing on the little metal label which said 'Melody' and had a Calcutta address. Anu's six-year-old son, Chaitanya, came and lay down on the bed with his head on his aunt Saroj's lap. A few minutes later, he jumped off and started pressing random keys on the harmonium. His mother playfully slapped the back of his hands but after some time, exasperated, closed up the harmonium with two abrupt clicks, as if it was time for her to turn back into a pumpkin.

Although she loved the music, Saroj was simultaneously pinched by a sensation of uncontrollable envy towards her sister-in-law, a natural and unwitting competitor in any family. She felt plain and untalented in comparison. When she applauded after the thumri, her face broke into a stiff, slightly contorted almost grudging smile.

But the singer did not notice the jealousy, for she was still radiant from the bliss of creating gorgeous sound.

When Anu got married to the biggest family in south Haryana, she was forced to shut out music forever. She was told that girls from good homes do not sing in public. She was allowed to perform only at family weddings and funerals. Or, she could closet herself in the pooja room and sing for the gods there, surrounded by the children and the gardener's children—a dramatically different audience from the appreciative connoisseurs of Curzon Road in Lutyens' Delhi. For her, it was as life altering as the clitoris nipping practised by many tribes in Africa, but she didn't have much choice.

Gradually, young Saroj began understanding the dynamics of her husband's family. People were not good or bad, they just were. If a family member was mean to her in some way, it was only because someone had been mean to them. No one really meant any harm. It was just action–reaction, misery begetting misery, and happiness spurring happiness. Everything was circumstantial and contagious.

At some point, she learned to understand that she could not have an individual personality and that it was a part of a larger whole, a giant family jigsaw, and each piece fitted inexorably into the other. She could not disconnect herself from someone else's mood swing. If Big Ma was having a bad morning because her husband had been out all night, she would reprimand Anu in the steaming kitchen in front of all the servants, with a comment about how she came from a family that encouraged hedonism by allowing singing girls into their home to teach their daughter. Later, Anu may sneakily try and win back her mother-in-law by offering to massage her hair, but in the process could potentially undercut Saroj. The young bride gradually started allowing herself to manipulate and be manipulated. Her way of thinking started to change. Now, no action or statement was straightforward or spontaneous but, rather, strategic, even if it were something as simple as saying, 'Big Ma, you are looking so nice in that sari.'

Indian families are like large overgrown bougainvillea bushes—overwhelming and tangled up with both pink flowers and sharp thorns on the same stem. No single individual was culpable. Everyone in the Mohan family had been handicapped in some way so that they would always be just slightly desperate. That's what kept them floundering within the courtyard. The brothers were never given as much money as they wanted, so they were constantly beholden to their father or his proxy, the munim. In the case of Big Ma, the family had done something particularly evil.

Big Ma was married to Bauji after he had lost his first wife to tuberculosis. When she came into the family—acquiring not just a husband but three miserable teenaged boys—two things happened. First, she was told to change her name to the name of her predecessor, Pratibha, the mother of the children. Second, she was told that she could not have any of her own for she had to raise her stepchildren. She was not much older than her daughters-in-law. So, every once in a while, she would slip into the role of being their girlfriend and giggle over some piece of jewellery or gossip. But this kind of thing was short-lived. Most of the time, the rules of the house prevailed.

There was only one person who was able to twirl Big Ma on her finger, around whom she melted like ice cream on a summer day, indeed the only man she was perhaps ever in love with—Dharmendra, Manu's elder brother whom he called Bade bhai. She saw in his wide, intelligent forehead her own father whom she adored, and the man she would have liked her husband to be. From the time she came into the house, the fifteen-year-old boy overruled her husband as the object of her attention; she detached herself from her husband, allowing the numerous arms and legs of the house to take over his daily duties, and doted entirely on this boy, spoiling him over the two others.

She went into deep depression when the family elders insisted on sending Dharmendra to a boarding school in England. It was important for him to get away from the women in the family, she was told, or he would never develop a moustache and learn how to be a man. She had been torn between her obsessive love for him and her desire to see him flourish. She gave in to the latter, on the condition that he come home during every vacation, so that she could feed him and make up for all the time they were away from each other.

This is how it went for years. The same conflicts arose when it was time for him to get married. On the one hand, a suitable bride was sought, on the other she was resented, ignored and, ever so slowly, crushed like a basra pearl under a beautiful brass pestle. She viewed Dharmendra's wife, Anu, as a threat—especially because she was so beautiful and talented and could distract her son from his mother's fawning attentions. So, from the day her competitor entered the big house, gingerly leaving fresh red imprints of her feet on the threshold, Big Ma ensured that Anu would lose traces of her former feisty self and turn into a glorified servant who had little time left to tickle her husband's fantasies. Unlimited chores were unleashed on the young bride—she had to empty out and restock cupboards filled with ancient stained sheets with sprinklings of mothballs and cloves, random brass objects, musty old books, extra steel utensils with family members' initials inscribed on them.

After Saroj got married, she was given the same treatment, but with less intensity. When Manu came home from the office in the evening, Big Ma would invariably develop aches and pains and make Saroj come to her room and press her legs instead of spending time with her husband. All her life she had controlled these boys, the wife was merely an extension of them. Their happiness was the last thing on her mind.

So, Anu was told that she could no longer do the thing she most loved. Every once in a while, some carrots were thrown her way and they would let her perform—for relatives or guests or at a pooja ceremony. But strictly not in a public concert or for the radio, even though the local programming head clamoured for her to come and record. As for Saroj, she could scarcely imagine what was to be her twisted fate, but her own personal purgatory would soon come.

It came a couple of years later and the instrument used was her little son Manoj—who had been lovingly named by his parents using bits of their own names. They had been sitting in the big room in the east wing of the haveli. Big Ma was fingering her rosary necklace, muttering her mantra, but simultaneously instructing the family jeweller who sat crouched by her feet, stringing a necklace of rubies under her watchful eye. Her three daughters-in-law Anu, Saroj, and Sita, were sitting around her. Anu was sewing on a shirt button, Sita was rubbing coconut oil into the child's hair, smacking him playfully every time he fidgeted, and Saroj was pressing her mother-in-law's feet and cutting her toenails.

'If even one stone is lost, I will have you hung by your pubic hair,' cackled Big Ma at the jeweller. Her curses were spectacularly sharp, but reserved only for women, servants and, in particular, for service providers such as jewellers and tailors. Around the men of the house, she would turn into a firm, but polite, matron, but even they knew better than to cross her. Her husband had developed a nervous tick around his mouth soon after he got married and, even though no one said it, she was probably responsible for the periodic contortions of his lower lip.

Little Manoj must have been three or four. He was thoroughly enjoying the oil being rubbed into his scalp by his childless aunt, when his grandmother said, 'So, who do you like more, little sparrow, your Ma or your chachi?'

Now, the child hardly knew that by innocently and playfully choosing, over his beloved mother, an aunt who spoiled him with balls of jaggery and little wooden toy trains from her visits to the bazaar, he would be irretrievably twisting his destiny.

'Sita chachi, Sita chachi. Mamma is too mean to me!' Manoj giggled and made a mock face at his mother, who smiled adoringly at him despite feeling a bit betrayed.

'Aah. I knew it. So, from now on, why don't you call your mother "Big Mummy" and your chachi "Mummy". And you can start sleeping in her room whenever you feel like. She will bathe you and dress you and feed you your milk in the morning. That will be fun, no, little poppet?'

Manoj looked a bit bewildered but, treating the whole thing as a game of snakes and ladders, sliding up and down the arms of the women of the house, said, 'Yippeee!' and ran off to play cricket with the cook's son.

His aunt Sita didn't say anything. She merely looked intently at the cap of the coconut oil bottle, trying not to reveal the rush of mixed emotion that was running through her head. It was that eternal conflict between instinct and survival where gradually, survival drowns out the inner voice. She knew that there was something vaguely wrong about this but she also knew that she longed, more than anything else, for the nights when her nephew did sleep with her, cuddling up into the crook of her stomach and letting his still-baby smell fill the bed. She had wanted a child so badly but it was not to be, and she could not tell anyone the reason it was not happening—that her husband was impotent. As a result, they were cursed with childlessness.

Sita decided on the easy option. She would agree to her mother-in-law's wishes. In family, you shared jewellery and you shared children. Everything belonged to everyone and to no one.

And Saroj did not say anything either, for she knew that if she did, Big Ma would make it worse, she would stand on her other toes as well. That had been the pattern. She looked at her curly-haired son, who was romping around the courtyard being a little lion. He was being taken away in that way where he was not really gone, but she had lost the cosy control that a mother cherishes over her offspring. He would be like the rubies that the man on the floor was stringing—precious, delicate, worn and shown off by all the women. While rubies and pearls shine more when they are worn, children are not the same. They need a sense of belonging, of coming home to one mother, one room, one smell.

She knew that this was the worst, most cruel, move that her mother-in-law had masterminded. And she also thought she knew the reason why it was happening. It was because Manu loved her so much and didn't listen to anyone else. When it came to naming their son, the family wanted to go with the astrologer's suggestion, but he had insisted on fusing their names instead. The two of them still went away on long, romantic business trips together, leaving the child in the care of the extended family. She had her husband, but she had to lose her son. Manu reassured her that it would make no difference to her. Besides, they were going to have another baby.

She made the choice.

In large families, these kinds of movements take place in insidious ways, like silent poisonous eels that glide deep inside the ocean leaving a trail of delicate destruction in their path. They are so insidious that no one really knows what is going on least of all the perpetrators themselves. It only comes to people's notice a generation or two later, when the damage has been done and people work their way backwards through a family album, trying to make sense of the missing persons in the pictures. That's when they begin to peel off the masks and gradually and painfully piece together the torn images.

Saroj didn't mind so much that her son was now staying in another room because he was always around, like a pet puppy for anyone to pamper. Besides, didn't she love spending time with her nephew, Chaitanya? But she was more concerned that Sita had begun to distance herself from her. She couldn't understand it. They were small, insignificant things, but they would hurt her—she would walk into the kitchen and Sita and Big Ma would stop talking mid-sentence; or, they would go to the big fair with Manoj, without telling her. It puzzled her, but she didn't want to seem petty and dwell on it. When she hinted to Anu that she was feeling funny about something in the house, her sister-in-law stared long and intently at her and then gave her a tight hug which left Saroj even more bewildered.

Then, one night it all came together, like a storm that had been quietly gathering force for months, only to lash out in one sudden destructive move. Saroj was five months' pregnant. Manu had not been sleeping well. One night, as Saroj got up to heave her way to the bathroom, she saw him sitting at his desk by the window, with his head in his hands, in the dark room. He looked up. A moonbeam suddenly lit him up and she recoiled. Just over thirty, and he looked like a finished man. He had dark rings around his eyes and an unkind stubble. He looked faintly ghoulish. Manu looked up and saw her expression.

'They wanted me to sign something which would have been a horrible lie and potentially criminal—it involved taking over some poor farmer's land. I just couldn't do it. Bade bhai and Devendra were perfectly comfortable with what was going on. Bauji has decided to keep me out of the business and wants me to sign over all my rights within the month. They have been planning this for a long time, and really put it all together when I was away in Europe with you the last time.'

'Hai bhagwan! But what about us, Manu? What will we do? Where will we go?'

'We can continue staying here, in the family house, because it is owned under the Hindu undivided family and belongs to all of us equally. But I have to relinquish control over the business. I have been given only the fort and the land around it. We will get some cash, but not a lot. We no longer have access to medical allowance and cannot send our bills to the office. And the cars will be divided up over the next few days. We will probably get the Ambassador, the one that doesn't have an air-conditioner.'

'And Big Ma?'

Manu was quiet, but Saroj could hear his silent roar of pain.

It didn't sink in just then. Saroj could not understand what was going on. She went back to bed and tried to shut her eyes so that sleep would take her away from this terrifying new reality. But it just wouldn't come. She thought she felt the baby inside her kicking angrily. It wouldn't stop. Manu came and lay down next to her and put his arm around her belly. She turned on her side and tried to stroke his hair. He was such a good man. Things had to get better. He fell asleep, but she lay awake for a long time after. There were all kinds of cross-connections going on in her head… An angry conversation she had overheard between Big Ma and Bauji where they were discussing something to do with the house; a look that she remembered flashing in her mother's eyes right after she met her brother-in-law and he spoke about the family land. Everyone had already known. She tried to shut her eyes and think of something good, of the Zurich lake, of the Ludhiana mustard fields. Why would sleep not come?

Saroj woke up groggy and felt that familiar lightning flash of panic which sets in before you remember why it's there. Manu was still sleeping, hugging his pillow. She held up the mosquito netting, bent and slowly got up. Because of the heat, she had slipped off her sari and slept in just the blouse and petticoat. She wrapped a fresh printed cotton sari around herself listlessly and went out to the family room to greet her husband's parents. Despite her protruding belly, she was expected to touch their feet every morning. As she dived down hesitantly, she felt sad. These were the people who were supposed to replace her parents. She wanted them to protect her, to tell her it was going to be all right. She actually knew that Big Ma loved her in her own way. But they, too, had betrayed her. Can money blind you so much? As she bent down in a final imploring move, Big Ma lightly touched her shoulder, then got up and left for the kitchen. Saroj went back and opened the door of her bedroom. The vents inside her had started closing, one by one by one. She sat at her husband's desk, looked out on to the leafy road that led to a dead end, and let her eyes fill up.

She sat there for at least an hour, staring out of the window. She saw her neighbour on the terrace, laying out wheat grains on old sheets so that the sun would kill the insects. Normally, she too would have been engaged in a similar task, or helping in the kitchen, organizing tea or making puris for breakfast, standing behind Big Ma while she gave orders to the servants on what was to be ground or marinaded, and then finally, when all the men were out of the house, she would bathe.

But today, Manu did not get up at his usual time, and she did not go into the kitchen. She felt strange, miserable. There is enormous comfort in routine; it lulls you into a rhythm in a life otherwise filled with inconsistent emotions and fragile relations. That had been broken. She felt like an alien in her husband's home. She wasn't sure of anything—did she have access to the same rooms that she would bustle in and out of with mistress-like poise, tucking her pallu into her waist, mindlessly ordering servants around and expressing fake irritation at their laziness? Would Anu still come and lie on her bed in the afternoon and talk about this and that and sing for her? Could she still open Big Ma's cupboard and pick a sari she wanted to wear? Saroj looked at her husband and was shocked to see that he was lying awake, but immobilized, his eyes staring blankly at the ceiling. She had never seen him like this. It was as if a pillar had cracked and the house around her was crumbling to dust, in slow motion. Her heart reached out to his pain. And momentarily, she forgot her own fright.

When she booked a call home later that morning, Saroj was filled with shame and dread, for she knew her mother would be shattered with this turn of events. Their prize catch had turned into a mirage and her smug plan for her daughter had backfired badly.

'Mummyji, jai Ram ji ki,' she spoke softly into the receiver.

'Jai jai Ram, beta, how are you? Are you keeping well? How is the morning sickness?'

'Yes. Everything is well.'

'I sent besan laddoos for your in-laws with your Bade bhai.'

There was silence. Then Saroj said, 'Ma...'

Mummyji instantly realized that it was not a routine call. Her daughter's voice sounded small and tinny. She heard fear. She instantly knew what script was being played out. Devendra had been very shifty and not looked her in the eye when he came over to pick up the food parcel she was sending to Pitampur. Her instincts about family dynamics had been so finely honed over the years that she picked up the smallest signals. The truth hit her like a flash: There was going to be a money blow-out and her son-in-law was going to get the short end. Even before her daughter said anything to her, she knew. Her own heart sank with the weight of her daughter's distress, because she knew this was the beginning of the end.

'Just come home,' she said. It was almost an order. 'I will send Rajan Papa to get you. You are pregnant and need a lot of care.' Neither of them brought up the subject of Manoj.

A few days later, Manu swallowed half a bottle of lethal rat poison he brought back from the market. That fateful, horrible day had not started well for Saroj. In the morning, she had seen a row of crows sitting on the neighbour's roof, menacing and mocking, when she woke up and drew open the curtain. She had found Manu unusually distracted and behaving very oddly when he woke up. He had not bothered having a bath, nor breakfast, and stepped out in his kurta pyjama, without telling her where he was going. He took the poison after lunch, and didn't wake up for tea. She thought he must be tired from a sleepless night. But when she tried to nudge him, he felt heavy and leaden. That's when she ran out and called for Big Ma.

Manu had to be taken to the hospital and the doctors and nurses were paid off to keep the entire episode quiet. It was a small town, where the most valuable tradeable commodity was family reputation. As Manu was brought home, Saroj began to make her preparations to return to Cozy Villa. She had argued with her mother, pleading that her husband needed her now but Mummyji, having heard of the latest developments, was more insistent than ever. Saroj, ever compliant and gentle, did not say no. She packed her bags robotically—taking most of her things. It was as if her marriage had been an extended holiday and now she was on her way back home.

Before leaving, Saroj had been spending more and more time in her dark bedroom, away from the family. They suddenly felt aloof, which may or may not have been true, but reality is merely a deceptive construct of perception and fear. Her only real friend was Anu, and Mita, Manu's young niece. Mita was an eighteen-year-old bright-eyed girl, who had adopted Saroj as her confidante and her conduit to the world outside Pitampur. Mita felt throttled by her family, the way they deftly swept all emotion under the big almirahs of the house, by the way they let their real feelings drift into the rice fields outside where they could find comfort in nature; she constantly felt like she wanted to run away, and the only people whom she trusted were Manu and Saroj, her uncle and aunt.

Saroj spent solitary afternoons in her bedroom with only the whirring fan and a rippling belly for company. When no one was around, Anu came and comforted her, expressing her helplessness over the situation. Sometimes Manoj bounded in and then left as quickly. When would she be back there? Would the room be the same? She didn't know the answers.

Rajan Papa arrived at the door of the haveli in a dusty rented Ambassador, wearing his usual crisp white kurta pyjama, with a grey sleeveless sweater. Manu came to the door and greeted his brother-in-law warmly, with a hug, and reached down halfway in the token feet-touch. Saroj stood a few feet behind her gaunt husband. Rajan Papa could not hide his eyes, though he quickly controlled himself. She was quick to notice his shock at seeing this ghostly vestige of the man his sister had married. Her eyes filled up and she widened them and lifted her chin slightly, clenching her jaw so that the tears did not spill.

She hugged her son tight and then let him wander back into the courtyard, where Sita was helping him string beads and make necklaces for the gods. She watched him throw a bead into the fountain in the centre and then turned and left.

Saroj sat next to her brother in the plane, heavy-bodied and heavy-hearted. As the Indian Airlines stewardess poured tea into her white plastic cup, she reflected on the last few weeks that had caused her more pain than the labour she was about to go through. She had been told that she would have to learn how to drive because they no longer had access to the company perks. She had also realized that the kitchen would now have two separate sections, and she would have to take charge of her own grocery bills. The bile now stayed with her all the time. She was never sure whether it came from the stomach juices that were being churned inside her by the new person waiting, feeding off a new diet of rage and pain.

Saroj woke up when the stewardess nudged her arm gently, saying that they were about to land and she would have to put her seat in an upright position; the bad feeling came back even before she could gather herself. Rajan Papa helped her manoeuvre as she tried to get the seat belt around her and winced as the baby kicked inside. A thought flashed across her mind. This child was going to cause her a lot of pain. Saroj was beginning to resent that she was now being forced to be an alert mother. She looked outside the window at the infinite sky and saw herself outside, a shapeless helium balloon with a protruding belly, drifting further and further away from herself.

Mummyji was sitting on her armchair doing the milk accounts with a slightly sodden Ratansingh, who had slipped out in the afternoon and had a quick swig, when the bell rang. The chair next to her had now been empty more than five years. Saroj walked in, went straight to the footstool in front of her, put her arms around her mother and they both wept. Ratansingh slunk out of the room looking miserable.

Rajan Papa kept mumbling, 'Don't worry. Don't worry. It's going to be all right,' but the two women howled louder every time he uttered a word of consolation, almost relishing their collective catharsis.

Saroj allowed her mother's smell to settle on to her like a salubrious balm—that mixture of her hair oil and sandalwood and light garlic—as she sat with her head on her lap. Finally, Mummyji lifted her daughter's head with her hands.

'Beti, I have cleared out the last cupboard for your things. Go, lie down now. I'll send Rajni with some tea and garam garam pakodas. We have to feed two of you now. I will come and massage your head later. You don't worry. You are home.'

Rajan Papa was tired from the long journey to Delhi and Pitampur and back. He lay down on the couch with his hands interlocked on his chest and dozed off. At some point, he heard the voice of Jassu who was making her routine obligatory visit to her mother-in-law, but didn't feel like getting up. He pretended to be asleep, while the voices droned on about the price of potatoes and Premsingh's chronic corns.

In the Fairy Room, Saroj lay on her back, staring at the floating cherubs. The room was comfortably the same. The almost opaque windows were shut. There were the same muffled shouts of the same boys playing cricket downstairs. Saroj wondered why the pink cherubs had not blessed this home. Perhaps they felt equally trapped as the inmates of the house. Or maybe they felt that it was deserved—for pain begets pain, and there was still a lot of unfinished karma. The cherubs had watched it all from above, for more than fifty years, from the time Khuba and Bimmo first procreated, the very first night they slept together.

Saroj suddenly missed Manu and his big warm body by her side, but then she slowly started melting into the shadowy memories with the ease of those who subconsciously will bad things to happen to them, then wait for the dull pain to start taking over and put them at ease.

She moved back into the Fairy Room as if she had never left it. She and Mummyji shared the king-sized bed, and they would both lie on their backs with their legs spread out, to ward off the terrible heat.

Within a few days, Saroj started emanating the same smells as her mother. She became her shadow, finding comfort in echoing all her activities. If Mummyji was doing crochet, or embroidering a table linen set with purple and pink flowers, Saroj would pick up the extra needles and start doing the edging. When Mummyji shelled peas, Saroj took a smaller plate and did the same, next to her. She was as non-confrontational as a person inside a photo frame. If visitors came around, they sometimes forgot she was there because she melted so comfortably into the background.

She was about to enter the living room when she stopped outside, then took a step back lest her belly was visible. She heard the voices of Swarno behenji and her mother speaking in that loud whisper they reserved for when they were talking about someone or gloating in another's misery.

'He has nothing to give her, behenji. You know very well what the position of a girl is in a house where her husband has been made impotent. She will be turned into a maidservant,' Mummyji said.

Swarno clicked her tongue sympathetically.

'I feel as if we've been tricked. This flower of a girl has been crushed before she could even bloom.'

'But Bimla, don't you think a girl's place is by her husband? Will she be happy here? Also, a question you must ask yourself is, will he let her come away?'

'Manu has no say in this,' Mummyji shot back. 'He should have thought about all this before allowing his family to steal the gold from under his eyes. I have heard from our relatives that the only thing he has been given is that fort in the middle of the fields. What are they going to do? Go and sell horses there? This is the limit. A husband has no use if he has no money. That is the only rule in life. Finished.'

'Well, you know best. Do what you think is right. She is a good girl. She will listen to you.'

There was a pause, then a loud farting sound which Saroj recognized as Mummyji's, almost a disgusting sound effect released for her son-in-law's benefit.

'Let's see what happens, Swarno behenji. For now, at least she should be comfortable and give birth without any tension. Then we will see.'

Saroj stood there, stupefied, terrified, almost instantly bereaved at what she had just heard. She couldn't believe it. Her mother had used her pregnancy as an excuse to take her away but actually she wanted her to never go back. She held her stomach protectively and thought she felt a small movement of protest inside. Half of this child belonged to Manu, to the Mohans. What was her mother doing? But she knew best. Maybe she was right, a man with no money had nothing more to give his family. Her eyes filled up and she slowly walked back to the room and lay down, allowing the conversation to prick her entire body like many tiny invisible needles.

Every few days, Saroj would go and visit her sister Suman for some change of scene. She sometimes accompanied her to her prayer meetings. She liked to listen to the little feel-good parables that her sister told her doting audiences. There was a strange sense of comfort in their philosophy, it was like rubbing a gentle balm on to a bruise that never really healed, but at least there was momentary respite.

Yesterday, the meeting took place in Cozy Villa, but on the third floor, in the home of one of the disciples. Suman had talked about the journey of water as it flows on earth, and how it mirrors our lives. Water is a great teacher. Like a flowing river, we move through life, encountering many twists and turns and obstacles along the way. We must move with grace, ease, determination and always adjust. When a river breaks at a waterfall, it gains energy and moves on. So, when we encounter our own waterfalls, we may fall hard, but we must learn to move. Water does not waste time clinging to its past. It flows on, adjusting its speed according to the circumstances. At the same time, if there is a hole to fill, or time to be passive and still, water does not run away but quietly fills the empty space and stays until it can move away. Eventually, the river flows into the sea, without fearing a loss of identity or control. It seamlessly and humbly tumbles into the ocean's vastness, merging without resistance.

'Each time we move beyond our individual ego to become something larger and join the universal space, we are becoming as wise as the river,' Suman said, to a loud applause of hands and murmurs of appreciation.

Saroj was sitting on a footstool at her mother's feet, resting her hands on her protruding belly, while Mummyji parted her hair bit by bit and rubbed coconut oil into her white scalp. She was gradually entering a lovely massage-induced stupor when Mummyji said, 'You know, I think you should just leave Manu.'

Mummyji continued massaging her daughter's scalp without breaking the rhythm, as if she had just said something as mundane as, 'Let's go shopping for saris to Kala Niketan.'

There was no response from Saroj. Mummyji continued, 'He has nothing to give you any more. You just stay on with us. The baby will be fine here.'

Saroj held her breath as a lightning flash of terror went through her. With one swift stroke, her mother had run a knife through her heart. She was torn, with her mother's approval on one side and love for her beloved husband on the other. She felt like a bulbous beetle being squashed, injured, and then left to fend for herself. Leave Manu? And Anu bhabhi and the smell of dusk in the haveli? Did her mother really mean it? Does that mean she would be—oh my god, she couldn't even mouth the word—a divorcee?

She did not allow her thoughts to continue. She put them on pause and decided that she would think about these things another time. For now, it was better to just turn into putty under her mother's imperious kneading hands, like a round gulab jamun that was about to be deep fried in a great big pot of hot oil.

Mummyji allowed Saroj to sleep and wake up as she pleased, as if she were a child on an extended holiday. Neither of them talked any more about Manu or future plans. They just pretended that Saroj was back home, like any other pregnant woman, to deliver her baby. Manu called every Saturday morning, through an operator who spoke in a nasal drone, announcing the trunk call. Sita called once in a while and made Manoj speak to her but the long pauses and the static left Saroj even more depressed.

One morning, long after the sun had moved high up in the sky, Saroj woke up and went into the balcony. There, she saw a row of large black crows, perched on the sill outside. She stared at them dementedly. They looked larger than usual. Surely these were the same ones she had seen in Pitampur, outside the window. Perhaps they were emissaries from her husband and had flown across the country to come and tell her that he was thinking of her. She waddled into the kitchen and asked Rajni for some roti. Rajni looked at her with a touch of pity, then reached into a steel box and pulled out some of last night's rotis that had been wrapped inside a damp napkin to help them stay fresh. Like a child, Saroj went into the balcony smiling, broke the roti into little pieces, and sprinkled them on the perch, next to the surprised crows that were more used to being shooed away than warmly welcomed thus. They nibbled at the offering, cawing absurdly, and then flew off, some carrying more bits of roti in their beaks to share with offspring and loved ones.

Saroj was thrilled, because she viewed them as her only connection with Manu and Pitampur. She made up her mind to feed them every day. For an hour every morning, after she had had her tea with Mummyji, she took leftover roti and walked slowly into the balcony. They were waiting. One of them had a fleshy bloody strand hanging out of his beak, but Saroj didn't care. Across the road, in the balcony of the neighbouring building an old man on a wicker chair who spent most of his time there, staring out at the sea, saw her feeding the birds and nodded approvingly. After all, these could have been his ancestors she was taking care of.

The crows began following Saroj around. She thought she saw them everywhere, swooping into her mind, cackling mercilessly inside her heart. But gradually, they became her friends and she felt she could trust them more than she could the people who walked in and out of her life, pretending to care. They were unconditionally around, without an agenda other than the bit of soggy bread they looked forward to. They brought her messages from her loved ones, and carried back invisible shards of her broken heart.

One night, she dreamed that the crows were telling her a story. She was not sleeping in the Fairy Room, where the cherubs protected you from nightmares because they are the last things you see before you leave the waking world. The air conditioner was not working there, so she and Mummyji had decided to sleep in the other bedroom, the one rarely used, where the creatures of the night freely entered and plotted chaos in people's lives. In her dream, Saroj had also become a crow and was sitting on the balcony railing. Because she was a fat pregnant crow, she kept losing her balance and almost falling down, and would be seized by sudden bouts of panic every time she almost fell. She had forgotten that she was a crow and could fly if she lost her balance. Anyway, this is what the other crows told her: After you left, Manu fell into a gradual stupor, spending more and more time in his bedroom, and emerging only for meals, unshaven and often unbathed. He wore loose white kurtas which sometimes bore a yellow stain, a pinch of curry spillover from the previous meal. They complained to her that the water in the courtyard fountain was drying up and they were parched with thirst. They whispered to her that his family was dissolving strange pink pills into his milk every morning which was gradually turning him into a zombie, someone who would not do something silly like attempt suicide again.

She woke up with a tremendous sense of unease, the bile from her stomach churning up into her throat. She looked at the clock next to the bed. It was late, almost lunchtime, but Mummyji had not woken her up. The heavy curtains shielded the room from sunlight and from reality. Saroj heaved herself off the bed and went into the bathroom. As she sat on the cold toilet seat, a passing thought about Manu flashed across her, as terse and unforgiving as a telegram. She knew he was in trouble. And, at that very moment, her water broke.

The crows treaded softly around Saroj in the hospital room, passing on comforting messages from Manu while she screamed with pain and held on to her mother's soft fleshy arm and breathed in the comforting scent of sandalwood. She kept muttering, tell the birds not to litter, tell the birds not to litter. But no one could see the crows and didn't pay attention to Saroj's babbling. Mummyji and the nurse kept stroking her hair and advised her to push hard. She herself had given birth to her children in the top room in Ludhiana or in the Fairy Room, except Rajan Papa, whose arrival into this world had been a miracle, for he was born on a train.

Saroj gave birth to a conglomerate of all the unhappy, malignant juices secreted by her body. Her child was stillborn. A boy with honey-coloured skin and long limbs and the fingers of a tabla player, fingers which would never play for an aunt who would never sing.

She spent the next few weeks reliving the baby's death,

living like a shadow that was scared of its body for fear of the damage it was capable of doing. Every morning she would feed the crows in the balcony bits of hard, stale roti. One morning, she saw a little boy the age of Manoj, his wet hair slicked back in a neat side parting, walking hand in hand with his mother. They were heading for the gate, where he would wait for the bus. She waved out to him and blew him a kiss and, when he waved back happily, her heart broke and she felt an enormous sense of bereavement. She had lost not one child, but two, and the pain was unbearable.

She wrote long letters to Anu and to Manu and Mita to get broken bits of information back from the women. Manoj was fine and would be starting school soon. Manu still wasn't well. He was being treated for depression. He was devastated that he couldn't be with his wife but he had very little control over anything right now. He had no money and no idea which direction his life was headed. He didn't speak much. He mourned for his dead child. He kept asking the others when Saroj was coming back but seemed too weak to do much about it.

Two months after her dead baby's birthday, the phone rang. It was late afternoon and Mummyji was napping. Mummyji stirred in her half-sleep as Saroj went to pick up the receiver.

'Yes, yes.' Then, a long pause, followed by, 'I will take care of it. Just let me know how much to send? It will still be a while before I come back, so please handle this…' She choked back a sob. 'And tell Manu not to worry. God will take care of us.'

'Who was that?' Mummyji mumbled, her curiosity eternally compulsive.

'Mita from Pitampur.'

'Who is that? Manu's niece? What was she saying?'

'Nothing, Ma,' said Saroj, a very faint wave of irritation in her voice. 'Go back to sleep.'

Saroj waited to hear her mother snoring again and then stealthily tiptoed out of the room, looking back only once to ensure that her mother had not woken up.

***

That fateful morning, Saroj woke up a little late and came into the living room as usual, expecting to see her mother sitting there, ordering the day's meals. But the seat was empty. Puzzled, she walked towards the kitchen, smelled milk burning and gagged. In the kitchen, the gas stove was switched off but the odour had remained. Obviously someone had let the milk burn. The smell followed her into the corridor and past the aquarium dining table. When she walked into the Fairy Room, she found her mother lying motionless on the bed, her eyes shut, and her two brothers, Rajan Papa and Sunny standing solemnly next to her.

'What happened?' The bile starting bubbling inside softly. She clenched her fist to stay steady.

'Nothing to worry, Saroj. She collapsed. The doctor will be here any minute.'

'Hai Ram. Why didn't Rajni wake me?' But no one answered that question, for they knew that the sick cannot help the sick.

She knelt beside her mother and started gently pressing her feet. They were unusually cold and she felt alarmed. She kept kneading them gently, rubbing the toes between her hands. A few minutes later, the bile receded and she put her head down on the bed next to her mother's feet, her hand outstretched along her mother's tall length. She didn't know it just then, but this was going to be the first day of the rest of her life.

Part Two

Three days before Diwali…

When Mummyji woke up, she was lying on her bed in the Fairy Room. She heard familiar voices circling above her and they gradually came into focus. She honed in on Rajan Papa and Sunny and dear old Dr Nadkarni, the family physician. They were talking to each other in whispers. Both her sons' brows were corrugated into that familiar three-wave frown that was a signature of their family. Even their father had died with that expression obstinately embedded on his face, though he was smiling.

'Beta, what happened?' she ventured weakly, frightened at how slurred her speech sounded.

'Nothing, Mummyji, nothing. You had a minor stroke but the doctor says you will be fine in no time. In no time,' Rajan Papa said.

Rajni came in with a glass of hot milk for Mummyji. She stared at the men who claimed to be her madam's loving sons and swallowed her anger. She could not fathom the sophisticated restraint exhibited by rich people in times of trouble. For her, illness meant difficult times—expenses, possible death, uncertainty. What if something happened to her Mummyji? Where would she go? She was her family, not the children and grandchildren whom she barely knew many train stations away and definitely not the wasted old man with teeth decaying from tobacco, whose stale odour had seeped into his skin and remained there forever. Mummyji was her mother, her benefactor, her friend. She had been with her more than fifteen years. What would happen to everything as she knew it?

Mummyji had slipped back to sleep and was snoring gently. Rajni carefully removed the two hair clips that were still clinging to the old woman's wispy hair, and pulled a crisp white sheet over her, tucking it under both shoulders.

'Sahib, have you told Suman behenji?' Rajni asked Rajan Papa hesitantly, aware that she was crossing a line.

'I called, but she was sleeping and the servant refused to wake her up. He has been given strict instructions not to disturb her.'

Rajan Papa was moved by her concern. He looked at her and gently touched her shoulder.

Sunny went into the balcony for a cigarette. He smoked half of it, stubbed it out on the railing, and came back into the room. He said he had to go to all three shops and would be back later. Diwali was the busiest time of the year for them and he had to ensure that the order flow went smoothly. Rajan Papa looked away when he heard his brother talk about the business, and busied himself with Dr Nadkarni.

'I don't think there is much reason to worry. Just call me any time,' the doctor said, patting Rajan Papa's back reassuringly.

Rajan Papa saw him out and went into the living room. He heaved himself on to the paisley couch and shut his eyes. After a few minutes, he opened them and looked around for the remote control and, when he couldn't find it, hollered for Ratansingh. The skinny servant scuttled in.

'Sahib, remote has no battery. I'll put on the TV for you.' He switched on the old box television which flickered and opened into the Hindi music and dance channel—the one Ratansingh watched for hours every night when Mummyji had gone to bed.

'Put on the news,' said Rajan Papa sharply. He was irritated that this foolish servant was calling the shots. He was also vaguely disturbed by the mustiness that creeps into a home whose owner no longer has the stamina for its upkeep. Because Mummyji was not sitting in the drawing room, it suddenly felt empty, as if it had not been inhabited for years, setting the stage for what the future would be. He knew that there were long-unopened drawers containing old buttons, a faded photograph of a young couple on the *Queen Elizabeth* ocean liner, a solitary knitting needle, the share certificate of a company that had gone bankrupt, and loose change that once added up to something. He knew that the curtains let off a cloud of sparkling dust when opened and that there were cracked crystal vases that lay inconsolably in forgotten corners. And then this impotent remote. That was the price he must pay for not living with his widowed mother. He quickly shoved the thought away and brought his attention back to the screen in front of him.

The news channel was reporting a feature on the Kumbh Mela. The camera swept across the millions of pilgrims and sadhus that had gathered on the banks of the holy river and then honed in on two toothless widows who were wailing uncontrollably. They were speaking in Bhojpuri. The English subtitles at the bottom of the screen translated their entreaties. One woman bleated: 'We woke up and found that they had all gone. My family left me. I don't even know where my village is, or how to get there. Oh why have I stayed alive to see this day?'

It was a gruesome story. The lost-and-found section at the holy mela had a huddle of elderly people whose families had abandoned them in the hope that a charitable ashram would take them in—a phenomenon, stated the news reporter dispassionately, that is disturbingly common among poor Indian families who couldn't afford to take care of their elderly.

Rajan Papa felt uncomfortable and frowned as he pushed away a fleeting sense of guilt. But the images of the wailing widows resurfaced and he lost control over his mental remote control. He jumped up and started pacing the room, his hands clasped behind his back. He badly wanted a drink but he knew it was too early in the day. It was only eleven in the morning. He'd have to wait at least several more hours for his Patiala peg. He picked up the phone to call Suman again. Her phone was busy, so he absent-mindedly dialled his house.

'Yes, Manju. We're not sure, but it could be that she has had a mild stroke. Yes, he was here and has just left after giving her an injection. Anyway, he says there's nothing to worry about. She just needs complete bedrest for the next couple of weeks. I think you should call Swarno behenji and Bindu masi and tell them. I suppose we should carry on with the Diwali pooja this week? Hahn, I'll be home soon…'

Saroj came into the room in her faded night salwar kameez, her hair still uncombed and coiled into the previous night's plait, with strands buzzing out to create a frizzy halo around her face. She looked at her brother and tried to break into a smile. Rajan Papa got up and gave his younger sister a comforting hug. She lay her head on his shoulder and turned it to one side, staring at Gandhiji's bare brown head in the painting on the wall.

'I'm leaving now, but I'll come back later,' she thought she heard him say. His voice was a distant echo that ricocheted with the other sounds in her head.

She then went and sat on the aquarium dining table, drinking her tea, waiting for the crows' cawing to begin. To her surprise, she didn't hear it. As she nibbled at her rusk biscuit, dipping it in the teacup so that the edges softened, she felt a calmness which she greeted with some hesitation and surprise. It was like meeting a stranger whom one instantly likes. Saroj finished her breakfast, washed up, and spent the rest of the morning sitting next to Mummyji, fanning her gently, keeping the flies away. Mid-morning, she and Rajni lifted her and helped her sip on a glass of freshly squeezed orange juice. She instructed Ratansingh to make a light khichdi and dry potatoes for lunch.

Suman arrived at Cozy Villa early in the afternoon, her face pale and puffy from sleep that had not fully run its course. Her mouth looked contorted, as if she had put her lipstick on in a hurry, for a bit of frosted fuchsia had gone over her right upper lip. She went straight to the Fairy Room and saw her mother sleeping, breathing heavily with her mouth slightly open. She sat next to her and started sobbing, softly first, then more dramatically, taking deep breaths in between. Saroj was sitting on the other side of the bed shelling a tray of peas. She came around and held Suman, stroking her back, surprised at her sister's frailty and her own sudden resilience.

'The doctor's said she will be okay, behenji. Please don't cry. We are all here for each other.' Saroj looked up at the cherubs on the ceiling and then started singing softly. Raghupati Raghav Raja Ram... Her dulcet murmur filled the room with an invisible mist of serenity.

***

Rajni overheard them talking in the other room. They were speaking in Punjabi, a language as alien to her as her native Marathi may be to them. But, over the years, to her own surprise, she had picked up bits here and there and could now catch the gist of what was being said, whether she liked it or not. She felt a desperate need to get out, away from these people.

She quietly opened the front door and went down the two flights of stairs. Instead of walking out of the building, she turned right behind the stairs, pushed open a sky-blue door, bent down and climbed into a cubbyhole in the wall. This is where her best friend, Babu, lived. He was squatting on the floor, smoking a beedi. Without saying a word, he pulled another one out and gave it to her. They both smoked in silence. Rajni then turned to him and said, 'Mummyji is a little better, but I just don't know what is going to happen. Something is not right.'

'Have faith in Krishna.' He pointed to the blue god smiling on a calendar above his bed.

'Babu, there is something going on with this family. I don't think Suman behenji or Sunny sahib have any control over their actions. Even Krishna may not be able to help them.'

Babu squeezed Rajni's hand. He watched a tear roll down her smooth dark cheek, but didn't reach out to wipe it or comfort her for he believed that pain was a part of life and must be allowed to flow naturally, without obstruction or protest. They finished their beedis in silence.

Babu was the presswallah, the man who ironed out creases for a living. He knew the intricacies of each customer's life based on the bundles that came to him. During the holidays the number of clothes piled into each lot would go up because that was when his clients' grandchildren and friends visited. During the wedding season, he would marvel at some of the expensive saris that came and would take extra care not to disturb the sequins and the embroidery while pressing them into shape. Babu had been living under Mummyji's building for almost twenty years, ever since Lochan brought him there from their village, around the time he had brought Ratansingh. He now managed the clothes and linen for not just Cozy Villa, but also the buildings around it, all the way down to Churchgate station. The room—large enough for an ironing board, a wooden box to sit on, a bedding roll, and a small cupboard—was his workplace, home, temple, and coffee shop, all in one. His work was done for the day and he had delivered all the bundles, like freshly baked cookies still warm from the touch of the flat iron.

He reached into a small glass bottle on the shelf above and pulled out a black-and-white Bullseye, a round boiled sweet flavoured with mint. He popped one into his mouth and gave one to Rajni. It was a regular ritual. Smoke followed by mouth freshener. They didn't speak much, but there was a sense of comfort they felt in each other's company—they had virtually grown up together and recreated family bonds in this home far away from a home that had turned into a memory frayed from repeated and tired reconstruction.

Two days before Diwali...

RAJAN PAPA WOKE UP WITH a sick feeling in the pit of his stomach and it took a few moments before he remembered what had happened the previous day. Mummyji! His head throbbed from the two extra stiff pegs he had drunk at night, sitting up late, alone in his living room. He sat on his bed and held his hand, pressing his thumbs against his temples. Through the haze of his hangover, he experienced an irritating mixture of emotion—why did Mummyji have to go and collapse like this now when he needed her the most; then, that gave way to a burst of love for his poor darling mother.

He would have to finally take things in his own hands and make that trip to Bhatija to get his money back. After that he would go straight to Cozy Villa. As he put his thoughts into neat compartments that would help him through the day, the flush in the bathroom exploded noisily and Manju came out of the bathroom smelling like a pink Lux rose, in a good mood, possibly because she had eluded her chronic constipation that morning.

'I have spoken to Saroj,' she said cheerily. 'Things are stable there. She slept through the night.'

Rajan Papa's head was now hurting. He felt as if a little man was sitting inside it with a hammer. He felt terrible and knew that the portents for the rest of the morning were not looking very good. He rolled back into bed and lay on his side for a few minutes but his wife's constant bustling in and out of the room made it impossible for him to go back to sleep. She was already on the phone with her mother discussing what she was wearing for the card session in her parents' house that evening, speaking just a bit too loudly for that time of the morning. Rajan Papa got up. It was another day and time to try, yet again, to get his money back.

The street on which Bhatija lived and worked was one of the oldest streets in Bombay. It housed a series of blistered buildings which should have been pulled down years ago, but they had obstinately stuck around because of the thousands of ant-like humans that buzzed in and out of their crevices and refused to budge. It was the story of rent control—a populist law that was slowly and systematically destroying the old parts of the city. There was no point taking a car in there, it would get stalled by the human flotsam and invite scratches from the handcarts that thrived there. Besides, parking was impossible. Rajan Papa decided to take a taxi.

Bhatija's office was in the worst building on the street—one that was permanently propped up by scaffolding and held together by god's good grace. The taxi inched its way along the street, until Rajan Papa saw the familiar Yunani medicine shop which had been there since he was a child. Next to it was the building which housed Bhatija's den.

When he got there, the taxi driver asked him if he should wait. Rajan Papa considered it for a moment and then said, 'No.' He had no idea how long it would take him and didn't want to hear a meter ticking in his already crowded, noisy head.

Rajan Papa had to bend under a loose bamboo which dangled precariously from above. Gagging at the powerful smell of what must have been a combination of urine and rotten eggs, and imagining all sorts of vermin crawling up his leg, he tentatively made his way up a rickety flight of wooden stairs to the first floor. He passed a shipping company, an insurance agent and a sub-broker's office before reaching Vensimal Bhatija's rooms. A thin woman with a harelip, Bhatija's only employee, was staring at her nails. She started when she saw Rajan Papa.

'Sir, Bhatija sir is not here today. Mother is not well.'

'I don't care. I'm going to wait here until he comes. That's that. He can't keep avoiding me like this. He just can't avoid me like this.'

Rajan Papa stormed into the inner cabin and baulked. Sitting inside, chewing a paan, with his legs crossed on the Formica tabletop in front of him, was the beak-nosed Bhatija. He was sourcing dandruff from his hair with one hand, while holding a telephone receiver in the other. He immediately threw his legs off the table and sat up straight. 'I'll speak to you later,' he mumbled into the receiver, in Sindhi.

‘Come, sir. Please come in. I was going to call you and tell you that everything is okay. You should get your money in a few weeks. Can I get you some tea?’ Bhatija reached across the table and pressed a buzzer for his receptionist.

At that moment, something came over Rajan Papa and he did something he never imagined he would do. He grabbed hold of Bhatija’s collar and said, ‘You bastard. You have been saying a couple of weeks for too long. I want my money. I want it now. You’d better watch out.’

Bhatija looked terror-stricken. He whimpered. ‘It’s coming, sir…it’s coming. Please…don’t hurt me.’ He did not dare push Rajan Papa away.

A combination of rage and frustration suddenly turned Rajan Papa’s grip flaccid and he fell back. He knew that he was helpless and no amount of threats would make a difference to this creature who sat whining before him. He had in his possession Rajan Papa’s unreported black money, so there was no question of bringing in a lawyer or the police. Rajan Papa suddenly let go, turned around, and walked out of the room, just as the receptionist entered. She took one look at her boss and hurried back to her table, not stopping to ask why he had buzzed for her.

As Rajan Papa entered the dank corridor, reality hit him like an overpowering stench. Half his life savings had been sunk into this dirty place and he was stuck. He had no idea what he should do next.

Rajan Papa blinked as he entered the scorching street after bumping his head against a piece of bamboo scaffolding.

As he started walking towards the main road, he heard someone shouting.

'Sahib. Come, I'll take you.' It was the taxi driver that had brought him here. He had obviously not found a customer and was still hanging around.

Rajan Papa climbed in. As the car inched its way out of the morass of humanity, Rajan Papa looked visibly stressed. The driver looked into his rear-view mirror and switched off the raucous Bhojpuri remix that blared into the stuffy taxi.

'Sahib, were you meeting one of those brokers? Money problems?'

Responding to the anonymity of a taxi driver, Rajan Papa volunteered, 'Yes.' He lifted his right trouser leg to scratch the back of his calf where a pink bite was spreading like an embossed design.

'He is not giving you your money back?'

'The bastard refuses to give me either the principal or interest. I have no way of getting it out of him.'

'Sahib, I think I can help you.' The car was now stalled at a traffic light and the driver leaned over the backrest to talk to his customer, face to face. 'My neighbour has connections with the bhai-log. They know exactly how to get anything out of anyone. They even use eunuchs to go and scare the defaulting people. You won't have to worry at all. It's a simple deal. They get ten per cent. You get the rest. You can trust me fully.'

Rajan Papa's head went blank for a minute and then everything came into focus again. He didn't think he would ever be having this conversation. Getting involved with the underworld? Not a good idea at all. What would Mummyji say? Manju would be hysterical if she found out. Rahul would be so ashamed of his father. Then again, if he didn't get the money back, he would be doomed. His life would be over. His mother would continue pretending that she didn't know what was going on. His father-in-law would not help him any more. And what about his son... Rahul wanted to go away to a design college in Bangalore and needed to be set up. How could he explain to him that he had lost his money to an oily cheater who treated him worse than dandruff?

Rajan Papa didn't reply. He slumped on the sunken back seat whose spring had given way. He vaguely saw the people who were in cars all around him and felt even worse when he thought about their busy, productive lives. It was hot and humid and his underarms had turned damp under his pale blue full-sleeved shirt.

The taxi driver was now pulling into Walkeshwar road, where Rajan Papa lived. He pulled a pen out of his glove compartment, and wrote the collection agent's name and number on the back of a petrol bill. Rajan Papa took the note and felt it go damp in his palm. He shoved it into his trouser pocket hurriedly, which is where it remained for weeks, surviving two intense sessions with the washerwoman and the heat of the ironing man.

Rajan Papa went back home to find that his wife had already left for her parents' home in Santacruz and his son was, as usual, locked up in his room.

He knocked and spoke to the plywood door. 'You should come and see your grandmother, son.'

'Okay, Papa.'

Rajan Papa rarely spoke to Rahul these days. He didn't understand his son. He didn't understand too many people besides his mother and now even she was going down before his eyes. Actually, he didn't understand her either—why she could not reach out and help him the way she was supposed to, why she did not fight his battles for him. He sat down in front of his friend, the television, and randomly switched channels. Then, he got up and did something he had never done during daylight hours. He poured himself a small drink. He was ashamed of what he was doing, but the stress was more than he could take.

His heart was reaching out to the golden water swirling in the glass in front of him, with big blocks of ice floating inside, and he imagined himself, like a cartoon figure drowning inside it. He had contemplated suicide a couple of times before, fleetingly. But he was too lazy to even entertain the thought beyond the initial mental foray. He shut his eyes in an attempt to block out the cruel world outside but found that his inner world was an even worse place to inhabit.

Then, just as the miniature cartoon figure was about to go glug glug glug into the yellow liquid, he saw a lifeboat. Oh god! This was the answer. Even if she was not well, he would figure out a way of getting cash from the Cozy Villa chorkhana. He was not stealing. This was his mother. She would understand completely and of course he would put the money back when he could. Besides, he needn't even tell her since she was now not too well. Why bother her. He drank the last sip and sprang up like a man with a mission. He would go there now. Rahul could come later.

The long afternoon shadows loped into the living room of Cozy Villa. Rajan Papa heaved himself off the chair and went back into the bedroom where Mummyji was sleeping. He lay down next to her and covered his eyes with his forearm. The whiskey and heavy lunch had made him nice and sleepy. Soon, he was snoring and Mummyji was wide awake.

While Rajan Papa's stomach rose and fell in a steady rhythmic growl, his mother stared blankly at the ceiling. The pink and blue cherubs etched into the plaster, which had silently watched her family for more than thirty years, drifted in and out of focus as she went from waking to a dreamy state. The drugs had made her heavy-lidded and her lips felt dry. She allowed herself to nod off and enter her sepia-toned world that had morphed from a combination of the odd photograph, memory, and imagination.

They were playing badminton in the courtyard of their old Ludhiana house. She was in her favourite lemon yellow salwar kameez, with her white chunni draped around one shoulder and tied at her waist like a sash. The person on the other side... Ah, yes, it was her cousin Phoolchand. She was fifteen and had just learned how to make luscious triangular aloo and mooli parathas, soaked in fresh ghee, ordained to turn any man into the maker's slave. This particular skill was the final qualifier for matrimony.

She wiped the sweat off her face with her chunni, grabbed Phoolchand and ran inside, playfully hitting her little sister Bindu on the way, and laughing loudly at her mother who shouted from the kitchen. 'Oye Nimmo, khasmakhan, if you keep running around like a drunken billy goat, how are you going to settle into a sari and be a coy wife? Your mother-in-law will reprimand you, and then also curse me, for bringing you up like this...'

Mummyji used to be Nirmala or Nimmo before she was married and before her husband's family changed her name to Bimla. It was the customary practice. When a woman entered her husband's home, she was given a new name.

She shot back to her mother. 'Oye, Chaiji. Any mother-in-law would be less cruel than you! Hee Hee.'

Her innocence blurred the realities that screamed at her from all around: the girl down the street who always looked sad. And the cousin whom no one discussed, who had disappeared mysteriously a few months after her wedding. And dear Geetan, the woman who used to empty the litter box every day. Her parents had given her to an old imbecile opium addict because they had no dowry. At thirty, after five children, she was already haggard.

Nimmo's prospects were good—her family was well-off, she was pretty enough, had large child-bearing hips, and had mastered the Great Paratha Secret.

Then, Bauji, her father's elder brother, dropped the bomb. Many years ago, he had promised Sundersingh Aggarwal, an old business associate from Amritsar, that he would give one of his girls to his family. When Aggarwal sahib's son was the right age, he sent a message to confirm the betrothal. The girl next in line for marriage at the time would be Nimmo. Her parents went to see the boy. To their horror, the Aggarwal women did not come out of their rooms. And when they did, to take Nimmo's mother for a darshan to the Golden Temple, two sheets were placed on either side of the driveway to create a purdah until the women had made their way to the closed horse buggy on the street.

On their way home, Chaiji said to her husband, 'Whatever happens, I cannot give my daughter here. They are way too conservative.'

'But what about Bauji? You know how he is about giving his word. There's no going back.'

'I don't care. You deal with him. But this marriage will take place only over my dead body.'

That evening, after dinner, when the women were clearing up, Nimmo's father sat in the courtyard and, filled with trepidation, ventured to bring up the subject. 'Bauji, I'm not quite sure that Nimmo is right for this family. You know how she is, like a butterfly who cannot be contained. She will suffocate.'

The elderly man took a deep drag from his hookah and did not answer. His younger brother tried again, started a sentence, and faltered. Then, Nimmo's mother came into the room. Without looking at her elder brother-in-law, she said, 'This marriage cannot take place.' Her husband stared at his wife.

No one spoke after that. Nimmo watched the scene unfold from behind a pillar, filled with both terror and admiration.

Bauji had to go back on his word and the entire community got to know of the broken promise. It was considered a deep insult and Nimmo's marriage stock nosedived. As their neighbour, Veena, put it, 'Who would want to associate with people who think their daughter is such a princess that they must break their promise over her. Shame.'

A few months later, Nimmo's mother's told her husband, 'We have got a proposal from a progressive family in Bombay. Phoolchand knows them well. I would like my daughter to go there.'

Kulbhushan's family was originally from Ludhiana but had settled in Bombay during the war, where they traded and speculated in grains. They were not that rich, and the groom was on the short side, but because of some sly bargaining on the part of the marriage broker, they were getting fresh curd for the price of wheat. Nimmo was gleeful at the prospect of moving to a strange new big city which she had only experienced in cinema—Ashok Kumar riding a tonga down the lovely long promenade by the sea.

The families met at a relative's house in Ludhiana, where the honey-skinned Nimmo wore a red-and-gold salwar kurta and served them—what else?—home-cooked parathas on a silver platter, and when her naughty smile twinkled at the young man who sat munching on her savouries, he felt a tidal wave rise inside him and gulped to curb its path. How could he not say 'Yes'?

And that is how Nirmala metamorphosed to Bimla, the name picked by her future mother-in-law when she put the gold chain around her neck, firmly obliterating her maiden identity and all those giggling days when she had swung into the sun, thrown her head back and let her hair almost touch the ground. She was sweet sixteen, seven years younger than her betrothed.

A little over a year after Nimmo and Kulbhushan got married, her father died of a sudden heart attack caused by the tension of going against the wishes of the family elders. She didn't get to go back for the funeral and her grief remained in limbo.

'Nimmo! Nimmo! How are you, behenji? Hai bhagwan! You look so pale. They phoned me in the morning, and luckily I could get a car to rush over, twadde kol.' It was Nimmo's younger sister Bindu from Pune, bustling into the room like a giant owl, her eyes barely visible behind the thick round spectacles that hid most of her face. Bindu masi was the last person alive to call Mummyji by her birth name. She was a much stouter version of her sister, and she dyed her hair with henna, but otherwise, the olive skin, the rosebud bow-and-arrow lips...they were all from the same mould.

Rajni followed her inside and asked if she could get her something to drink. She involuntarily began pressing Mummyji's feet while waiting for Bindu masi to reply. Mummyji slowly sat up, wincing slightly. On cue, Rajni promptly jumped up and propped some pillows behind her. Mummyji sighed as she sank back into them.

'Yes, Rajni beti,' said Bindu masi. 'Please get me a glass of cold sherbet. It is unbearably hot outside.' She turned to her sister, 'Behenji, Rajni may be a servant, but she really looks after you like a daughter. I don't know what you would do without her.'

Rajni left the room beaming to herself. 'And what would I do without Mummyji,' she said to herself. 'Dear god, please make her better. I will not eat eggs until she has recovered and I will light a lamp in front of Krishna all day.'

She made a glass of sparkling crimson rose-flavoured sherbet, wiped the rim with the tip of her sari and went back into the room, where Mummyji and Bindu masi were talking in whispers because Rajan Papa, who had turned from his back on to his side, was now in deep slumber, curled up like a child who sleeps most soundly when he is by his mother's side.

'Sunny still has so much anger inside him,' said Mummyji weakly. 'My heart breaks when I see how he speaks, in dull monosyllables, to his elder brother. I can't understand these boys. Where did I go wrong, Bindu? Girls go away, but at least my boys were supposed to be the two pillars on whom I could rest in my old age. But they are both so weak.'

'Don't worry yourself with all this,' said Bindu masi. 'You have done your best as a mother. The rest is up to them. If they are going to keep behaving like this, then it's their problem, not yours. We all do our best as mothers.' She knew, even as she spoke, that this wasn't true. How could a mother detach herself from her children? What could she tell her dear sister—that her children had been bred on a diet of greed and ignorance, that it had destroyed their family? Her heart moved with the futility of her sister's pain.

Mummyji turned her head towards the wall. She didn't want her younger sister to see her tears. Her thin, frail body twitched gently as she controlled her sobs, overwhelmed with self-pity.

Just then, Rahul entered the room and her fears suddenly vanished. She loved him so much, her beloved curly-haired grandson with gentle brown eyes, her renewed hope, her legacy. Grandchildren offer what children cannot. He was also her son of sorts, but in that distant way, which is sometimes the prerequisite for unconditional love.

Rahul sat on the floor, kneeling next to his grandmother's bed, holding her hand, stroking it softly. He looked sad when he felt her raised blue-green veins and the papery wrinkled skin that you see on an ancient elephant. His beloved Dadima suddenly seemed so fragile.

He used to find great comfort in the way she used to order and organize her life, the way she managed to coordinate the drop-offs of goodies to all her children, remembering that Rajan Papa had to have less salt, or that Diya loved extra-sweet boondi laddoos. For him, Cozy Villa was the place where he would drop in after school, laze around, eat a lot, drink Thums Up crackling with big cubes of ice, and never be questioned. She would chat with him about mithais and about the magic of milk. Whenever his parents travelled, he came and stayed with his grandmother. He felt miserable at the thought of not having her boss him around and order his favourite snack of sweet bhel from the vendor down the road, or sneak him a few rupees so he could go down and buy Bullseyes from the old man with the sweet basket. Most of all, he loved her smell. It was her peculiar musty, old-fashioned scent, a combination of burped-up food and sandalwood and stale hair oil. It gave him solace and helped him cope with his own confusions. Rahul saw his father stirring next to her and felt a tinge of anger towards him for no apparent reason.

With her grandson next to her, Mummyji felt a surge of strength course through her, as if her limbs had been injected with a gentle love potion. She decided that she didn't want to go just yet. There was more to be done. She wanted to see Rahul's children. She wanted to spend more Diwalis with all the little ones around her. Her old self came back and suddenly she was greedy for life. She had things to say about Bimz, the quality of the pista barfis had gone down, the kulchas were not being stuffed properly. She was still the main signatory on the cheques.

By the time Suman came over with Smriti and Sumit, Mummyji was almost back to being Mummyji and even remembered to give an annual pre-Diwali command to the servant: 'Ratansingh, clear the ceiling cobwebs in both the bathrooms and don't be lazy about polishing all the silver.'

Hearing her instructional, even if slurry, voice was more reassuring to the family than anything the doctor could have said.

Rajan Papa returned home with Rahul, feeling terrible. The thought of money had now begun to overpower him in a manner he had never before experienced. Panic enveloped him and eclipsed all other feelings. Just before leaving, he had asked Rajni for Mummyji's bunch of keys. She said she didn't know where they were. He had hoped to look under the pillow where she usually kept them, but did not have a chance for there was always someone or the other in the Fairy Room.

He had three whiskeys that night, crunching into several roasted Amritsari papads on the side to soften the blow to his stomach. An hour later, his head buzzed and he felt an enormous sense of loss. Through his haze he came to an important realization—that his mother would not really be there for him, whether she was alive or dead. She had known of his trouble with Bhatija and remained silent, and she had sided with Sunny. He had no control over the next thought that buzzed through his head like an angry insect. He blinked several times to fight it back but it buzzed louder. How could he allow such a gruesome thought, but no, it was there... he wanted her to die.

Luckily for him, the phone rang, cutting short the thought and bringing him back to his comfort zone of vagueness. It was Gurnath Advani, calling to say 'Happy Diwali'. Rajan Papa spoke slowly, measuring his words, so that his new friend didn't catch on to the fact that he was inexorably drunk.

'Wish you the same...the same. I will see you next week at Shraddhashram. Hari Om.' He put the phone down and felt even sadder at the great betrayal of his mind. He wished there was someone he could talk to, but he had very few friends. There were the Lion's Club couples he and Manju used to meet once a month at the club, but he could hardly talk to them about these things. You don't go around telling people you are sad. You can talk about the weather, or corruption in the Congress party, or why you think the Americans are corrupting your country, but you cannot talk about sad thoughts. You certainly cannot tell them that you momentarily wished your mother dead.

Rajan Papa's dinner had been laid out a while back. But the plastic hot pots had not managed to keep the food warm and he felt sorry for himself as he dipped his roti into the tepid toor daal and cold baingan bharta. As usual, the servant had forgotten to keep his favourite gobhi-shalgam pickle out. He ate listlessly, alone, aware that he was dropping bits of daal on the plastic table cover every time he served himself. As he munched slowly on the aloo paratha, his numb taste buds could not even savour the ajwain and coriander that punctuated the potatoes.

Rahul had eaten in his room as usual. Manju was not home. Why should she be? Her parents were having their annual card party that evening and she wanted to be there, with her brothers and sisters and cousins and lots of film stars, all of whom were rich—unlike him.

Down the corridor from him, Rahul lay on a futon on the floor, smoking his second stick of marijuana. He knew that he was getting into trouble, but this made life much easier. He had just masturbated, in urgent, restless hand movements, to a blurry, pirated orgy of men on screen, until his wrist hurt. Back and forth, back and forth, he had gone, for he had no other recourse. In a few years, his parents would be busy scouting around for a wife—a woman who was suitably semi-educated and suitably semi-obedient—and he would get entrenched in their world of lies. He had to escape.

Rahul could not physically run away. So he had started altering his reality. He was introduced to the perfect escape route by his school friend Barun, who lived a few buildings down from him and had been his chaddi buddy. They were walking near Chowpatty late one night when Barun said, 'Yaar, I am going to get you stoned tonight. I have some great maal, fresh from paradise.'

'Yo!' said Rahul, enthusiastic about the novelty of this adventure.

Barun pulled out a tightly rolled cigarette from his pocket. Its tip was pinched together like an elongated nipple. He held it up as if it were a wand about to work its magic.

'You have to drag deep on this cigarette and wait a few seconds before blowing out.' He demonstrated how to do it, dramatically. Then, forgetting his original mission of initiation, he continued to smoke on his own.

'Hey, hey! What about me, bandhu?' said Rahul.

'Okay, here. Go for it. Say a prayer before you start so that you get it right. Ha ha! Welcome to Manali, my friend. We prefer to call it Manwali.'

They had sat cross-legged on the parapet facing the silvery ocean, letting the sweet marijuana smoke mingle with the fishy smell below. Rahul sputtered and coughed and made sincere efforts to inhale. An enormous rat disappeared into the giant stone tetrapods below. The tetrapods may have been placed against the wall to break the force of the waves against the land, but they doubled as safe hiding places and hid many of the city's secrets.

'Did you know where we are sitting was once all part of the sea? The waves went all the way up to the railway tracks,' said Barun, his speech slowing down. He was entering that hazy space where a beaded curtain opens up and seemingly irrelevant things suddenly find meaning. Rahul was following close behind.

'Really? That's very wild, yaar!'

Soon, the queen's necklace turned into a happy blur of twinkle twinkle little stars. Rahul smiled at the ocean, then turned around to face the world, a new man.

It was as if some unwanted baggage was sliding off his back and being absorbed by the water. He would soon be free to run. He did just that a few minutes later—sprinted down the pavement a few metres and back. No one seemed to notice anything odd about his behaviour. The people around them seemed to be absorbed in finding their own freedom away from their lives.

Barun stopped a cyclist who tinkled past them with his canister of hot tea and little plastic cups. 'Hey bhau. Give us two!'

They sipped the sweet tea and felt light-headed and giddy, watching the speeding cars that now seemed like timeless moments in a video game.

It soon became a weekly ritual. They started out on the pavement on the Nariman Point end, where the horse carriages with flashy lights and emaciated animals stood around waiting for business, and walked all the way down to the point where the flyover sloped down to the main concourse. They then perched themselves somewhere along the parapet. Sometimes, Barun brought a friend from his building, Bawari, a nonchalant girl with a wiry nose ring who didn't speak much and smoked joints with great flair—or at least Rahul thought so. He tried to copy the way she held the cigarette, with her thumb and index finger, her eyes just slightly narrowing as she dragged.

One evening, just a few days before Diwali, he came unaccompanied. He slapped his friend on the back. 'I have another surprise in store for you, Rahul beta. You are going to thank me for the rest of your life.'

They smoked in silence, ignoring a policeman who strolled past them, looking for cuddling couples to harass. Two teenaged boys would be relatively profitless in comparison to the bounties that could be made from the young men and women whom he caught in the middle of their ecstacies.

When they were done with their smoke, Barun jumped off the ledge in a deft manoeuvre, using one hand, the way they had been taught on the pommel horse in the school gym.

'Follow me, my friend!' He laughed.

They walked down towards Chowpatty beach and reached a dark, unlit garden just before the sandy stretch that housed the food stalls. Barun jumped over the turnstile and went inside with practised ease. Rahul hesitated, then followed. It took him a while to get used to the shadowy movements of branches and limbs inside the secret garden. They walked into a gazebo which smelled of dank bird shit. A neon light from a hoarding on high blinked on and off, lighting up a small patch of grass.

'Now just wait,' whispered Barun. He then whistled softly.

A few minutes later, a tall woman in a sari appeared out of the darkness and walked into the gazebo. Mouth job, he said in crude Hindi to her. Two hundred, she replied, in a deep, husky voice. The deal was clinched and the money paid—beforehand, always.

He pushed Rahul towards her, and said, 'Go on!' As Rahul stepped off the gazebo step, Barun added, in a loud whisper, 'Enjoy!'

Another woman glided in like a ghost and Barun followed her in the opposite direction.

Rahul followed his partner to the other side of an enormous tangle of bougainvillea bushes which shrouded them from the other clandestine operations that may have been taking place in the garden. The woman laid out a mat she was carrying with her and told him to lie on it, a little abruptly. Then, in a more gentle tone, she told him to pull down his jeans and underpants. He did, grimacing at the thought of who—and what—else had seeped into the furry fabric that now touched his naked backside. As she knelt over him, he was disgusted by her cheap scent but then simultaneously comforted by the more natural aroma of coconut hair oil reminding him that she was an ordinary girl making her living. Gradually, and with extraordinary talent, she worked on him, holding him tight at the base, teasing and enveloping him with her tongue, pushing down his outer casing and leading him, finally, into a state of blankness.

He had touched heaven.

Rahul's partner generously let him lie there a few minutes while she turned the other way, slit open a packet of gutka and poured the contents into her mouth. Almost in slow motion, he got up and walked away, still a virgin at sixteen, but initiated.

Barun was still not back from his pleasure spot. Rahul leaned against the gazebo column, oblivious now of the pigeon crap, of the neon light, the grass, or the night shadows. He heard Barun laughing and the sound of twigs crunching.

As they walked out of the garden and towards Marine Drive, now much quieter, Barun slapped Rahul on the back and said, 'Well?'

Rahul merely laughed. 'Yaar, that was real.'

They walked further in silence until Barun said, 'Okay, I may as well tell you.'

'What?'

'The women were both men.'

Barun thought that Rahul would clobber him playfully or at least express shock over the he-woman who had just squeezed his private juices out of him. Little did he know that this detail actually made the whole experience even more erotic for his friend.

One day before Diwali…

AFTER LEAVING MUMMYJI'S HOUSE, SUNNY went straight to the Kalbadevi shop. He was edgy and sat on a corner table, his leg involuntarily drumming the ground beneath it. One of the workers brought a cup of tea and a glass beer mug of mixed fruit juice, the colour of pomegranate, and set it in front of him, followed by a plate of fresh chhole and fluffy bhature. Sunny bit into a whole green chilli and munched on it, staring at the circular puddles of oil that danced in the dish in front of him. He continued to sit there for a while, absent-mindedly sipping the tea, unaware about the clamour and clutter that the brisk pre-Diwali business was generating behind him. The store manager, Phoolchand's son, brought a copy of *The Times of India* folded to the page which carried a small advertisement they had inserted. Above a drawing of a big bowl of laddoos it read:

For your sweet tooth this Diwali, come to BIMZ.
To avoid disappointment, book your purchase now!
20% discount on early orders
Free home delivery!
Phone: 237265

His eye ran over the box and the rest of the page. Next to the advertisement was a picture of a still from the film *Sagar,* with the caption: Look who's back together: Rishi and Dimple.

He got up suddenly and, without finishing his juice or snack, left for the office next to the shop. He went into his cabin, shutting the door behind him. He sat there with his elbows on the desk, his head in his hands looking morosely at a short grey steel cupboard in the corner which had been there right from the early days of the shop, when it was still Bimmo di Barfi. The door of the cupboard still bore a faint remnant of the red swastika that had been imprinted on it, year after year during the Diwali pooja. The cupboard contained not just money, but promissory notes, valuable papers and a red diary bound in white thread that everyone knew was important but no one had bothered opening since Daddyji's death.

It was five in the evening. Most people were getting ready to leave the office. Sunny suddenly felt aroused, which had become his instinctive response to depression or stress. It was his escape route. He got up and walked out, leaving a small white towel folded neatly on the right hand corner of his table. This was a cue for Lolita, who sat outside. They had worked out a system of cues and secret codes to communicate with each other so that it did not compromise the professional space of the office. The white towel—her suggestion—meant that he wanted her to meet him for a quickie. Most times, it led to a coordinated ritual. He would leave a little earlier and go to Mummyji's house and she would follow a little later.

But because he was so preoccupied that day, what his code language failed to communicate to her was that she should not go to Cozy Villa, where his mother lay dying, but to their old haunt, Ocean Breeze hotel.

So, about an hour later, Lolita arrived at Cozy Villa at exactly the same time as Jassu. Both arrived in an intoxicating cloud of Poison, a perfume which had been gifted to them by the same person. Lolita was wearing a long black skirt with a tight-fitting red T-shirt, her breasts protruding. Jassu was in a pale blue chiffon sari, her long hair still damp from a recent wash. She rang the bell and threw her hair back with a flourish.

Inside, Mummyji was deep inside the folds of her life. The past seemed real and alive now. She was fifteen years old, married just about four months. She woke up early that morning with a faint sense of excitement followed by homesickness. It was her birthday. She turned around and looked at Kulbhushan who was sleeping on his side, and gently lifted his arm off her stomach, where it had come to rest, almost proprietorially. This was the time she loved him the most—when he was hers, unencumbered by ritual, undistracted by pesky family, unconditionally devoted to her and her young, yearning body. She rolled out of bed, braiding her hair with quick practised finger movements and, on reaching the end, threw back the long thick rope. She picked up the sari that was lying crumpled in a heap on the floor where it had been thrown the previous night, amidst hushed whispers and shuffles. She stood in front of the full-length mirror and looked at herself. She cupped her hands under her breasts and admired them. She ran her hands down to her waist and gently touched her pelvis through her petticoat. She winced mildly at the soreness in her groin and remembered her conversation with her mother, Chaiji.

'You must give your husband whatever he wants, kudiye. From now on, you belong to him—body, mind, and soul. Do everything he says, even if it doesn't suit you at the time. Forget about your free days, they got left behind with Nimmo. You are now Bimmo and you must learn to walk on the razor's edge. After a while, you will get very good at it.' Nimmo had scowled at her mother when she lectured her while massaging oil into her long hair and braiding it into two tight plaits. But deep down, she knew the truth. A few seconds later, as if she suddenly grew up in those moments, she had turned around and nestled her head in her mother's bosom. Both had tears in their eyes, in which swam foreboding for a future that was fearful, inevitable.

Bimmo turned around and looked at her husband, who was still snoring. She walked to the foot of the bed and touched his feet and then her forehead. She started humming the title song from one of her favourite films in which the heroine sings of worshipping the dust from her husband's feet. Bimmo enjoyed these romantic ideas.

A loud bellowing suddenly emanated from the room adjoining theirs in the chawl. Ma was up. Kulbhushan's mother had this infuriating habit of getting up and, first thing in the morning, singing hymns in praise of various gods out loud, with complete disrespect to the sleeping members of her family or her neighbours. Besides giving the gods an earful, it was a stentorian wake-up call for the household. No one dared admonish her, least of all her husband, who would use this time to go for his early morning walk to the beach—a sensible escapist route he thereafter adopted for most matters in life.

Kulbhushan stirred and groaned. He reached out for his bride and pulled her back into the bed with him. She feigned protest and then lay down for a few minutes to indulge him. But Ma's crackling voice overwhelmed the room and there was no space left for love.

Bimmo forgot that it was her birthday. She quickly bathed, wore one of the saris her in-laws had given her, pulled her hair into a tight bun, and ran out of the room into the room next door where her in-laws lived. The minute she saw her mother-in-law, she pulled her sari over her head and touched her feet. 'Bless you,' said Ma, warmly. 'May you live a long life and bear many healthy sons. Now come with me.'

Bimmo shyly followed her to the other side of the room which was separated into two by a thick curtain. Ma plucked the keys from her waist, where they were always securely fastened, and opened her creaky steel cupboard. She pulled a drawer. From its innards, she pulled out a large red-and-gold pouch and shoved it into Bimmo's palm.

'Open it,' she ordered.

Bimmo did, unable to hide her girlish excitement and even letting her sari fall from her head. It was a gold necklace, intricately crafted in the old style, with semi-precious stones inlaid along the neckline. This was to be the first of many trinkets which Bimmo would receive only to realize that, while she could wear them freely, they never really belonged to her; they were part of the family's community assets that could be called upon any time.

'Thank you, Maji,' mumbled Bimmo shyly, once again bending to touch her feet. For a brief moment, she allowed herself to love her new family.

'Cover your head, Bimla,' said Ma, in a tone that made Bimmo remember that this was never going to be her mother.

The most unnerving thing about Ma was that she was unpredictable. Her moods swung from benign to vicious at the drop of a pallu and there was no telling where one stood with her. Bimmo slunk out of the room and went straight into the small kitchen space in her room to start the preparations for the morning. There was tea to be made, and kachoris to be fried for breakfast. After that, lunch would be cooked—at least two vegetables, a daal and some rice and roti. That was then packed into tiffins for the men. After all that was over, the women would have to knead dough for puris, which would be served up at teatime.

Bimmo sighed as she reached for the oil jar. Was this what marriage was all about? Slaving in the kitchen with an old woman breathing down her neck? Having a husband who forgot about her during daylight hours? Not being allowed to go out and play a game of badminton with the other children in the chawl?

It was only at about eleven in the morning that she again remembered, when the bell to her room rang and her uncle's servant stood at the door, holding a box of sweets for her birthday. Bimmo took one look at it and stifled a deep sob and ran into her room. She flung herself on her bed, thrust her face into the pillow and started sobbing. A few minutes later, she sensed Ma's presence in the room and pretended to be asleep. Ma stood there quietly for a few moments and then, without saying a word, walked out. Both pretended as though the bedroom scene had never taken place.

Kulbhushan came home at six that evening. He had asked his father's permission to leave early because it was his wife's birthday and Bauji had instantly agreed, even though they were in the middle of Navratra and business was brisk. Bimmo had no idea about the celebration plans—they did not have a telephone in their rooms and they could only use the neighbour's phone down the corridor for important matters. She was still sulking about how no one really loved her in this new place and how she longed to go back home. She arranged her hair with two curlers on either side of her temple to get that cute little swivel, like Madhubala. By the time Kulbhushan would arrive, an hour later, she would be perfectly dressed for him to admire, with her hair done, and maybe a jasmine flower in it, if the flower vendor showed up. Every evening, this was the time she used to dabble with the cosmetic tray that had come in her bridal trousseau. Today, she would wear not just the usual kohl, but also some pink rouge.

When she heard the familiar three-tone ring of the cycle bell that announced Kulbhushan's arrival, she ran to the balcony.

He stood there and said, 'You thought I had forgotten! We are going to celebrate, my pretty one. Go get dressed.' Bimmo was about to hug her husband when she remembered where she was and The Rules: No public affection. Not allowed to utter her husband's name, she could only refer to him in the third person. Her head had to be covered in front of him when any of the elders were present. And if she wanted to call him, it had to be: 'Sunoji!'

He hollered, 'Maaaaa! We are going to a see a film and we won't be eating dinner at home.'

Kulbhushan's niece and nephew scampered out of their grandparents' room and hugged their uncle. 'Chachu, Chachu. We want to come too.'

Kulbhushan and Bimmo watched *Tansen* starring K.L. Saigal, which she found dreadfully boring, and they ate idli and dosa in a small restaurant next to Liberty movie hall. After the movie, they went to Chowpatty beach, where they ate bhelpuri and creamy kulfi and sat on the cool sand, hardly speaking, just watching the waves kiss each other. Bimmo nestled her head against Kulbhushan's shoulder and softly imitated Saigal's nasal pitch.

Later that night, when they were back in their room, and the household was quiet, Kulbhushan surprised his wife. He reached into his coat pocket and pulled out a packet.

'This is something that no one can take away from you. It does not belong to the family. It is yours and no one can stake a claim on it. Keep it carefully. Don't tell Ma, or even anyone in your family about it. It is from my personal earnings. I went and picked it from Motilal today. In a few years, when I have made enough, I will get you a second one so you will have a pair, my dear wife.'

Bimmo stared at Kulbhushan's hand in awe. Cradled in his palm lay an enormous diamond, almost the size of a laddoo, sparkling magnificently in the light of the bedside lamp. It was the most beautiful thing she had ever seen. She picked one up and walked to the mirror. She stood in front of it, and placed it on her neck, then on one of her ear lobes, laughing. 'What shall I make with it?'

Kulbhushan put the jewel back into its little cloth bag and instructed her on where she should hide it. In a large family, the vault is like the in-house whore, which anyone can use at any time. Instead, he told her to stitch the stone into the crimson sari draped around the lovely marble statue of Laxmi that sat in a corner of the room occupied by his parents. It was a brilliant suggestion. No one would find it there. He then pulled Bimmo to him, pushing them both back on the bed. She wished he would be a little gentler, but didn't know how to tell him. Then her thoughts went to the evening, the sea and the movie, and the lovely gift, and she felt happy.

Forty years later, Mummyji could hear the same ocean outside her balcony and she fell asleep, disoriented.

Jassu and Lolita stood on the landing, waiting for the door to be opened. There was a hint of a strain in the air, but neither of them caught on why. How would they have imagined that they were both sleeping with the same man—or, rather, one of them was. Jassu was still distracted by her anger and was plotting ways in which she could squeeze the diamonds out of her mother-in-law. Lolita was wondering why on earth Sunny had told her to come to Cozy Villa, if there were going to be other people there. She waited respectfully, behind Jassu.

They continued to stand outside, avoiding eye contact, until Ratansingh opened the door. He looked at the two women, puzzled for a moment, then looked down and became expressionless in the way that servants do when they know they are not supposed to react to the strange things their employers do or say.

Jasmeen walked in first, and Lolita followed. They took off their sandals together outside the living room. Both were wearing high heels. Lolita's slightly frayed black heels fell to their side. There were two other pairs of women's shoes there. Jassu walked past the kitchen into the Fairy Room to see Mummyji who, at that point in her dream sequence, was admiring the jewel her husband had placed on her palm and was about to hide it away, almost as if she instinctively knew that the predators had started to surround her.

Sure enough, when Mummyji opened her eyes, she saw Jassu hovering around her and the first thing that came into her head was the image of a vulture waiting for its prey to die. Next to her was her other daughter-in-law, Manju. As soon as they saw her wake up, they both came and said with exaggerated concern, 'Mummyji...' and, at that moment, the only person she really wanted was Rajni—and a bedpan.

The drugs were still heavy on her and she felt wooden. She heard their voices ordering Rajni around and, instead of feeling relieved that there were three women in the room fussing over her, she felt strangely insecure. This was, perhaps, the first time in her life, other than the time her mother died, when she felt completely out of control. That was worse than death.

Lolita waited in the living room for a few minutes. Where was Sunny? Where was his mother? Something was clearly going on. Either way, she didn't feel comfortable. She walked towards the Fairy Room and stopped at the door when she saw Mummyji lying there, with the two well-dressed women sitting next to her. She thought she saw Mummyji look at her with an expression of faint disgust and suddenly she felt like an intruder. She knew there was something wrong. She quickly walked back to the living room, her heart beating faster. *Where was Sunny?* What kind of cruel joke was he playing? She was sure he had wanted her to meet him. He had given her the look as he left the office and the towel had been put in position. She suddenly felt paranoid that something had happened to him. She sat as still as the Mirabai statue, staring at a family wedding picture, zooming in and out on the overdressed people in the frame, looking for Sunny, and then the hideous realization struck her. Oh god! The woman next to Sunny was the one she had just seen, in the blue sari. She had walked in with her lover's wife. This was their home. The picture in front of her was taken at their wedding reception. He actually looked happy.

She quietly got up, slipped on her sandals and left the house. She went to Churchgate station next door and took a fast train home, standing all the way, her thoughts as sodden as the damp, tired armpits all around her. The next morning, she would be on the bus to Jabalpur, to celebrate the festival, where she would sit at the feet of her blind grandmother and listen to her retell tales from the Ramayana and remind her that even if your father had brushed his fingers across your breasts when you were a little girl, you must control the anger and pray. Bad things happen. You can't allow that moment to dictate the rest of your life. She felt comforted at the thought of seeing her beloved grandmother.

In another part of the city, Sunny lay on his back on a purple-and-pink velvet machine-made blanket in a corner room on the second floor of a hotel, the green glazed windows shut, waiting, masturbating, sweating, miserable.

It was that time of day when the sound of children's voices playing downstairs starts tapering off as they all make their way back home. Rajni and Ratansingh were performing their evening ritual of pulling at a washed sari that crackled with starch. It was the last sari that Mummyji had worn before she slipped reluctantly into one of her daughter's nighties which fell loosely around her skinny shoulders.

After she had pulled the rest of the clothes off the blue nylon clothesline in the balcony, Rajni came into the Fairy Room. It was silent, except for the soft clickety-clack of the needles. Saroj was knitting, determined to complete

Rahul's sleeveless sweater before winter, on behalf of her mother.

It was getting dark outside. From downstairs, and all around, there came sounds of happiness—of children squealing and the heady buzz of fireworks and upbeat film music on someone's radio. Rajni switched on the light. As the tube light flickered on and lit up the ceiling cherubs, Saroj plunged momentarily into that black space that had become her favoured hideout. Then, she heard her mother sigh and was grateful for the distraction of having to take care of her.

Mummyji was breathing heavily and kept clenching her forehead as if she was struggling with something. She pointed feebly to the ground and her loyal helper immediately reached out to the bedpan beneath the bed. With the help of Saroj, she gently lifted Mummyji and laid it beneath her. After she was done, Rajni got a comb and ran it through Mummyji's hair, then redid her thin silvery braid and placed it on the side as if she were a little girl.

Mummyji spoke in a hoarse whisper, stopping between sentences to get her breath.

'Is there enough oil in the diyas to last through the night? Did you get the Campa Colas?'

'Don't you worry, Mummyji,' said Saroj, caressing her mother's cheek as if she were a baby. 'Everything is organized. Everyone is coming. Everything is going to go just the way it always does. And you will be better soon.'

She was mouthing the words but she knew in her heart that all of what she was saying was untrue. Mummyji was fading, and every flicker of life was just a teaser before the tube light went out.

After sitting with Mummyji for some time, Jassu had started prowling around the house. She briefly wondered who the attractive woman was who had come in with her and then disappeared. She must have come to sell something, or maybe she was from the office. She went into the kitchen storeroom and ran her eye over the cupboards. She opened one and was assailed by a smell of stale oil from the sticky raw mango pickle. She lifted the jar and put it back down. Now the smell entered her fingertips. She then went into the second bedroom, the one that adjoined the Fairy Room. It was the one she had stayed in briefly after returning from America. A small photograph of Mummyji and Daddyji inside a blackened silver frame rested on the sideboard. Jassu picked it up and looked at the father-in-law whom she had never met, and decided that she liked him. He would have been her ally.

She sat on the large king-sized bed that sprawled awkwardly across most of the space—soon after their marriage, an astrologer had told them to shift the headboard to the south side so that they could have a happy life together. She remembered the Sunday mornings when they would lie there, without drawing the curtains, so that they could prolong the night. Her insides felt tousled. She thought of Sunny. She thought of his lover who had begun to encroach on her thoughts all the time. She had become the default option in Jassu's headspace, this woman she had never met, an imagined creature, playing footsie with her sanity. The tenderness Jassu briefly felt towards her husband and the happy memories of their time in the room once again dissolved into rage. She got up and went into the living room. She opened one of the drawers in the cabinet, felt exhausted on seeing the medley of household rubbish that it contained, and shut it again. She decided to sit and wait, to plan her next move.

A little while later, Suman arrived at Cozy Villa. Seeing that Mummyji was sleeping, she came and sat in the living room and asked Rajni for tea and rusks.

'She's sleeping,' she said to Jassu.

'Shouldn't we get her a nurse?' Jassu said. 'When my grandfather had a stroke, we arranged a day–night nurse for him. It really made him feel more comfortable.'

'We could, but what are daughters-in-law there for?' Suman said. She realized how rude she sounded and then spoke in a more placating voice. 'We could get someone. But Rajni seems capable of handling things,' she said, smiling at Rajni, who had just walked in carrying a big teapot gloved inside a white lace filigreed tea cosy to keep it hot.

Suman and Jassu didn't speak to each other for a few minutes. Both were not ready to leave. They independently had plans of sifting through the chorkhana and looking for the diamonds. Each one thought the jewels rightfully belonged to her, Suman for being the eldest beloved daughter, Jassu for being the wronged daughter-in-law. Suman had carved out an elaborate plan to get Rajni involved in this exercise. Jassu was still not sure how she would go about it.

Rajan Papa arrived and now the three of them continued to sit there in silence.

Jassu suddenly felt emboldened. Rajan Papa was her enemy's enemy, so she could confide in him, complain.

'Rajan Papa, why can't you speak to Sunny? He is not bothered about his family. You are his elder brother,' she said. She sounded nasal and desperate.

Rajan Papa looked at his sister-in-law, taken aback at her manipulative outburst. He didn't reply. He was in no position to take on his brother's family issues. He got up and helped himself to a cup of tea. He stared at a large portrait of Daddyji that hung on the wall and suddenly realized how much he missed his father. He would have taken care of so many things that had gone horribly wrong in their lives. He was now the eldest male in the family but he didn't feel like he could take on such a mantle.

A few minutes later, he got up and went to the Fairy Room. The two women followed him. They both looked tense, poised to do something big. It was their time to strike.

Mummyji's eyes were now open, but she wasn't looking at anything in particular. It was as if door after door inside her was slowly closing. A few old rooms were opening up, but only so that she could enter them to say goodbye to old times. Then, they were gone. The more recent doors had already turned into blank white spaces as she navigated the corridors of her subconscious. She could hear distant voices rising and falling around her.

'Mummyji,' said Jassu softly, 'we really want to sort out your things. Do please give us the keys. With you in this condition, it is not safe to leave things at home, especially your diamonds. They should be taken to the bank locker.'

'Don't talk rubbish, Jassu. How can they be taken to the bank?' Suman snapped. 'They are not declared to the tax department. You should know better than that.'

'Well, either way, we should know where they are, right?' Jassu said, the softness in her voice suddenly gone. 'Mummyji…'

'What are you people doing? This is hardly the time to bring this up,' said Rajan Papa. His voice emerged as a low growl.

'Please don't talk to me in that tone,' said Jassu.

Saroj instinctively started stroking Mummyji's hand. She silently wondered where the diamonds, in fact, were. The last time she had seen them was at her wedding, when her mother had worn them and elicited many envious stares. It was not something she had even thought about since. She was quite certain she had not seen them inside the locker. She looked at her sister and, after a long time, felt enormous anger towards her. How insensitive could a person be? How could she be so selfish at a time like this? All those great speeches she gave to others, why couldn't she apply them to herself? Suman got up and walked out of the room, shaking slightly.

While they argued, Mummyji's head ached and she felt dizzy. She was scared and fatigued, tired of a lifetime of mediating between her husband, in-laws, and now children, holding back her own emotions to let others volcanically release theirs. It was only duties, no rights. The constitution did not apply to her. Why should she bother any more? If her release could only come in the form of death, so be it. At least it would take her to the other side.

The voices around her stopped making any sense; they sounded like barks and growls and whimpers and chirps. Suddenly, she felt her left arm tingle and then go numb. She tried to speak, to alert the family that something was going on with her body, but her mouth was refusing to listen to her. It opened but nothing came out. The words remained in her head and then swam away in front of her eyes in a jumble of letters. They were too busy to notice the pathological alarm in her eyes.

That was when Mummyji had her second stroke, at eight that evening, but no one found out till the next morning. They realized it only when she was unable to lift her left hand and when her words came out as empty balloons.

Diwali...

On Diwali morning, Saroj woke up to the sound of a knife-sharpener's grating machine downstairs. She saw that Mummyji had curled up on her side and was still sleeping. Saroj raised herself from the bed and gently shut the tinted windows so that the noises of the morning would not disturb her mother.

The room became dark again, the way she liked it to be. She went back and lay next to her mother, sliding up close to her until their bodies melded into each other like a spoon. She drifted back into a deep sleep and started dreaming vividly. She was in Pitampur and could see the brown faded hills that surrounded the haveli. Today was Diwali, the most important day in the year. She heard Anu bhabhi singing '*Babul mora*' in her beautiful plaintive voice and she was magically backed by a full orchestra of tanpuras and a sarangi. She saw Anu bhabhi emerge from her room, but the music didn't stop, it became like a haunting background score. She bustled into the courtyard and told the servants to pick up the empty diyas laid in front of every room, which had flickered late into the night and then suddenly died, one by one, the way fireflies do.

Anu bhabhi swished around organizing the house in that lovely efficient way that Saroj admired and envied. Chhotu the youngest servant put all the dead lamps on a tray and took them into the kitchen, for the oil to be replenished and to be dressed in fresh wicks made from a long roll of cotton wool. There was a clanging sound as the cook took out the biggest pots to make the special meals of the day. She smelt the fragrance of fresh flowers. Kaku gardener had brought in a basket of fresh buds to lay around the rangoli patterns that were painted around the chowk like a pretty sari border. Then, Big Ma was up, and Saroj felt happy to see her. She started directing the cooks to make halwa for the pooja. Oh and there was little Manoj, the sleep still in his eyes, but the excitement too great for him to stay in bed. He was gathering his fireworks and running all over the courtyard in the new silk kurta bought for him by his grandfather. Finally, the men got up to bathe before heading to the factory for the pooja.

And Manu? Her beloved? Would he too change into his chikan kurta, the one they had bought together from Laluchand's in the market, and head to the factory? Yes of course. He would not be left behind. The family was crisp and fresh and laughing and forgetting, for a short while, their contempt and collusion. Munimji had arrived in his starched dhoti and was getting ready for a small pooja in the room where he sat. He would then hand out the sweets that his wife was famous for—the melt-in-your-mouth chocolate barfi. The men would return by lunchtime with bundles of crackling notes which would be flung around on clean white sheets later that night during the gambling session. Even if Big Ma shouted at the servants today, it would be taken lightly and in the spirit of hustle-bustle. Saroj woke up smelling the dhoop, smelling the smoky dusty haveli, and ran her palm across her face, not wanting the feeling to go away.

Seeing her mother lying immobile, she felt sad but strangely liberated. She pulled the blanket over herself. Saroj's hand involuntarily went to a reclusive place between her legs that had shuttered down ever since she had spewed out a bundle of cold flesh. She felt aroused, as if some deeply slumbering animal inside her had been woken, brought back to life. Her thoughts went to her husband and his lovely strong hands that had wrapped themselves around her, inside her, filling her up with the only joy she had ever really experienced.

When she got up for the second time that morning, Saroj waited for the crows to begin their cawing, carrying their mean missives, but they didn't utter a sound. Their cackling had stopped and she could hear a man downstairs bellowing 'batli-pepaaaaaar' and the muffled sounds from the upstairs flat and the sound of the door creaking open as Rajni entered the room.

'How is Mummyji, Saroj behenji?' she whispered.

'She had a decent night. Didn't move around too much. Let her sleep. Is Bindu masi up?'

'Yes, she has gone to get ready. She is going back to Pune in a little while.'

Rajni asked if she should get them both tea and Marie biscuits. Saroj gently dabbed at a small bubble of froth that had gathered at the edge of her mother's mouth and said that she should wait, and bring just hers for now. After her tea, she asked Rajni to sit with Mummyji and said she was going to the seafront for a walk.

She smiled into the mirror, ignoring the discoloured blotch on the corner of the silver surface as she splashed water on her face. She dipped her middle finger into a little box of kohl and lined her eyes. She blinked a few times. It was as if she had been in a dream state for two long years and the dream she had just dreamt was reality. She couldn't understand that lightness in her being, but the heart's infinite impulses are outside one's control.

When she came back into the room, she realized that something had gone wrong. Her mother was not well. Mummyji had woken up and was looking at her helplessly, shaking her head, not speaking. She panicked and ran out of the room. To her relief, Dr Nadkarni rang the bell just then for his routine morning visit. She ushered him into the room. He smiled at his patient and took her pulse and blood pressure. Then he moved her arms one by one, let them hang, and frowned slightly.

'Mataji?'

Mummyji didn't answer. She stared at him; her eyes wide open with fright.

The doctor turned to Saroj and spoke calmly.

'She has had another mild stroke. There is some blockage of blood flow to her brain that is why she cannot speak.

Her left arm is paralysed. Her condition is worsening, but not serious. Nothing to worry about. Let her rest and she will be better.'

He gave her a high dose of restive medicine and beckoned to Saroj to step outside. He shut the door quietly behind him.

'Saroj, I think she is more serious than we thought. It may be time to take her to hospital and keep her constantly monitored. I didn't expect this, but it almost feels as if she is giving up. Speak to the others and let me know what you decide.'

After seeing him out, Saroj went and sat in the living room. She felt the same old bile emerging inside her but this time it didn't take over. She was able to watch it and wish it away. Saroj then called Rajan Papa and found out that he was already on his way to Cozy Villa. She then called Suman to ask her to come over but was told that she and Shyam were still sleeping. She left a message with Smriti. She went back inside and found Mummyji fast asleep again. Bindu masi was now up and she gave her the lowdown on Mummyji's condition.

The bell rang. Rajan Papa and Rahul arrived at Cozy Villa, dressed in crisp kurtas, just as they did every Diwali morning. Sunny came a few minutes later. Rahul greeted his Sunny chacha with a hug but the two older men did not address each other. Saroj beckoned them into the living room and told them about the second stroke, the paralysed arm, and her loss of speech.

'Oh god,' said Rajan Papa softly.

'Shouldn't we take her to the hospital?' asked Rahul.

Sunny didn't speak, but looked upset.

'Right now, the most important thing is for us not to let her realize that she is more sick, she must not see us looking worried,' said Rajan Papa, with a sudden tone of authority. 'Today is Diwali. Let us make her feel that everything will be alright. Mummyji is a very strong lady, she will pull through.'

The brothers walked into the Fairy Room where Mummyji was now sitting propped up on pillows, while her sister fed her tea, using a white-and-gold china soup spoon.

Everyone inside the room could smell the scent of sickness. A tray of assorted medicines lay on a table next to her and the room smelled faintly antiseptic. A stand with the facility for a glucose drip had been placed in a corner in case she needed it.

'Jai Ram ji ki, Mausiji,' said Rajan Papa to Bindu masi. 'Diwali mubarak. Mummyji, don't worry, your arm will be back in shape again. You just need a little rest.'

'We are going to the shop, Ma. It's almost time for the chopdis,' Sunny said, with some tenderness. He pulled out a dog-eared yellow postcard from his pocket, which is what the stationers sent to all their customers just before Diwali, confirming their order and naming an auspicious time for them to come and pick up the ledgers. 'The muhurat for pick up is 9:04 am. We should leave now.'

'Jai Ram ji ki, puttar,' Bindu masi replied. 'Are you both all set for the office pooja? Carry on. Carry on. I am here. Doctor sahib just gave her an injection.'

Mummyji's face cracked into a tired, weak smile. This would be the first time in her life that she would not be presiding over the pooja in Bimz, bossing over the pandit, placing the bundle of fresh cash at the altar, and later handing out the envelopes and blankets to the staff, while they touched her feet one by one. She felt as though the ground was slipping underneath her and she was already floating somewhere between life and death.

As the two men walked out of the door, their uncle Phoolchand emerged up the stairs in a grey safari suit, carrying a big basket filled with fruit, his drooping moustache glistening with Brylcream. A few minutes later, Saroj opened the front door, and disappeared, clutching the little brown paper packet that she took to a secret place in the last week of every month.

Sunny and Rajan Papa drove in their separate cars towards Kalbadevi. While most people had barely bestirred themselves after a night of cards or deep-fried decadence, the business district was wide awake, shiny, happy, with strings of marigold and tinsel covering the grime, like an overdressed whore waiting for her customer.

The two cars pulled into Bhatia Wadi, a block away from Bimz, and entered an ancient gateway that bore the inscription: Ramchand Sethia. Established in 1932. The city's oldest stationer was best known for its impeccably crafted crimson chopdi books and pre-folded desi Marwari bahis, ledgers where each page is hand-folded to make it easier to differentiate the debits from the credits.

Inside the courtyard, an old salesman recognized them immediately. He bustled up to them and greeted Rajan Papa, Rahul and Sunny with folded hands. In an enormous veranda alongside, accounting books in all shapes and sizes lay stacked in differently sized piles, with the order number scribbled on top. Merchants wearing their stiff Marwari topis browsed through the piles, trying to find their pre-ordered package, some bigger than others depending on the size of business, before they headed to their shops, offices, and factories.

Rajan Papa greeted his old friend Moinuddin, a coloured-glass dealer whose store was on the same street as the sweet shop and set up around the same time. 'Ready for the pooja, Lalaji? We can't wait to dive into your boondi laddoos. Ammi asked me to order four dozen yesterday!' he said, slapping Rajan on the back.

Kalbadevi had become a symbol of secular India. Although the Diwali pooja was traditionally a Hindu ritual, the goddess Laxmi had been adopted by merchants and traders of all communities with equal deference because of what she represented. Parsi shopowners, Muslim merchants, Sikh traders all started their new year on the day after Diwali.

At the heaven-appointed time of 9:04, just after the morning siren's wailing had died down and given way to the grating sounds of the street, Sunny picked up the bundle of books wrapped in a coarse red cloth and signed on the receipt. At the gate, a young flower girl dressed in a pink-and-gold skirt and blouse, symbolizing Laxmi, handed him the slim hollow bamboo kalam or pen, sharpened on one side, painted in diagonal stripes, which would be used for the inaugural notation in the books. No one questioned her credibility. She was part of the ritual.

Sunny touched the bundle to his head and then told his nephew Rahul to carry it out. The boy carried it gingerly, as if it were a Ganpati idol, not a bunch of accounting ledgers. The sentiment was the same. The difference was that this was an ode to wealth, not wisdom. But very few understood the secret that the little flower girl may or may not have whispered to them that morning—that one cannot exist without the other.

Around the same time, Saroj was heading to the other side of Kalbadevi in hurried steps. She stopped only when she reached Bhatija's soiled building. Halfway there, it struck her that today would be a holiday and the office may be closed, but she continued to walk briskly past the Parsi Dairy Farm and then turned left for the filthy street where Bhatija sat, entering numbers into two distinct categories—borrowers and lenders. The office was open. An old man was sweeping the floor. As soon as he saw Saroj, he straightened up, saluted her and wished her a happy Diwali, a cue for a small baksheesh. She gave him five rupees.

'Where is Bhatija?'

'I don't know, Bhabhi sahib. I was told to clean the office by the lady who sits here,' he said, pointing to the secretary's desk. 'She has gone to buy some things for their office pooja.'

Saroj left and decided to come back the next day. It was already late for her secret remittance, the package she would send with a kiss and a blessing. She had been consistent about it over the last three months. But things did get delayed during Diwali and everyone would understand.

A little later, she was back outside Cozy Villa, but didn't want to go upstairs right away. Instead, she crossed the street and sat, for a long time, on the parapet overlooking the ocean, a few feet away from where her nephew had his first hit of weed. The parapet had experienced life in its many motions. It had survived the tidal lashes of the monsoon, absorbed the footsteps of so many strangers and offered a resting place for those who wanted to contemplate the infinite or drown their sorrows. A solitary fishing boat lurched in the distance.

Saroj's mind was operating in a different gear today. Instead of drifting in slow motion, it seemed to take charge. She thought about all the things she had to organize for Diwali in the house. The family would be over by the evening so she must make sure that the usual fare of rassedar aloo, pithhi di puri, boondi raita, deep-fried bhindi and of course the jewel in the crown, the halwa, would get organized. She didn't have to worry because Ratansingh had been superbly trained by Mummyji and knew how to replicate all her recipes to perfection. He had become her clone in the kitchen.

She slipped off the ledge and walked back towards Cozy Villa. After peeping in to see her mother, she went into the other room and opened the cupboard. She decided that she would wear one of her old beautiful saris that evening. She selected one that she had bought with Anu bhabhi on one of those hot afternoons where the two of them had gone to the market after haggling with the munim for some spending money, and she ran her hand over it. A line of dust had comfortably settled into the fold created by the hanger. She lay down the sari and the matching blouse out on the bed. She then rummaged around the drawers and pulled out a small aluminium box, her mother's sewing kit. She licked a thread and squinted to get it into the eye of a slightly rusty needle. She remembed how her mother would stitch for hours, crafting blank white hankies and napkins into beautiful works of art. She recalled, with some sadness, that morning after her wedding, when she came home to say goodbye to her, before leaving for Pitampur, and found her on her three-legged stool, stitching the seams of the goddess Laxmi's sari. A few seconds later, the thread was in the eye and Saroj sat down to open the seams on the sleeves of the blouse that had grown too tight for her depressed bulging body.

When Suman woke up, she found her daughter squatting outside the door, painting a red-and-yellow floral pattern.

'Nani has had another stroke,' her daughter said, without looking up.

'What do you mean?' Suman held on to the door for support.

'Call Cozy.'

'Oh god! Okay, Papa will be leaving for the office soon. I will get dropped off there. That is a beautiful design, Smriti. Make sure you wash your hair today.'

Her daughter didn't answer.

Suman did not believe in poojas and attended them with grudging condescension. Her cult looked down on all forms of ritual, oblivious that they indulged in their own. She had long stopped accompanying Shyam to his Marine Lines office where every year, the typewriters and computers would be marked with a small red swastika for luck. The only thing that was exciting about Diwali was that Sumit and Smriti were both home and so was Shyam, and they could all pretend that they were a happy family, even though she sensed deep in her heart that there was an unnatural deadness to their interactions.

She knew both her children viewed her with some amount of irritation. She tried to win them over by reading out little sayings from a spiritual handbook—little stories about 'how to be good' or 'why everything happens for a reason'. When they were younger, they would listen blindly to the tales, try and live up to their ideals. As they grew, they would blink back at her, and form a jumble of contrary stories in their head because children learn from what they see around them, not from what they are told. They had begun to see that their mother lived in a land of fairy tales and there was no prince charming or fairy godmother who could come and rescue them from their loneliness.

It hurt her that she did not feel close to either of the twins, but she had no idea how to rectify it. Sumit, in any case, was away most of the time at a boarding school in Panchgani and Suman had become the vacation mother. She had tried to reach out to him but it was now too late. She was part of a composite parent which included his friends and his school headmaster and his father. He had many parents and yet none, really. She was a shadowy mother. She did love Smriti but not quite the same way as she loved what she didn't have. That self-absorbed, righteous anger, over not getting what she wanted, wanting what she couldn't have had been Suman's constant companion, her defence against the world. A small part of her revelled in her martyrdom.

By the evening, she was already exhausted. Being at Cozy Villa and seeing the state of her mother left her emotionally drained. She lay down on her bed and thought about the disastrous way this Diwali was turning out. She had never seen her mother look so vulnerable. Her mind was a blur of emotion. She was anxious about her mother. She also wanted to start organizing things at Cozy Villa. Who was handling Mummyji's little-little things that lay in cupboards all over the house? More than anything, Suman kept agonizing over what would happen if Mummyji couldn't speak, how could she find out where her jewels were? It was going to get more complicated now. She heard Shyam holler at the servant for a cup of tea and pulled herself up. It was time for them to start getting ready for the evening.

She turned the key, opened her cupboard and gingerly lifted a delicate kundan necklace with tiny pearls that hung like dew drops from the pendant for Smriti to wear for the Diwali pooja. For herself, she unscrewed a pair of solitaire earrings carefully, screwed them into her delicate ear lobes and vainly turned her head this way and that, to watch them dazzle as the light sliced through the stones. Nice, she thought to herself.

But Mummyji had the real sparklers, the ones that were three times the size of these ones. Her mind continued to search for the secret hiding place. She was determined. Perhaps she could give Rajni some money to help her on her treasure hunt. Maybe, just maybe, Mummyji had already set them aside for her this Diwali. She was the elder daughter. Who else would she give them to? Manju had enough from her family and Jassu was a hopeless wife whom no one really trusted. Saroj had stopped wearing jewellery. Suman lost herself in her fantasies.

The servant knocked. She hurriedly closed the cupboard and regained her poise. 'Come in,' she hollered.

He walked in, carrying two beige kurtas, embroidered with brown flowers at the breast and cuffs, and laid them on the bed, ironed and ready for Shyam and Sumit. They would first drop in at the old haveli to wish Babaji's ghost and Sweety bua, now a widow, who rattled around in the crumbling house alone. Shyam had abandoned it, but his sister had refused to leave because it had been both her maternal and her marital home and it was all she knew.

Sumit had asked his parents if he could spend one night there, in his favourite room in the attic above his Babaji's room, where some of his childhood toys were still stored under the bed and a faded poster of Bruce Lee remained plastered on the wall. It always irritated her when he asked to go back there. She felt that familiar sense of jealousy and helplessness.

Suman held her stomach in and tucked the pleats of her off-white Banarasi sari into her petticoat and then evened out the bottom. Her large white stomach spilled out again, spreading against the diaphanous fabric.

'Are my clothes ready, Suman? And are you people getting ready?' Shyam's voice jolted her back into the more immediate matter of rounding up her family.

'Yes. You need to take out your diamond kurta buttons.'

This was the one habit that Suman found most hurtful in her husband—they had been married almost twenty years but he still kept his own set of cupboard keys, his own jewellery box, and did not trust her with his money. He made her keep meticulous accounts of household expenses and if the numbers didn't tally, he would get irritable. It was not personal, but an eccentricity that he had inherited from his father—just like his flared nose. As a result, from the time they were married, Suman always felt nervous when it came to money. She felt as though she never had enough. Even though she had created her secret coffer, she was broke in her mind—a malaise that has very little do with the actual wealth on hand. She was, therefore, eternally covetous.

Smriti came into the room looking very pretty in a pink embroidered kurta offset by a purple churidar. Suman lifted her hair and clasped the pearls around her neck. Shyam held his daughter's cheeks and kissed her forehead. 'You will always be my little princess, even if you look like your mother...ha ha!'

Later that evening, the entire Todarmal family gathered in the pooja room at Cozy Villa. The only person missing was the upright matriarch who used to sit on the three-legged steel stool, her back to them, directing the half-hour long ritual, scolding the panditji for not cleaning the coins properly, lighting the big five-pronged silver lamp that stood on the side of the altar. Today, she was fast asleep, and that tenuous link that had threaded her family together had also retreated under the blanket with her.

'Rajan Papa, you are the eldest son. You sit on Mummyji's stool and preside today,' said Suman to Rajan Papa, slyly, throwing out the dice and watching the game begin.

'No no, let Shyam sit, na. Let Shyam sit. He is the eldest person here.'

'Why don't we make the youngest person, Diya, sit there,' piped in Jassu, in an unnaturally high-pitched voice. Suman and Saroj looked at each other. Sunny looked the other way.

The goddess stood mute, watching the family with her ancient painted marble eyes. How badly misunderstood she was, yet again. Like her pet owl that doesn't see during the day, these people were blind. She was not the goddess of wealth but of well-being. She was the other side of Narayan, the god of right thinking and right action, but they worshipped only her, desperate, ignorant.

The goddess decided then that she would not reveal the secret that lay hidden inside the folds of her red-and-gold sari. It would remain there, like the many undiscovered pearls lying deep in the ocean which keep man's quest alive. These people had a long way to go and they must be allowed to experience the exploration or she would be cheating them. Truth lay in the journey and sometimes it came as quietly as a leaf falling on your head, sometimes it took generations.

And so, while the priest muttered incomprehensible mantras, yet another Diwali unfolded before the Todarmal family.

Pandit Purshottam always said a few words before he began the pooja, either a mythical story from the Ramlila, or a parable with a lesson in it. It was a ritual Daddyji had started. He cleared his throat and started. 'Brothers and sisters, today you must hold your emotions back. There is a reason that Diwali falls on a day when there is no moon in the sky. The moon controls tides and your emotions. It is the opposite of the sun, of light and truth. It represents maya and delusion because it reflects the sun's light, it is not light itself. Therefore, see the light of the sun within yourselves. Let good prevail. This is the day that the goodness of Lord Ram was celebrated because he fought and vanquished the ten senses.'

But he knew from his discussions with sadhus during his retreats in the mountains that human beings have an uncanny way of recreating mythologies to suit their selfish needs. Diwali happened to fall during the harvest of the kharif crop so it had become a celebration of prosperity. This overshadows the myth of goodness and, without warning, the world had started rotating in the opposite direction. He didn't have the energy to explain this to these people any more. He had another family to visit right after this and another pooja to conduct. He blew the conch long and loud with a dramatic flourish and started the ritual.

Inside the room, Mummyji heard the conch and receded into the day she heard a similar shrieking sound—only it was the honking of a peacock in the woods behind her house. She was in Ludhiana for Suman's delivery. She was breast-feeding her, admiring her fair creamy skin and lovely brown eyes and she heard the bird honk, followed by something sadder. It was her mother sobbing softly. What had happened? It couldn't be that she was mourning the birth of a girl child, could it? No, her mother did not think like that. Maybe she was missing her husband, who had been reduced to a fistful of ash floated deep inside the Ganges. She closed her kurta buttons, picked up the sleeping baby gently and came outside. Chaiji was sitting on a stool, tears streaming down her face. Baby Rajan was crawling around in the courtyard, playing with a wooden bullock cart toy, his face covered with mud. The sun was setting. It was cold and she shivered slightly.

'Nimmo beti, we are doomed,' said her mother. 'Bauji wants me to move to the outhouse.' She continued to cry. Rajan looked at her quizzically for a minute, then went back to scraping the mud with a twig.

Nimmo stood silently, absorbing what her mother had just said, slowly rocking her baby. It didn't fully sink in. It could not really be true. Was her mother hyperventilating as usual? No, she had sensed something different in her elder uncle's attitude even towards her since she had been home this past month. He was more distant. She had been a bit hurt, but then let it pass. Obviously it was true. She felt terribly pained at the thought of his betrayal. This was the man she had worshipped and loved even more than her father. She called him Bauji and her own father Chachaji. Then, a slow rage started boiling inside her. She would never allow herself to be financially dependent on anyone. When it came to money, there were no relationships.

Mummyji moaned in her sleep, fighting off the pain of past and present.

In Cozy Villa, the pooja was now almost over and had reached the climactic arti. Everyone stood up to sing and clap and praise the goddess. Suddenly, Smriti started sobbing. She ran into the living room. Her mother raised her eyebrows and, for a brief moment, the pain shone in her eyes. Then, the mask slowly came on. When the prayers were over and everyone had taken drops of the milky charanamrit in their cupped hands, touched their foreheads and swallowed it, Suman said, 'Children, come into the living room. I am going to tell you some stories.'

Rahul and Sumit protested. It was time for fireworks. No, not today she said, out of respect for their grandmother's condition. Saroj took little Diya's hand and led her to the living room. Smriti was already there, but no longer crying. She was holding, close to her tear-stained face, a slightly discoloured laminated photograph of her grandparents surrounded by the family, taken on the farm. Mummyji was holding her in her arms, and Rajan Papa was hugging them both from behind. Saroj masi was holding Rahul.

The dashing Sunny mama had Sumit on his shoulder. Her parents, wearing bell bottoms, had their arms around each other. The cousins crowded around the picture.

'Unbelievable moment,' murmured Rahul. They then hugged each other, embarrassed by the intensity of their emotions.

Suman sat on Mummyji's chair, ready to declaim, but her stories never came out because at that moment, Saroj walked in and handed out the velvet jewellery boxes that Mummyji had sorted the day before she collapsed. That was enough of a distraction.

Suman tensed up as she opened hers and her face fell. There was a lovely bangle set with alternating rubies and emeralds. It sparkled invitingly, but the stones that she had fantasized about were not there. Perhaps it was silly of her to think that she would get them, why should she be singled out, right? But now, she had to find out where they were and how she could stake her claim.

A few minutes later, Ratansingh announced that dinner was ready. The family sat around the aquarium dining table. The food was delicious, even though Mummyji had not garnished it with her personal love commandments.

Manju supervised the making of puris, ensuring that they ballooned up nicely in the bubbling oil before being placed on a newspaper to absorb the excess. She stood there with the end of her pallu tucked into her petticoat, periodically touching her damp forehead with the back of her palm.

Suman came into the kitchen, but she could not bear to be there more than a minute. The heat had made her upper lip and the tip of her nose break into little balls of sweat.

'Where is Jassu?' she asked sharply.

'I don't know, behenji!' said Manju, looking disappointed over a puri that was obstinately staying flat despite being submerged in the oil.

Jassu had pointedly decided not to help in the kitchen. She was sitting defiantly with the others at the table, waiting to be served, already imagining a world without Mummyji's rules of governance.

Everyone was distracted by the delicious food. Since there were not enough places on the table, Saroj had pulled up a stool and sat next to her favourite niece, Diya, feeding her with her hands in between feeding herself. Shyam and Sunny shared business tales of woe. The children passed on secret coded messages to each other. Everyone was used to the forced gaiety of this annual meal. As soon as he had wiped his plate clean, Rahul disappeared downstairs for about ten minutes, without telling anyone where he was going.

Phoolchand arrived with his son and nephew in time for the grand finale of halwa. The warm dish swam in a lake of ghee and the diced almonds floated like little fish in the centre.

'She is sleeping,' said Rajan Papa, answering his uncle's question even before he asked it. 'Come, Phoolchand mama, join us, join us.'

'Hello everyone. Hello Shyam. How nice to see you after so long! Looks like we only meet on Diwali. And great to see the twins. They've grown so tall. Where is our young Rahul?'

'Jai Ram ji ki, Phoolchand mama. What good news do you bring?'

'Not good, only depressing news everywhere. Things are getting very bad in Punjab. The grain trucks are not making it to Bombay in time. I just heard from Aggarwal uncle in Amritsar. There are constant rumblings that there is going to be trouble. The Akalis are up in arms over being thrown out. They have been protesting inside the Golden Temple precinct. The shops continue to remain closed on and off in the lanes outside. Jassu beta, I hope things are okay with your grandfather's family in Jalandhar?'

'It's unsafe everywhere. My cousin sisters are not allowed out after it is dark. It is so sad and so terrifying,' said Jassu.

There was a brief silence while everyone pretended to feel concern for the people of Punjab.

In the living room, Ratansingh had laid out clean white sheets on the floor for the card session. Two packs of cards with the Bimz logo on the cover were placed in the centre. It had been the last of Mummyji's brilliant ideas. She had suggested that they make these packs as a bonus gift to be given to those who ordered more than five kilos of sweets from the shop during Diwali.

Diya had already curled up and gone to sleep on a sofa. Manju and Saroj were talking to each other in whispers. The men sat on the sheet on the floor but no one began the game.

'Jassu says that she wants to come and live here for a few days to take care of Mummyji and the house,' said Saroj quietly.

Manju looked taken aback. She knew that there was some ulterior motive here which could potentially jeopardize her son's inheritance. Sunny, who had been absent-mindedly shuffling and reshuffling the cards, put them down and looked at her. He reached into his pocket and pulled out a cigarette.

No one spoke. The card game never began.

Right after the pooja, while everyone was sitting in the living room, Rajan Papa had slipped into the Fairy Room, turning the door handle as quietly as he could. He cringed when the door creaked. No one saw him go in except Rajni, who was clearing the dining table. She had seen one odd piece of behaviour in the sahib a little earlier. Just before dinner, he had gone into the living room, pulled out a plastic bottle of Chyavanprash from a plastic bag tied up with a rubber band, and drunk out of it. She would never imagine that it contained, instead of the gooey black churan, three generous measures of neat whiskey. He didn't see Rajni pass by the door. Rajan Papa had looked around to make sure no one was there, put the bottle to his mouth and then smacked his lips. It was the first time that he had carried alcohol with him to Cozy Villa. And it was the first time he was drinking on the auspicious day of Diwali. At the time of pouring the whiskey into the bottle, he had felt ashamed and miserable, like a sneaky drug addict, but after he drank it, his nerves felt soothed and he was relieved he had brought it with him.

Inside the Fairy Room, he did not switch on the light, for fear of waking his mother up. He groped around in the dark, yelping softly as he bumped his knee on the dresser. He held his breath. The movement had jolted a musical box which carried her hair pins and a few seconds of 'Fur Elise' played out in slow motion. Rajan Papa was mortified. By now his eyes had got used to the dark and he could see his mother's shape like a shroud. He went near her, took a deep breath, and reached under her pillow. She groaned softly and her head turned. She could not make out who was there. She grabbed the hand that was fumbling around under her pillow with a surprisingly forceful grip.

'Mummyji, it is me, Rajan. It is late. Go back to sleep,' he hissed.

She turned and slipped right back into the moving pictures, her in-between world, where dream and reality, life and death, past and future, merged into each other and she could float through and pick flowers and swim in the ocean and cook enormous vats of sweet halwa and then meet her mother, her husband, her little children, sitting around watching the fish dart inside the dining table, while they were eating gol gappa and ice cream and crunchy malpuas, nibbling at the crisp caramelized edges. Everything lies in the remembered experience and when these memories begin to fade, life slips away

Rajan tried groping under her pillow once more. His mind was swirling vigorously from the liquor he had gulped down in a hurry. He wasn't doing anything wrong. He was merely borrowing something and he would definitely return it. He felt the cold metallic bunch of keys and gently dragged it out. He had no idea which key would work. He stood in front of the cavernous cupboard and saw his own sorry reflection silhouetted in the mirror on its door. The cherubs on the ceiling were now laughing at him and he felt dizzy. He put one key in the keyhole but it didn't work. He was about to put the second one when he heard the door open and a triangular slice of light from the outside came in. He froze.

Saroj came to the Fairy Room to check on Mummyji. When she saw her brother standing with the keys in front of the cupboard, she whispered, 'What are you looking for, Rajan Papa? I've already taken out the jewellery boxes and handed them out.'

'Nothing, nothing, Saroj. Just wanted to see if there were any papers that we should be looking at, with Mummyji being like this. Come. Let's not disturb her. She is not doing well, she is not doing well.'

'Yes, I have been thinking about that too. Let's talk to Phoolchand mama? He will have some good suggestions about what we should do. I will tell Rajni to sit here until I come back to sleep next to her.'

Rajan Papa followed her out, shutting the door as quietly as he could. He was amazed at his sister's innocence and trust in him, her elder brother. It made him feel even worse.

The older children had finally got their way and gone down to light fireworks by the oceanfront, supervised by Phoolchand's amiable son and Ratansingh. The rest of the family was sitting around the living room looking somewhat ghostly in the pale fluorescent glow of the tube light. They requested Phoolchand to sit on Mummyji's presiding chair.

'Why don't you take Diya home?' said Sunny to Jassu with a hint of tenderness in his voice, an afterglow of the pooja and the food.

'Please carry her downstairs, Sunny,' said Jassu. 'And phone Premsingh. Tell him to wait down at home so that he can carry her up.'

Shyam was still jet-lagged and said his goodbye, offering to drop Manju home even though he would have to go in the opposite direction. Rajan Papa requested Manju to stay but she smiled her warm betel nut-stained smile, said it would be better for the brothers and sisters to be alone with one another and disappeared. Besides, she would be meeting her card friends in the building a little later and she knew that would be far more entertaining than listening to her husband's family battle it out in their dying mother's living room.

In the end, there were just the four Todarmal siblings and their uncle. Sunny lit a cigarette, filling the room with a thin haze. Saroj went to the door to tell Rajni to bring five glasses of water and also some silver-coated cardamom, which she liked to chew at night.

'Well,' said Suman, pursing her lips. 'There are two things we need to think about. The first is whether it is time to hospitalize Mummyji. The second is to make sure that we know where everything is.'

'Let me be frank,' said Phoolchand, always meticulous in his thought process. He stroked his walrus moustache thoughtfully for a few seconds before continuing. 'Mummyji may not be around long. In my view, we should get her to the hospital where she can be in the care of good doctors.'

He paused again, gulping down a glass of water in one shot. He looked around him and made sure he was addressing each person.

'Now, for the family assets. There are essentially three-four big ones to think about. Of course, the big one is Bimmo di...I mean, Bimz. As you know, Mummyji is still the chairman. I assume that when she is no more the company will have to somehow be divided up between the two of you...' He pointed at Rajan Papa and Sunny. 'Since Sunny does not have a son, that will have to be taken into account in the division. Either that, or Sunny can buy Rajan's share and I can help you come up with a fair valuation... Frankly, the best thing would be not to divide anything and for you two boys to work together and take advantage of each other's talents. Two is always better than one.'

Phoolchand watched his nephews carefully. He knew these boys better than his own. He had watched them grow up and fall apart. He felt sorry for both of them, for their blindness and their foolishness, but there was nothing he could do about it.

Rajan and Sunny did not look at each other. Silence can be the cruellest form of communication. There was so much that hadn't been said—about the business, about its vague ownership, about the fight, about Sunny's guilt and Rajan Papa's hurt. The business was doing well—it had an annual turnover of seventy lakh. As long as all petrol and medical and electricity bills were being paid by the company, no one wanted to rock the boat. Everyone owned everything and there were no clear lines of demarcation or control.

Sunny frowned. He had never really thought about inheritance, nor the fact that he didn't have a son. He suddenly got up, walked to the door then back inside, and sat down, as if he had been jolted. He lit up another cigarette. Suman started coughing pointedly.

'Now,' said Phoolchand. 'Most of her jewellery she has given away to all of you over the years, except for a few things and the two seven carat diamonds which are still with her. Then, there is the farmland. And finally, some cash.'

Phoolchand waited for his words to sink in.

Rajan Papa looked crestfallen. The subject of money did that to him. He preferred not to talk about it even under the most extreme circumstances. He wanted to go home, to get under his sheets, to shut out the world, and dream simple dreams. Like the one he had a few nights ago. He and his cousin were in the Ludhiana courtyard downstairs, sneaking a look up through the wire mesh into the room upstairs where their Big Breast Chachi had just emerged from her bath. If they were lucky, they would catch a sight of her lovely milk jugs and then giggle about it all afternoon. Sunny was so young, they would send him up to distract her. He looked at Sunny and longed to reach out and hug him. He thought he saw his brother look back at him with some pain and confusion, but that was where their silent dialogue stopped.

'And what about Cozy Villa?' Sunny said.

'Ah yes. That is there. It has been put in a trust and the beneficiary is Rahul—but only once he gets married.' He didn't need to justify this. In Mummyji's eyes, only a son's son qualified as an inheritor of family property. The rest of the grandchildren were like pets, to be loved and fed.

'When did Mummyji do that?' asked Sunny, sounding surprised. He had not been privy to this move.

'A few years ago, son. She made me the trustee,' said Phoolchand, observing the expressions on each of the four faces in a detached manner, as if he were watching a family drama being enacted at his favourite theatre, Bhaidas Hall. 'She also once mentioned to me that if ever something happens to her, Rajni and Ratansingh must continue to stay in Cozy Villa and receive their salaries. If they retire or prefer to leave, they should get fifty thousand rupees each.'

'Oh, and I think she had talked about giving Rajni some gold bangles,' he added.

'Ah! That's who those two bangles were for,' said Suman. 'I was wondering, because there was no name inside the pouch but they had been kept aside. Yes, now I do remember that she had spoken to me about it once.'

'So, where are those diamonds?' asked Saroj softly.

'Actually, I don't know.' He looked at Suman, anticipating suspicion to cloud her face and he was right. But he really did not have a clue about the whereabouts of the monolithic sparklers and, for the first time, wondered where they would be.

'And...the land papers?' Rajan Papa asked.

'Well, many years ago, just before he died, your father sent them to a secret bank account in Switzerland for safekeeping, along with a big chunk of gold in the form of bricks and some coins, and also some cash. Rajan beta, do you remember, when you were sent to study catering there? Almost twenty years ago, no? That's when Daddyji opened the account. I think he must have taken you with him? You were probably too excited and nervous to pay attention to what he was doing.'

Rajan Papa looked up with surprise, recalling the innocuous visit to the bank, being greeted by the grey-suited man. He had completely forgotten the incident. Sunny looked at him, how many more such matters had Mummyji kept to herself? There were probably so many things about the business he still didn't know.

'The thing is, it's a numbered account and only Mummyji knows the code,' said Phoolchand.

He paused again, contemplating how easy it was for a family to be oblivious about matters of such importance. There had been too much dependence on the head of the family—first Daddyji, then Mummyji. There were no systems in place to handle sudden or unforeseen situations like this. He had seen it again and again around him and it was the greatest and most repetitive mistake that family elders made. It came from their delusions of immortality as well as their desire to control and protect. But it led to chaos and hurt and insecurity and eventually to destruction. Because when money matters are left vague and inconclusive, just as happens with unresolved emotions, they lead to complete breakdowns. Phoolchand made a mental note to speak to his two sons and daughter about his assets and his secret locker in the nationalized bank down the road.

The four Todarmal children were bemused by this sudden new information about an old bank account that none of them knew anything about. It was like discovering that many years ago, your father had a secret child by someone else who was now grown up and ready to meet them. The evening suddenly felt heavy, weighing on all of them.

'But...but...how do we find out about this?' said Suman, her voice faltering. 'I mean, the farmland will be of no value unless we have the papers.' She turned to Rajan Papa and spoke in a sharp, accusing voice. 'You are the eldest brother. How come you never paid attention to such important things? Or maybe you do know and are pretending! Are you hiding things from the family, Rajan? This is the limit, really.'

Saroj stared at her sister in disbelief. She couldn't believe how low she had fallen. Sunny lit up another cigarette and his face grew dark. Suman was suddenly sobbing. A few minutes later, she got up and left the room, saying, 'I'll just be back.'

Phoolchand started pacing the room slowly, his hands behind his back, like a senator who was addressing his crew. He waited for Suman to return and then spoke, carefully measuring his words. He suddenly felt tired and wanted to go home to his record player, to soothe himself with some ethereal Begum Akhtar, who knew how to turn pain into something sublimely beautiful. But he was a man of conviction. He knew how much rested on his sound advice at this point. He had nothing at stake here other than his love for his beloved old friend Kulbhushan and his cousin Bimla. They went back such a long way. This was the least he could do for the family.

'Look, let us leave these matters for the time being and focus on organizing Mummyji's medical attention. That is the most important job at hand. Rajan, why don't you get in touch with Dr Nadkarni and Suman you should call Breach Candy Hospital to book a room. Try for the new wing, it's a little more expensive, but better equipped. Let's get her to the hospital tomorrow.'

'Oh, by the way...' Phoolchand continued, 'there is a diary that your father used to keep many years ago. He would make copious notes about many things. Try and locate it. You may just find the name of the Swiss bank and the account number inside it and a lot of other useful information.'

Sunny looked up. An image of the squat grey cupboard in his office flashed before his eyes. He knew exactly where the diary was. He had seen it in the cupboard only a few days ago, the faded red book bound together with white thread. 'I think I know where it is. I'll look for it,' he said to the group as he extinguished his cigarette and got up to leave, suddenly feeling tired. The thought struck him for the first time, would his mother return from the hospital? His brother and sisters were thinking the same.

Outside, the sound of a whooshing rocket ended in a loud explosion.

The day after Diwali...

THE NEXT MORNING, SUMAN WOKE up a little before six in the morning, heard the birds stirring and continued to lie in bed, flat on her back. After a few minutes, she rose and fumbled around for Shyam's coat. She reached into his pocket and pulled out a cigarette and a box of matches with a picture of an iron on the cover. She tiptoed into the bathroom, put the toilet seat cover down and sat on it. She lit the cigarette and then realized that, in the dark, she had lit the wrong end. She sighed, got up, threw it into the toilet and pulled the flush. She went back to her bed and pulled the blanket around her. She could now hear the splashing sound of cars being washed downstairs.

When Shyam was around, she tried to avoid taking her sleeping pills so she could get up at a decent hour and join him for breakfast. Besides, it was Bhai Dooj, the festival of brothers and sisters, and she had to organize the small lunch at home before leaving for Cozy Villa. Shyam's sister Sweety and his two cousin sisters would be coming to put a big red mark on their brother's forehead and collect their stuffed envelopes.

She watched her husband eat his poached eggs in meticulous bites with thin slices of toast. When he was done, she told the servant to call a taxi. The driver was not going to come today. Bhai Dooj was a big festival in their community. She picked up a vase of yellow roses, took it into the kitchen, and trimmed the stems so that the flowers would last longer. She peered out of the balcony and there, on the road opposite the big maidan, her taxi waited. She repeated instructions to the cook for the third time that morning and went down.

Suman cringed as she slipped into the taxi even though it was warm with the scent of fresh jasmine incense. She hardly ever took public transport and hoped no one would see her. On the dashboard, she noticed a peeling sticker of a stricken woman sitting with her head bent into her lap with the caption 'Tum kab aaoge'. She realized, with a shock, that it was how she felt most of the time, but quickly pushed that thought out. She told the driver the way to Cozy Villa, and also told him to make one stop at a stationery shop on the way.

Rajni opened the door to Suman. The maid looked like she hadn't slept all night—and she hadn't. She had tossed and turned on the floor next to her beloved mistress, getting up every hour or so and touching her to ensure that she was still alive. She intuitively knew that once Mummyji left for the hospital, it was the end. She wasn't coming back. The thought had shaken her.

The doctor and the ambulance with the stretcher would arrive in an hour. Rajan Papa would meet them in the hospital. Saroj had gone to bathe. In the Fairy Room,

Mummyji was lying with her eyes shut, barely conscious. Suman told Rajni to leave her alone with her mother for a few minutes and shut the door.

Suman then got to work. She sat next to Mummyji and pulled out two sheets of paper and a Camel inkpad from her purse. She looked at her mother, how pale and frail she looked, and her eyes filled up. She loved her. Mummyji was her best friend, her consistent provider, her unconditional confidante. Filled with these thoughts of genuine belovedness, Suman gently lifted her mother's left thumb and pressed it on to the soft wet indigo ink. Somewhere in her mind, she had stored an important legal factoid that with women the left thumb impression was required. One of Shyam's aunts had willed everything to her stepson and her children managed to dispute it and win because she had used her right thumbprint.

Suman placed her mother's thumb on the bottom half of the paper and pressed it down. She then did it again on another paper, knowing that the second one would be less smudgy than the first.

That was the last time Mummyji opened her eyes. They looked vacantly in front of her like a dead fish. And then they shut. In that brief moment, she witnessed everything that she had done—and not done—to her children. She saw the beautifully disguised monsters that she had created, how her indulgences had been destructive, and her patronage so selfish. She had placed in her children her own fears and insecurities and desires, turning them into craven, calculating creatures. She had not helped them understand that, as you die, each breath becomes more valuable than a diamond. She had participated in cruelly emasculating her eldest son. She had turned Suman into a covetous fool, who could resort to the most foolish means to get what she thought she wanted; what she had done to Saroj, however, was the worst. She had wrenched the girl from what mattered most to her. She had placed money before love. It was only now that it all came to her, like a film seen backwards in fast motion. And Sunny? The one they never even gave a proper name? Sunny was the legacy she had left behind. He was becoming her.

Then again, she had done what all parents do—their best. She thought of the crimson-clad goddess in the prayer room and left it to her to take care of the rest. And, with that reassuring thought, she lapsed into a state of no memory where the world was pure, devoid of thought. Where there was no taste. And, no aftertaste.

The ambulance arrived a little later. Most of the family had assembled to see her off. They stood inside the Fairy Room while Rajni packed a small bag, putting in Mummyji's comb, her Vicco Vajradanti toothpowder, a pink Lux soap, a change of clothes, a towel, a soft thin worn pillow mildly stained with her hair oil, and an invisible sachet of hope.

Manju reached over, and whispered into Mummyji's ear, 'We are taking you to hospital. You will be comfortable there. And you will be home very soon, Mummyji.'

The sleeping body did not flinch.

Saroj held on to Manju's arm as the ward boys entered the room.

Sunny tried to vaguely direct them when they lay a stretcher on the floor next to the bed. 'Be careful of her arm. Put the sheet on top of her.' He looked irritated. He was used to sucking strength from his mother rather than the other way around.

The two boys lifted Mummyji with practised efficiency and placed her on the stretcher, while a third held the glucose drip and walked alongside. Rajni opened the door for them and followed them down. As they descended the stairs, Rajni broke into loud sobs, muffled by the end of her sari. Babu came rushing out of his little room to comfort her.

The family followed the matriarch down. Mummyji didn't open her eyes even when the stretcher came out into the blazing noonday sun. The ambulance stood outside the building doorway, its siren ready to start wailing. Standing next to it, Ratansingh was dabbing his eyes with the duster that hung on his shoulder. He had grown up in front of Mummyji. She had screamed at him for getting drunk on country hooch, had tolerated the times he would mix water in the milk he brought back from the farm so that he could pay for his small gambling debts. When he had suffered from acute jaundice and thought he was going to die, she had taken him to the hospital herself and bribed the ward boy to take special care of him. She suddenly looked so frail and ineffectual, the opposite of everything she had been when she was alive. It frightened him.

The watchman and a couple of the building drivers stood in deference, looking morose, as the stretcher was slipped into the back of the van. Everyone was behaving as if she were already dead.

'Should I come?' Rajni asked Saroj hopefully.

'No, Rajni, better you take care of things at home. Maybe you can come during the visiting hours later today or tomorrow.'

'Please behenji, tell the doctor to make her better.'

Ratansingh carried the small leather bag that Rajni had packed. He handed it over to Suman and went back upstairs. For the first time, he didn't feel excited about getting undisputed television time or freedom from his chores.

Just as the ambulance door was being pulled shut, Rajni suddenly ran up to the vehicle. No one stopped her. She climbed into it, kneeled besides Mummyji, and whispered into her ear: 'Barfi…boondi…kulcha…kachori.' In her village, there was a belief that if you whispered things that really matter to a person while he or she is in a coma, they hear you and wake up.

Rajni waited until the ambulance had pulled away and then disappeared with Babu into his room for a bereavement beedi and a Bullseye.

After settling her mother into the hospital, and leaving her with Rajan Papa, Saroj went back to Cozy Villa, picked up her packet and went to find Bhatija in his smelly den.

The man was sitting with his feet crossed on his table, his white socks tinged grey from overuse. He swung them to the ground the minute she walked in and spoke in that fawning way that she particularly hated.

'Arre, come, come, Saroj didi. Welcome. Your packet is ready? Let us send it right away. It has to be addressed to...ah let me see if I remember...Anu Devendra Mohan, correct? Yes. Five thousand rupees, plus my five hundred on that. Great. I will tell the girl to count. Please sit. Have a cold drink, at least. Pa-yaaal. Gold Spot.' He yelled for his secretary in a glutinous voice.

'How is Mummyji? All fine I hope? Give her my regards.'

Saroj did not tell him that her mother was fighting for her life in the intensive care unit on the third-floor hospital room. She didn't want him hovering visiting, pretending to be concerned, and then rushing back to check his ledgers and see what the impact of her death would be on his fortunes.

She turned around and left, happy to leave the room, the dandruff, the secretary with the dangling silver earrings, and her own clandestine transaction. For the last three months, ever since she received the call from Pitampur, she had been sending her husband money to help him recover and regain confidence. She used the money that her mother would give her every month. A ghost, especially a ghost with no children, had no use for cash. She wanted to rehabilitate her husband, to help him get back on his feet, so that he could work towards setting something up on his own.

Anu and Manu's niece Mita had been secretly taking him to some kind of mind doctor near Delhi every week, which Saroj didn't quite understand. How could a doctor treat your mind? Body she could understand, but mind? Did he do some sort of black magic on her husband? Then, why would he have had to take blood tests. She was told that he asked Manu a lot of questions, gently, like a kindergarten schoolteacher. She found it strange, and a little amusing, but mostly reassuring.

She trusted Mita and she heard that he was doing better and better, smiling and laughing more, spending time with his son. What would she do without her and Anu bhabhi. They really were her family.

As she walked down towards the old graveyard on Charni Road, Saroj suddenly missed the haveli and little Manoj more than she ever had in the last six months. She heard his pearly laughter in the cries of imaginary children playing hopscotch and cricket somewhere. She remembered the warm satisfying scent of the boondi laddoo being heated up for him, which is how he loved it, warm and slightly crusty.

Saroj absentmindedly turned into the graveyard and stopped in her tracks, realizing where she was. She was surrounded by broken tombstones overgrown with grass and weeds. An old man sat on his haunches next to a small tombstone, holding his head in his hands. He didn't look up at her. As she turned around to walk back out, she passed a beautiful mausoleum covered with blood-red rose petals and the truth suddenly came to her. Oh god, she thought, staring at the local train that clackety-clacked in a hasty noisy blur in front of her on the other side of the road. She had to go back. Now, even Mummyji would not be able to stop her. She was shocked at the realization that came to her like a clear whisper cutting through the cacophony: She wanted her mother dead.

BY THE EVENING, MOST OF the family had gathered in the hospital waiting room. Rajan Papa and Manju sat next to each other. Jassu and Sunny sat on either side of them. Sunny's eyes were sunken. He looked as if he had not been sleeping well. His skin had taken on a darkish blue hue that extended from his eyes into his cheeks.

Suman arrived a little later with Shyam and the twins.

'How is she?'

No one answered Suman. Rajan Papa nodded. Everyone looked serious and nervous and spoke in whispers. This was the first serious medical situation that had confronted the family and they really didn't know how to handle it. At times like this, Mummyji would have been the one telling them what to do, parcelling out roles and responsibilities to each of them in her instructional voice, sending packed lunches to those who waited in the hospital waiting room, turn by turn.

The nurses only allowed one person at a time inside the room where Mummyji lay along with three other seriously ill patients. She was still not conscious.

Rajan Papa went in first. He held his mother's hand—(at which point he was puzzled to see a strange blue stain on her left thumb)—but there was no flicker of movement from her. He came out of the room dabbing his eyes with a hanky. He couldn't bear the smell, or the endless tubes that stuck out of the listless bodies, nor the hushed staccato beeps that emanated from the various monitors. It was all very overwhelming. It reminded him of a horror film he had recently watched at Eros Cinema, called *Coma*.

Sunny was next to go inside. He stayed for quite a while. When he came out, he looked even more ashen. He felt like a bewildered child seeing her on her hospital bed, half expecting that she would open her eyes and smile faintly upon seeing him. But Mummyji seemed to be in another world, where she no longer heeded her son's wishes. It was the first time he understood that she was on her way out.

Suman went into the room and came out very quickly. She made a gesture to Saroj saying that it was her turn, but her sister shook her head slowly. She knew there was no point and that it was better for Mummyji to rest until it was time for the final resting place. She was being stoic, composed, but new emotions swirled around inside her.

Saroj declined Suman's offer to come and stay with her. She wanted to be alone in Cozy Villa with herself, in her old room, where the corner shadows would now change. As she walked out of the hospital gates, after waving goodbye to her sister, she saw Rahul standing on the corner.

'Hello, beta. Are you on your way in? Better not to go now. Mummyji is not even conscious. Everyone has left. And you will just get depressed.'

'Hi Saroj bua...I'm feeling so horrible about this. It has all happened so suddenly.'

'No, no. Don't be. Chalo, let's go for a walk.'

They stopped outside the hospital gates, bought peanuts from a vendor and proceeded slowly towards a garden further down by the sea, munching and talking. They reached the spot where worn-out ponies trotted up and down, their heads bowed, carrying squealing children who would grow up to be oblivious to the pain of others. They walked into an old unkempt garden and sat on a broken stone bench facing the ocean.

Neither of them spoke for a while.

'How are your studies going, Rahul?'

'Fine...fine, Saroj bua.'

'You have to be strong for your father right now. He is very tense.'

'Yes.'

Rahul looked into the distance and bit his lip. He spoke a few minutes later just as the last sliver of orange sun was about to dip into the horizon.

'Saroj bua...'

'Yes, son.'

'I don't know if I've been a good son.'

'Don't say that, beta. You are a very good boy.'

'I have been a bit distracted, Saroj bua.' He paused. 'There are things going on in my life that I don't seem to have any control over.'

'Just pray to God and everything will be fine. Sometimes, it is fine not to have any control, you know. It's fine to surrender to whatever it is that is happening to you, with grace. That may be half the battle. Then, slowly, the answers come to you.'

He turned to his aunt with a look of gratitude and she continued.

'And sometimes, there are no answers. When you ask yourself why. Why did this happen to me, dear God? But then you have to just embrace the pain and look for the little blessings around you. And do the right thing, whatever that may be.'

'What if the right thing is something that your parents would not understand? What if they think it's the wrong thing, even though it feels right to you? What if something that is taking place inside you doesn't agree with them?'

'I think...' Saroj paused to really think through what she wanted to say. 'I think then you have to be true to yourself. You'd be surprised how much your parents and grandmother love you, Rahul. They may take time, but they will understand whatever it is that you want to share. Don't underestimate the value of family. They are the ones who are there, in their own funny way, at the end of it all. You stumble through life, sometimes not understanding one another, sometimes even hurting each other, but at the end of it all, you are there for each other. And even just being there counts for something.'

Rahul found tears making their way down the contours of his cheeks, like a slow trickling stream that was bumping along trying to find its way. It just didn't stop. He licked the bits that reached the corners of his mouth, tasting the salt.

Saroj was surprised at what she was saying. She rarely articulated things in such a way. It was as if the years of quiet contemplation were suddenly flowering and she was making an affirmation to herself.

It was dark, and she couldn't see Rahul's tears, but she knew. She let him have his little catharsis and didn't speak again. She was reaching out to the son she was missing, and he needed a mother who was not his own. They continued to sit there for ten or fifteen minutes. Then, she gave her nephew a tight hug.

'I have also been thinking about so many things, my son. We must all learn and grow from our mistakes. Come on, let me drop you to your house.'

'Gosh. I'm sorry. I can't believe I'm crying... I guess I am feeling terrible about Dadi.'

Both knew that wasn't the reason for his tears.

Rahul said that he would get off on the way, at the Chowpatty crossing, which was a few minutes away from his building. After getting out, he leaned into the window of the cab and said, 'Thank you, bua. I guess I'll see you in the hospital tomorrow.'

The taxi carried on down Marine Drive to Cozy Villa.

Rajni was waiting downstairs, sitting on a stool, next to the watchman. It was where she often came and sat, just to get a breather. As soon as she saw Saroj she got up and walked up the stairs to open the door. Saroj went into the living room and flopped into Mummyji's chair. She shut her eyes for a few minutes. Then, she picked up the phone and booked a call to Pitampur, dialling the three digits to get to the long-distance operator with careful predetermination.

'PP,' she said, when the woman on the other end asked her the nature of the call. 'Mahendra Mohan.

She placed the handset back on the phone. A few minutes later a shrill ring ran through the room. Saroj's body tensed and then relaxed. She picked it up and said, 'Hello.'

Pause.

'How are you, Manu?'

Her eyes lit up when she heard his slow drawl.

'Soon, yes very soon. It will all be fine.'

Tears streamed down her face. They didn't stop. But they were not tears of sorrow. She suddenly missed Mummyji and wanted her to be there to see.

The next morning, the family was back in the waiting room, as tense and uncomfortable as the previous day. No one spoke much. Sunny's eyes were even more sunken. Rajan Papa looked sad and helpless. When the two grandsons, Rahul and Sumit, walked in, everyone turned their attention to them. Jassu asked Rahul about his board examinations and how his studies were going.

Manju pounced on Sumit. 'You've lost so much weight! Do you get good food in boarding? How is the non-veg fare? Mostly Indian or continental?'

Phoolchand tried to lighten the atmosphere and cracked one of Daddyji's favourite old jokes about the Sindhi man who calls a newspaper to print the death of his grandfather. The clerk tells him that it would cost fifty rupees per word. The Sindhi says, 'Dada dead.' The clerk says, 'Sorry, minimum five words'. The Sindhi replies, 'Dada dead wheelchair for sale.'

Rajan Papa looked at his uncle with gratitude. Sunny smiled. Manju giggled nervously. When a nurse came and announced, in a monotone, that visiting hours were over, everyone left in a cloud of relief.

But human beings have an uncanny ability to adapt. By the next day, they all seemed more at ease and were back to chatting with one another about the heat and the cricket match score. The hospital guard watching them was perplexed by their strange dynamics. He knew something was amiss. Under their amiable banter, each of the Todarmals seemed to desire something he couldn't quite fathom.

Four days after Diwali…

SUNNY'S OFFICE ROOM AT BIMZ contained a large wooden table covered with green felt, on top of that protective glass. Under the glass there were a few old photographs—there was one of young Daddyji and Mummyji standing in front of the store on the opening day, holding a marigold garland to hang up on the awning, with little Sunny next to them, making a face at the camera. He smiled when he saw the big black purse that always hung on Mummyji's forearm. As a child, he loved sifting through the purse's pockets and ferreting out coins or looking for the little box that would be filled with cardamom and cloves. Once, when he was travelling with her on the train, he found inside the purse half a blunt Natraj pencil and he had used it to draw a picture of Ganpati with a big curly trunk, which she had kept with her for long after.

There was also a picture of Daddyji and Mummyji on the Queen Victoria, both looking very posh—she in a jaamewar shawl and he in a three-piece button-down suit. On another side of the table, there was a picture of a fierce-looking holy man who used to visit Cozy Villa during the time Daddyji lost his money and stayed home a lot. Sunny had hated something about him, the way he had entered their household and preyed on its vulnerabilities. He vaguely remembered him opening the door of a cupboard that he shouldn't have been touching. There were a few scattered visiting cards—including an old one of 'Khurana Melody', the store next door. On one corner of the desk, there was a faded picture of the goddess Laxmi.

Sunny sat at his desk with his father's red diary in front of him. He suddenly missed his father, the man who would allow him to fiddle with his big radio, and to play on his stomach, who would take him on his shoulders as he strode through the streets of Kalbadevi and get him little pieces of diced coconut from the temple complex.

He slowly opened it, as if he were unravelling a treasure box, not sure what to expect. The first page had a couplet which he remembered reading on the back of a truck. The rest of the pages contained little notes his father had made to himself. He settled down to read, straining to understand the Devanagari script that had become so unfamiliar to him.

Barely able to focus, his thoughts wandered to Lolita. She wouldn't be back for at least another week. He missed her vaguely synthetic green apple shampoo smell. He thought lustily of his mouth on her breast. He then thought of Jassu and Diya and a recent Sunday they had spent together with his old childhood friend Vishwas along with his wife and little daughter. They had gone to the Radio Club and watched the boats bob in the ocean while eating french fries and chutney sandwiches. The two little girls had exchanged hair clips.

Sunny put the diary down for a minute and looked at the photograph of his father and mother under the thick glass. He blinked. It was the first time he was seeing it. He blinked again and tilted his head. Rajan Papa looked so much like the man in the picture. He must have been around the same age as his father was then. He was shocked. His brother had become his father—the same paunch and curly hair and serene smile. He froze at the realization. He had mutilated his father, his second father, a man who was still alive and cared for him. His heart felt like lead when he thought about the horror of it all.

Sunny suddenly started sobbing, letting loose a teary medley of confusion, frustration, guilt, and fear. Why was he like this? Why did he feel so much anger all the time? Why did Mummyji not help him figure out right from wrong? What if she really died? How would he be able to manage? Why wasn't his father alive to help him find his way in the world? He felt ambushed.

A few minutes later, he opened the drawer and took out the small towel that he used to keep there. He wiped his face and felt lighter.

The red diary lay open before him and he began to read. Over the next hour, he entered the mind of a young entrepreneur called Kulbhushan Todarmal and learned all about how he had started a business called Bimmo di Barfi when he was still a little boy, playing cricket downstairs and burning holes in his mother's saris.

The writing was unemotional and contained matter-of-fact things, interspersed with musings and comments. Today, Rajan did me proud by bringing home so much business. Tomorrow is the first anniversary of the shop, it feels so good. Spoke to Hansraj Gupta regarding giving Suman in marriage to Shyam. Today, gave Jain babu four thousand rupees, needed to pay rent on the new premises next door...

Something came back to him—one of the few times he saw his father lose his temper... Sunny had gone straight from school to the shop and was eating his lunch on one of the side tables, while finishing his Hindi homework, which was to write a short commentary on 'Idgaah', a story by Munshi Premchand. He heard his father's voice rise and saw Jain babu, a moneylender, in the shop standing next to him, in his black coat, black cap, and white dhoti. Jain babu suddenly started screaming in Marwari, accusing Daddyji of being a cheat. A few customers turned around and looked askance at this rude interruption to their gastronomic bliss. Sunny looked nervous. He felt the same way he would feel when he knew there was going to be a fight in the schoolyard and he was somehow involved. He looked at Rajan Papa who was standing next to the cash register and got a reassuring look from him.

'Jain babu, this is preposterous,' Daddyji said, stepping out from behind the counter and gently nudging the moneylender to step outside.

'It is impossible that you have paid me back, Todarmal sahib. I have not been in the city for the last one year. You know very well that I would have made a note of it if I had taken the money.'

'Why are you lying? Why are you doing this?' Daddyji looked hurt. He stared at Jain babu. Then, he turned around and walked back inside.

The story of the corrupt moneylender and what ensued in the following few months became family lore and was repeated many times over at close gatherings, on the dining table, or on holidays. It was the Todarmal story of triumph. Jain babu, who insisted that Daddyji had not paid him a certain amount he had borrowed, took the case to the magistrate's court claiming that he had not seen Kulbhushan Todarmal for a year and that fifty thousand rupees had been lying with him. Since neither had any written proof of the transaction, Daddyji had a genuine problem on his hands. It was not a small amount. Phoolchand had said at the time, 'Khuba, you are stuck. When a man gets desperate, all values and relationships go for a toss. And Jain babu is in that condition. You'd better start planning on how you are going to settle with him.'

It was then that the young Rajan Papa pulled out an obscure trump card. He went through his father's red diary and found an entry dated four months earlier. It stated that Jain babu had visited the shop. Daddyji happened to make a note that he had ordered special Banarasi meetha paans from Muchhad paanwallah for his esteemed guest and that he had never had such a mouth-watering, satisfying paan in a long time. 'The juice of the paan freshened our palate and our moods and stayed with us for the rest of the day...Jain babu left feeling most satisfied' is what he had written.

The diary was produced in court and accepted as evidence. Although there was no explicit mention of the money being returned, it proved that Jain babu was a liar—and extrapolating from that, the magistrate declared, 'It would have been impossible for the defendant to make a back entry of such a nature to generate false evidence. The plaintiff is probably lying. This is proof that he had visited the shop a few months ago and probably did take his money.'

The case was dismissed and no one heard from Jain babu again. A few years later, Bhatija entered their lives and became the family moneylender, bringing with him his own vile set of unethics.

Sunny found that very page, with the jottings about the paan, and marvelled at its value in their lives. He flipped through the diary, eyes partially glazing over. He had forgotten about his earlier mission, which was to look for information about a bank account in Switzerland and a series of numbers that would help him get to it.

He put the book into his briefcase and decided to take it home with him. He wanted to have some private time with it, to explore the world his father occupied. While he was driving, his mind was a jumble of thoughts, moving about like a kaleidoscope that was slowly being turned. They didn't quite tell a story just then, but the colours were changing and he was beginning to see a different picture in the frame.

Sunny sat on his armchair at home, watching Diya play Ludo with Premsingh. A fishy smell drifted up from the oceanfront across the street. Jassu had just returned from the hospital and was watching *Hum Log*, a new television serial, on the other side of the room, munching on fried onion bhajias. There was an air of calm in the house, but the Kashmiri carpet in the living room covered the dustballs of pain and lies.

Sunny continued to browse through the diary and watched different scenes in Kalbadevi emerge and unfold before him. He had blocked out so much. He saw the gentle meanderings of his father's mind and his interests. There was so much about food and people in there, so little about money. As if for Daddyji the business was about relationships as much as profit. It was not unlike Rajan Papa.

He was amused by the detailed descriptions on each of the sweets that Daddyji had added to the shop and the way he would tweak and experiment with the recipes.

On the second-last page, he read: 'I am worried about Sunny because I don't think he understands that relationships are more important than wealth. He has too much of Bimla in him. It is going to destroy the family.'

He read it over and over. He couldn't believe that his father had spelt it out, and wondered why he had never told him this. Or had he? He wished he had got more time with his father. He had always been Mummyji's little squirrel.

Below that, the following verse:

Maut, mukadma, maandgi
Manda aur makaan

Yeh pancho mamme bure
Path rakhe bhagwan

(Death, legal battles, illness, business slowdown, and property. These five M's are all bad; the only thing that protects you in the end is God.)

Sunny was stunned. He turned the page. He realized that there were only blank sheafs after that. This was it.

Sunny looked at his watch. It was past nine. Diya was fast asleep in her room, dreaming of fairies and demons that were sometimes interchangeable. Jassu continued to watch the next programme on television, *Chhaya Geet*, which played song after song and lulled its viewers into a state of virtual romance. Amitabh Bachchan was riding a horse cart down a beach with Parveen Babi in *Amar Akbar Anthony*. Jassu had comfortably nudged herself on to the horse cart, her hair flying in the wind dreamily, humming the song. The real world had become irrelevant.

Sunny remembered going to see the film as a young bachelor with Rajan Papa, Manju bhabhi, and Saroj some years ago at Metro cinema. Manju bhabhi used to get tickets for every new film on the night of the release. She was competitive about her films—she had to watch them before any of her friends did. All of them had laughed and laughed over the scene where the drunk Anthony put a band-aid on the mirror. Saroj said he had behaved like a taller version of Ratansingh, only he had a funnier accent. Later that night, they ate paan and Manju bhabhi had got dizzy because the paanwallah had laced all their paan with tobacco. Sunny had held her hand all the way home, comforting her and making fun of her at the same time. When he met Jassu a year later, she was wearing the same big hoops in her ears that Neetu Singh wore in the film and he had loved them instantly.

'Do you want to come to bed, Jassu?' Sunny asked in a soft growl, as if he had swallowed his pride but it had caught in his throat.

Jassu looked up from her television and smiled without really smiling. She didn't answer.

Sunny left his wife to her fantasy and decided to go to bed early. He felt incredibly fatigued. He lay in bed hour after hour, his mind racing, slowing down, picking up pace again, a medley relay of anxious thoughts. He thought about Jassu and what she had become, a rapacious ungainly woman. Had he turned her into that? He thought about the telephone conversation he had had a few weeks back with her father, the night of Karva Chauth, when she had cried and cried and called her parents in a protest fuelled by hunger and anger.

'You have no business treating my daughter like this, Sunny. Please take your responsibilities a little more seriously. She has no one in Bombay.' The conversation ran over and over in his head. Then his father-in-law was replaced by Rajan Papa talking to him, telling him that he had no right to treat him like that.

Jassu lay sleeping next to him, on her stomach, her long hair all over the pillow. Sunny suddenly threw his blanket off, jumped up and went into the living room. It was dark.

He saw Premsingh lying on the floor, next to the dining table, fully covered from head to toe with one of the old bedroom curtains. He envied the poor man's ability to sleep so soundly. He went to the window and lit a cigarette. He smoked it to the very end, then lit another and noticed, with slight panic, that it was his last. He looked down. The watchman was fast asleep on his white plastic chair, his head lolled to one side. The garden was still and the mango tree looked iridescent in the moonlight. He heard the door handle turn. He rubbed his eyes and turned around. Jassu was standing, framed against the bedroom doorway, her white satin nightie making her look faintly ghostly. He walked towards her and put his head on her shoulder. A few moments later she lifted her arm and put it around him. Her touch was light, it neither confirmed, nor forgave, just offered comfort for the moment, an act of decency. It was the first time she had seen her husband cry.

Sunny slept through most of the next day, waking up late in the afternoon, ravenous. There was no one home when he ate his lunch silently, his head blank. He felt unusually drained and limp, as if the juice had been sucked out of him. He did not have the energy to go to the hospital. Instead, he went back to his bed and picked up the red diary that lay at his bedside. But he found himself reading the first page over and over again without making any sense of it. He fell into a light sleep, his fingers resting on his stomach, intertwined in supplication.

At night, it was the same. The ghosts came back and did not allow him to sleep. Or, maybe he was sleeping.

This time, Mummyji was chatting with him about the price of sugar. She then gave Lolita a present, a naughty smile on her face. It looked like they were the diamonds that everyone had been looking for. Lolita hugged her. He noticed Rajni standing there, in a corner, looking at him disapprovingly. Next thing he knew, his father-in-law was in the room, speaking to Mummyji. He couldn't hear what they were saying; their voices rose and fell in a blurry murmur that lulled him to sleep.

Sunny slept through the next day and the next and stayed up at night, wandering around the house, smoking cigarette after cigarette, first in the living room, then in the bathroom. The towels, his pyjamas, the bedsheets started reeking of the stale smell of smoke. He heard his wife telling him that she had been to the hospital and that things were status quo.

On the third morning of his self-imposed exile from the world, the office called twice, but he did not return the call. He knew that there was a problem. He felt completely immobilized and didn't have the strength to speak to anyone.

Just after noon, his cousin who managed the main shop came over to the house. Sunny was sitting in front of the television, which was not on, his feet tucked beneath him on one side. He was still in his kurta pyjama, unshaven. A cup of tea lay untouched in front of him, covered in a film of dark malai which shivered under the fan. He looked up, surprised.

'Sunny bhai, I heard you were not too well. So I thought I'd come over and see you. I have just been to the hospital to see Bimla buaji.'

'Come, come. I have been a little unwell, yes. Is everything all right in Kalbadevi?'

'Well…not really. Pooran has disappeared. We have no idea where he has gone. And the thing is that we have to deliver a jalebi order by the weekend. It is for Sundar Singh, the biggest bicycle manufacturer in town. He is having a dealer conference.'

'Why can't someone else make the jalebis?' asked Sunny, frowning over the ongoing saga that the business had to endure thanks to the ups and downs of their star chef.

'Well, the thing is that Sundar Singh can tell the difference. He sends his car all the way to Bimz just with specific instructions for Pooran's jalebis. Otherwise he will go elsewhere. He is a very particular man. He has specified that he wants those and if we don't deliver, he will throw a fit.'

Sunny's heart sank. Most days, his temper would have taken over, but today he did not have the stamina even to get angry. The staff of Bimz was an area he had never really been able to handle. He didn't understand the mindset of these village people who would run home even if some distant relative died, or give each other loans that no one paid back, and they found him in turn distant and foreign. He shook his head and without saying a word, switched on the television. His cousin realized that he was going to have to sort this one on his own.

Before leaving, he said, 'Should we speak to Rajan Papa? He may know where to find Pooran. I think he knows where his elder brother is employed. Pooran listens to him.'

Sunny grunted. He saw his wife looking at him with a mixture of scorn and sympathy and wanted to go back to sleep. Later that afternoon, his daughter came into the room and gave him a light hug which made him feel like a king and he longed for more of that feeling.

The next morning, Sunny forced himself to get up, bathe, and go to the hospital. Phoolchand, Saroj, and Rajan Papa were in the waiting room. He could tell from their expression that nothing had changed in Mummyji's condition.

The doctor came in and started explaining that the clots in her thickened arteries were preventing a free flow of blood supply to her brain and the damage might be irreversible. Rajan Papa listened carefully and Sunny watched his brother while he listened and asked questions. He didn't want to make sense of any medical details. He knew that his mother was already gone and he was frightened, the way he had felt when he was pulled out of school and left at his sister's house. Then, it came out.

'Rajan Papa.' A long pause. 'Papaji, I...I need your help with a small matter.'

It was the first time in four years that he had addressed his elder brother the way he used to as a child.

Phoolchand looked momentarily surprised, but then did not allow his feelings to show. He instinctively knew that something magical was about to take place and did not want to jeopardize it. He got up and walked to the balcony, leaving his two nephews to a private moment of reconciliation.

Rajan Papa stared at his brother, looking slightly fearful as if there were going to be more rebukes coming his way.

'It's about Pooran...'

Rajan Papa smiled. He said, 'Yes, puttar, I heard. I have already spoken to Pooran's brother who thrashed him and sent him right back with a warning that he had better not act up again. Things are under control. I know exactly how to handle those fellows.'

'Thank you, Papaji, you are always so good at dealing with these issues,' said Sunny softly, but his eyes said much more.

Rajan Papa's eyes flashed with an entire universe of hurt, understanding, compassion, and forgiveness.

'Thank you,' Sunny repeated.

Sometimes, one moment is all it takes. It can catalyse a war or stop one from taking place. Rajan Papa didn't say a word. He got up, lifting Sunny by the shoulders, and hugged him tight. They were both crying but didn't reveal their faces to each other. Some people were looking at them but such scenes were routine in hospital waiting rooms, and everyone was respectful of heightened emotions.

'Please come and sit in the Kalbadevi shop every day, Rajan Papa,' said Sunny, his voice muffled on his brother's shoulder. 'I know you have been having issues with Bhatija. I can speak to him on your behalf. In any case, there is enough money in the company for you to draw from.'

'Yes, yes. I don't care about all that. It will be fine, be fine.'

Phoolchand winked at Saroj.

She couldn't believe it. Her brothers had broken free of the chains they had wound around themselves. Life could turn at any point. She knew instantly that things would be fine in Pitampur too. Faith was an important prerequisite for survival and she had started carrying it everywhere with her.

Later that evening, Rajan Papa left the hospital smiling. Although no one had remembered to wish him that day, he knew that this was the best birthday present he had received in a very long time.

Rajan Papa had just one drink that night. He didn't feel like having any more. He sat down earlier than usual for dinner and looked amiably at the spread before him.

'Ah! My favourite chana-paneer today. And also lobia. Double treat, what?'

Manju smiled, passing him a warm paratha. Rajan Papa complimented the cook on the food. He started speaking about the shop, about how he wanted to get more involved with the old customers, cater to their needs. She did not interrupt him, but listened with care, watching the expression on her husband's face, seeing him glow the way he did when he felt good about things—about the birth of his son, about a growth spurt in the business, about a delicious shaded milk cake that Mummyji had made especially for him. Finally, he said, 'I think Sunny needs me to be there more.'

'Did he say something?' she asked, tentatively.

'Well, yes. We had a nice chat,' he said casually, in a guarded way.

'I can't believe it. God is great,' she murmured, more to herself.

Rajan Papa didn't give her any more details about the conversation in the hospital. It was a man thing, between brothers. He burped loud and long like a satiated king and pushed the chair back, ready to get up from the table.

'I feel so happy, Manju...I want you to know that I love you very much.'

Manju looked at her husband and smiled. It was the first time in years that he had said something like this to her. She brushed it aside coquettishly. 'Leave it, ji. Come let us go to sit with Rahul.' She then made a sign to the cook and mouthed something, pointing towards Rahul's room.

They knocked on Rahul's room door. He opened it, looking surprised to see his parents standing there in their nightclothes.

'What are you doing, son? Come on, put the television off. Let us spend some time together. You have to grace your parents that much, at least today.'

'Of course, Mom,' said Rahul, smiling, and turning the television on mute. 'Don't act as if I'm doing you some big favour.' He then turned to his father. 'How was Dadi today, Papa?'

'It's the same. The same. I don't think it's going to get any better. We now have to pray that she finds comfort, and that she is not in any pain. That is all we can hope for. She is too strong a person to suffer like this.'

'I can't bear to see Dadi like this. She looks so...'

'I think times like this can only help us understand that more than money, it is our family that matters,' said Manju, snuggling up to Rahul.

He looked at her quizzically and then responded with a hug, enjoying the familiar sweet, musty smell of her kaftan.

The door opened and the cook walked in carrying a small chocolate cake on a white plate, with a single candle on it. He placed it on the table in front of the bed. Rahul pulled out a matchbox from his pocket, and lit the candle. He and his mother started singing in loud sing-song. 'Happy birthday to you!'

'Arre! What is this! You people are so silly! I am not a child, you know.' Rajan Papa laughed.

'Of course you are! A child who will always love sweet things.'

'Yes, sweet things like you! What a lovely way to start my fortieth year, Manju.'

Rahul looked at his parents and felt a little embarrassed about the way they were flirting with each other. But he liked it.

The cake had a message in white icing scrawled across it. It said: 'Happy Birthday Listen!'

Around the same time, Suman was sitting on the balcony of her flat, staring at the Rajabai Tower that loomed across the park like a tall dark shadow. There had been some talk about lighting up these monuments, but for now they stood there like hoary dead British soldiers watching over the city they had built. Shyam sat with her for a little while, sipping on a brandy, and then went to bed. Sumit and Smriti were both out with their friends. Suman sat alone for a long time, surrounded by stunted bonsai plants. She decided to smoke a cigarette. She went into the bedroom and rummaged through Shyam's things. She found his pack of 555 and pulled one out. She took it back into the balcony, looked behind her once to ensure that no servant was watching, and lit it. She coughed a little and then got into the rhythm of the inhalation.

She thought about the story of the man without the shirt and wondered whether she would ever find happiness. But did she know what made her happy? Was it Shyam? Was it the adulation she got from the people in the chanting group? Was it money? Was it those diamonds? Was it the love of her children? She thought about the thin purplish impression of her mother's thumb on the piece of blank paper that lay inside her purse. What should she do with that? Was there anything she could do with it? Did she really need to do anything with it? She would think about it in the morning. She was surprised to find tears streaming down her face. They were sad, soft tears. It was just the beginning of the grief that she knew she was going to feel for a very long time. It was that sense that she may never be able to say that one last thing to someone she loved very much. It was the death of her past. Now she had only the possibility of a lit-up Rajabai Tower to look forward to, but even that was not certain.

She went inside, swallowed a pill, glugged down a glass of cold water and flopped on to the bed hoping that she wouldn't dream.

A week after Diwali…

On the last day of October. Phoolchand's son went to the Kalbadevi shop and stuck a chart paper on the shuttered door. It carried, in bold black letters, the following notice:

WITH PROFOUND GRIEF,
WE REGRET TO ANNOUNCE THE DEMISE OF OUR CHAIRMAN
BIMLA KULBHUSHAN TODARMAL (1924–84)
(WIFE OF LATE KULBHUSHAN MOOLCHAND TODARMAL)

THE SHOP WILL REMAIN CLOSED FOR TWO DAYS

Pooran had just come to the store. He stood there, staring at the notice, and then realized what it meant. He immediately sat down on his haunches and started dabbing his eyes. A few minutes later, he was joined by two other staffers of Bimz. The mourning had begun.

While they were huddled on the pavement outside Bimz, Khurana came running out of his shop next door.

Have you heard the news about Indira Gandhi?'

'No. What happened?'

'She has been shot dead by her own bodyguards. They were sardarjis. She was walking down the garden in front of her house. It's absolutely shocking. They've taken her to the hospital. It's on the radio. I think there is going to be real trouble. They will not forgive the sardars.'

'Hai Ram. I guess now two great ladies have died,' Phoolchand's son said.

Later that afternoon, Rajni woke up after a long afternoon nap. She had not slept properly since the funeral. Her limbs ached with exhaustion. From the time Mummyji's body was brought home to the time it went to the crematorium, she had been on her feet. She had bathed her mistress, rubbed her body with ghee and dressed her in her favourite white kota sari, starched to perfection. She had stuffed her nostrils with cotton. She polished her nose ring so that it sparkled as if she were a young bride, and finally laid her on top of the aquarium dining table so that everyone could come and pay their respects, just as they had done many years ago to her husband.

She stood in deference, sobbing silently, as she watched each of Mummyji's children, and then other relatives and business associates, touch the shroud's feet and lay garlands on top of her until she was fully covered in a thick suffocating blanket of flowers, with only her face visible. She was moved by young Rahul who had knelt next to his dead grandmother, laid his head on her stomach and wept and wept. The other grandchildren looked frightened.

Diya had not been brought to the house because she was too young to witness death.

Purshottam, the priest, sat in a corner with professional detachment, muttering verses from the Bhagavad Gita as the final rituals took place. A group of women sat huddled in a corner of the room, their jewels sparkling, their clothes unnaturally white. Just as a stack of incense sticks were placed at Mummyji's feet, Suman started wailing loudly, drowning out all the platitudes that she had mouthed all her life, about death and attachment and the ephemeral body versus the eternal soul. Sunny cried softly and so did Jassu and they stood next to each other, not quite touching, finding comfort in proximity.

Mummyji had entered this home as a bride and she left as a shroud. After the body went to the crematorium with the men of the house, Rajni went back inside and stood in the balcony for a long time, just staring out of the window, thoughtless, allowing her grief to gradually evaporate into the universe. By evening, everyone had left. Saroj didn't want to be in Cozy Villa and breathe the smell of death. She went to spend the night with Suman. In any case, a part of her was already in her bedroom in Pitampur.

Rajni went into the Fairy Room and switched on the light. She looked up at the cherubs and sighed. She started fiddling with some of Mummyji's things, absent-mindedly arranging her hair curlers and clips in a neat pile. She picked up the little music box and twisted the key. It crackled out the last slow turn of 'Fur Elise'. She then went to the kitchen and made herself a cup of tea. Ratansingh had gone down.

Rajni hardly slept that night. Her mind raced back and forth, thinking deep fearful thoughts about her own children, about Mummyji's children. She felt profoundly lonely. When she woke the next morning, she didn't know what to do next. She went into the prayer room and lit an incense stick in front of the Laxmi statue, the way Mummyji used to do.

By early afternoon, she was so exhausted that she fell into a deep slumber. When she woke up three hours later, she decided to take a snack and some tea down to Babu and have a few smokes with him. She pulled out a round stainless steel box filled with homemade kachoris, waited until the tea had boiled for a few minutes, and then carried the box and the tea down the stairs, the pallu of her sari wrapped around the steaming hot glass so that she didn't burn her hands.

She poured half the tea into one of Babu's stainless steel mugs. They sat, as usual, in silence, sipping tea in slow, loud slurps. She opened the box to take out a kachori for her friend and left the box open.

'Hmm. Wonder what this is.' Babu picked up the lid of the box and peered at it. There, engraved on the inside of the lid were six digits in a neat row. This was followed by three letters, SBC, and then ZUR. Below that, a swastika. Lost in her thoughts, Rajni looked vaguely at the lid.

'God knows,' she said, and reached for the jar of Bullseye.

ACKNOWLEDGEMENTS

THERE IS ONE PERSON WITHOUT whom this book would not have been possible—my beloved father, Bhagwat Devidayal. He introduced me to delicious details about business families, took me into the bylanes of Kalbadevi, and brought alive the mouth-watering world of mithai.

I must thank, above all, my dear friend and editor Chiki Sarkar, who pushed me to make each draft better, even if deadlines were being flouted.

Among those who offered valuable suggestions are Mohammed Hanif, Nikhil Rao, Meenal Baghel, Parmesh Shahani, Gita Mehta, Gautam Khandelwal, Nilanjana Roy, Vikramaditya Motwane, Ishika Mohan, Naheed Carrimjee and my mother Meera. I am grateful to Girish Aggarwal of Bengali Sweet House for his insights into the mithai business and to Jaikishan Somani for taking me into the intricate world of Marwaris. A big thank you also to my editor Jaideep Bose at *The Times of India* who gave me time off to write, and to my agent David Godwin.

Finally, thank you to my family who patiently endured my obsession with this book and allowed me to steal ideas from all their secret cupboards. My in-laws, especially

Hardevi Motwane, Shobha Motwane and Chintu, for enduring my eccentricities. Gauri, for the eagle-eyed proofing. Rachana, for letting me turn her Morocco home into my writing retreat. Pratish, for giving me so much space, and Chaitanya for graciously permitting my laptop to become an extension of me.

A NOTE ON THE AUTHOR

NAMITA DEVIDAYAL IS A JOURNALIST based in Mumbai. Her first book *The Music Room* was a winner of the Vodafone Crossword Popular Book Award 2007 and named an *Outlook* book of the year.

A NOTE ON THE TYPE

Berling is an old-style typeface based on the classical Venetian model used by Aldus Manutius at the end of the fifteenth century. Berling was first cut by the Berling foundry in 1951 with further weights released in 1958.